I0593160

THE REALITY OF US

THE WATTLE JUNCTION SERIES

EMMA MUGGLESTONE

Cover design: Sam Palencia at Ink & Laurel

Structural edit: Penny Carroll

Proofreader: Jo Speirs at Nurturing Words

Paperback ISBN: 978-0-6458225-4-0

Ebook ISBN: 978-0-6458225-3-3

For Gorgeous,
because our love story is my favourite.

And for me,
because it's okay to want something that's just yours
and to celebrate your achievements.

AUTHOR'S NOTE

Hi there!

The Reality of Us is a spicy, small town, opposites attract romance written in Australian English so depending where in the world you're reading from there might occasionally be an 's' where you're expecting to see a 'z', along with a couple of other differences in spelling and slang.

Thanks so much for giving Owen and Alice's story a chance! I hope you love them as much as I do.

- Em

Trigger warnings: mentions of illegal drug use and overdose (not shown on the page), and past gambling addiction (not shown on the page).

1

The warning lights on the dash blurred as Alice blinked, her newly ringless left hand swiping at the tears threatening to spill. She sucked in a few deep breaths. Crying wouldn't achieve anything other than ruining her smoky eye make-up. And today *wasn't* the day to try and make the sad clown look popular.

Alice fiddled with the radio, desperate to find a pounding beat to drown out her thoughts, but the plastic knob snapped off. Heavy static saturated the air like humidity right before a summer storm. She tossed the broken piece into the backseat, where the remnants of her old life swallowed it whole. Half her wardrobe was shoved into suitcases and bin bags in the back of the old Volvo AWD she'd inherited from her grandfather.

Alice drove on, the white noise somehow magically speeding up to mimic the way her heart rate increased every time she glanced at Google Maps. Not because she was worried about getting lost on a straight road with no traffic, which, *okay, fine,* had happened before, but rather because of the banner notifications rolling across the top of the screen. The avalanche of missed calls, text messages and social media alerts made her empty stomach roll. Two years ago, this would've filled her with joy. Now she just wanted to hide.

Her mother's piercing gaze flashed up on the screen—again—but she let the call ring out. What was the point in answering when she knew how the conversation would go? Marguerite Aspinall would demand Alice return to Melbourne and follow whatever plan her parents had decided on, like they always did when she messed up. Then Alice would lash out and say something she'd end up regretting. They'd been doing this dance for twenty-four years.

When Alice couldn't take the buzzing any longer, her fingers itching to tear her hair out of its elaborate crown braid, she pulled over. The car bumped off the smooth bitumen onto the loose dirt and gravel, and Alice killed the engine.

Silence—blissful nothingness—surrounded her. She threw the door open. The dusky coolness of the mid-April evening settled against her bare legs. Her phone lit up again, her brother's big brown eyes and watermelon-sized grin appearing. Her finger hovered over the accept icon. Maybe if she told him she was fine, her family would leave her be? Dougie was also the least likely to say, "I told you so". He'd think it, sure, but he wouldn't verbalise the thought, something neither of her parents was capable of. And if he did say something, his boyfriend Rico would be there to run interference.

Alice answered the video call with a heavy sigh. "Hey."

"Thank God!" Rico crowed, pushing Dougie out of the shot. "Where are you? Are you okay? Obviously, you're not okay. That asshole ..."

"I'm ..." Alice's puffy, red eyes were still dangerously close to sad-clown territory.

"Come over. We'll eat carbs, drink an appropriately dry white wine and plot Fuckface's demise," Rico said.

"You think I could talk to my sister?" Dougie reappeared on the screen. "I've spoken to Mum and Dad. They've got a plan."

No surprises there.

"And I'd be happy to help you get a divorce. All free of charge for my favourite sister, of course," Dougie said.

Alice rolled her eyes. She was his only sister. Telling her brother, the mega-successful lawyer, just what a train wreck she was didn't appeal. She looked out across the vast, open plains. Some distance right now was a good idea. "I need a few days. To figure out what I'm going to do. And be alone."

"No, Alley Cat." Dougie was busting out the big guns using Alice's childhood nickname, ignoring that she'd always hated it. Who wants to be called something that skulks around dark places filled with rubbish? "Let us handle this for you. Please? You know Mum and Dad will feel better if they can help."

If Alice had a dollar for every time she'd done something to make someone else happy, she'd never have been tempted to make the bad decision that led to this mess in the first place.

"We'll make sure you're protected. Is your laptop handy? Can you flick me all your financial information?"

She could imagine Dougie's face if he saw her and Phoenix's bank statements. But first, she'd have to know how to access them. They'd lived an extravagant lifestyle, and that shit wasn't cheap. Not that she'd ever really paid much attention to it. Alice had always been allergic to details.

"I just need a few days to get my head together."

As soon as she hung up, her phone rang again. Phoenix's haunting blue eyes replaced her brother's face, and she tossed her mobile onto the dash.

Pushing out of her seat, despite the protest from her heavy limbs and heart, Alice squinted across the fields scattered with gum trees, weathered sheds that slumped sideways and feeding troughs. Soon night would swallow the dusty ground and the property fences made from wooden posts with rows of wire strung between them.

Alice shivered, rubbing her arms. Now everyone knew about all the lies, she'd have to be honest. Admit she went along with it. The thought of confessing the truth made her stomach twist, and she sucked her bottom lip into her mouth, smeared lipstick be damned. Her carefully curated appearance suddenly seemed so trivial ... so *stupid*. Her fitted top sprinkled with tiny sequins was as much of a joke as she was. She should put on a pair of jeans and a plain shirt. And Alice never felt like wearing jeans and a plain shirt, even if it was organic cotton. Well, maybe organic cotton with a sweet flutter sleeve. But the sleeve would have to be *really* cute. She'd always been so careful about making sure the Alice Aspinall everyone saw was the one she desperately wanted to be. Which was no help now that everything had gone to hell.

A large green road sign for Wattle Junction stood out like a beacon, and Alice smoothed her hands over her tutu skirt, pulled at a loose thread and bent over to wipe the road dust off her favourite rose gold brogues. Now the initial adrenaline dump was behind her, all she wanted to do was sleep. Wattle Junction it was, then.

Once she was buckled back in, she ignored the low battery warning on her phone and a quick internet search revealed there were rooms available at the Wattle Junction

Hotel. Two minutes later, she had the skeleton of a plan and a booking confirmation thanks to her parents' emergency credit card.

Alice turned the key in the ignition, and the car clicked once … twice … before the engine whimpered pitifully and died. She thumped her hands against the steering wheel. What else could go wrong?

She'd have to call Rico, beg him to drive all the way out here to rescue her and then not tell Dougie. Another Google News alert flashed up on her phone, and Alice froze.

Married Rockstar Live Streams Sex Fest with Mistress.

Her finger hovered above the link, and then her phone died.

As the sun dipped below the horizon, the last bit of colour leaching from the day, Alice threw her car door open and screamed at the sky.

It was all over, and it was all her fault.

"Mum," Owen sighed.

"What?" Lulu's voice crackled through the car speakers. "Darling, it's one little dinner. Denise is lovely. She's moved home from Sydney. You remember her, don't you?"

Owen's palms tightened around the steering wheel. Hard to forget someone who had been called 'Horse Face' for most of high school. Not by him, of course. He'd been so wrapped up in his girlfriend and getting the marks he needed to get them out of Wattle Junction that other girls hadn't registered on his radar. Owen tried to think of another excuse as he flicked his headlights on to high beam. The road to Wattle Junction was deserted.

"She'd love to hear from you."

The nonchalance in his mum's tone set off a series of warning bells. "Is she expecting to hear from me?"

The silence on the other end of the phone spoke volumes.

"I might've mentioned you'd been asking after her ..."

He took a steadying breath. "Mum."

Lulu cleared her throat, and someone chuckled in the background. Probably his dad, Wilbur. Probably with a beer in one hand, his gaze glued to the cricket. "Technically, you did."

Owen shook his head even though his mother couldn't see him. So much for letting him settle back in at his own pace. "You said you'd run into a Denise, and I asked if it was Denise Matherson. Hardly the same thing."

"Technically—"

"Mum."

"Leave him be, Lu," Wilbur said. "He argues all day for a living. You won't beat him on a technicality."

Lulu grumbled before she lobbed a final shot at him. "Fine. Don't call her. Be alone forever. I thought the point of turning your life upside down was actually to have a life, but perhaps I misunderstood."

Despite the theatrics, Lulu wasn't telling Owen anything he didn't already know. He exhaled slowly. This reminder of how empty his life had been for so long was unnecessary. The endless hours of corporate ladder climbing and lonely nights in a beige apartment. He'd just never expected the emptiness to follow him back here. All his friends had moved away or were married or in long-term relationships, busy in different life stages that were years away for him. And, truthfully, he'd done a piss-poor job of staying in touch with them. At least his three brothers were still single, so they were around a bit.

"Darling ..." Lulu said.

"Why don't you come see the office on Wednesday once I've finished repainting it," he suggested, steering the conversation away from bad memories towards safer ground.

"Fine, and we'll see you at trivia tomorrow night?"

"Maybe."

If Owen hadn't drained his savings and then some moving home three weeks ago, he'd have been tempted to bet Denise would be sitting next to his parents at their weekly pub trivia table the following night. He rubbed his face with his left hand.

His headlights bounced off something—not a roo, but a car—in the distance. In the shadowy darkness, a woman stood with her arms folded across her body, leaning against the side of a pale-coloured AWD.

"I've got to go, Mum. Someone's broken down."

He slowed, flicking his high beams off and left a few car lengths between his white Jeep and the Volvo. In the headlights, the stranger's blonde hair looked like a halo, twisted around her head in some sort of complicated plait.

Owen left his car running and hopped out, his mobile held up in one hand. "Are you alright?"

"Who are you?" the woman yelled back, her hands shielding her eyes from the bright lights of his car.

"I'm Owen." He stepped clear of the door so she could see him better.

"Don't come any closer!"

He stopped, his hands raised in surrender.

"Are you filming me?" She threw her arms in the air. "God. You people will stop at nothing!"

What was she on about? Then he realised his phone was pointed at her.

"I'm not ... Did you break down? Why would I be filming you?"

"I'm fine." She tossed her head.

"Then why's your bonnet up?"

The woman rubbed her hands up and down her arms. "Are you a murderer?"

A laugh caught in his throat. "Do you think murderers introduce themselves as murderers?"

Her eyes narrowed, and her chin jutted forward. One perfectly shaped eyebrow lifted. She probably flattened people daily with the ferocity of her glare. "Whatever."

Owen edged forward until he was only a few metres away. Her face was red, the skin under her eyes dark, almost bruised.

Oh, shit. Now he couldn't leave until he knew she was safely on her way to wherever she was heading, and he was pretty sure he knew where that was.

He held his phone up again, the camera pointed at him this time. "I've got the number for Kathleen's Place. You can ring them. They'll vouch for me, and I can give you a lift if you'd like."

The woman's brows pulled together, and she stood up even taller. "Whose place?"

The community home his great-grandmother had started in the sixties had a long official name, but it had always been called Kathleen's Place. Owen's fingers clenched around his phone. If he ever caught the bastard who'd hurt her, he'd ... add them to the long list of assholes who deserved what they had coming to them. But Owen wasn't a vigilante; he was a lawyer who drank too much coffee and tried to notch up a few wins for the good guys. At least, that was the plan now he was his own boss. His way of righting the ledger after too many years of helping the wrong people.

"Isn't that where you're headed?" He took a tentative step forward, pausing when she backed away. "They can help you with ..." He didn't want to embarrass her by pointing out he'd noticed her bruises.

The woman's arms dropped to her side, eyes flashing. "Why does everyone always assume I need help?"

"Because you're standing by the side of the road ..."

She pushed away from her car. "Is that illegal?"

Was he in a parallel universe or something? This was why he didn't date. Who had the time for all this drama?

"Listen, I can't leave you out here. It's not safe, and it looks like you need"—he contemplated the best word to use —"assistance. This road doesn't get much traffic at night."

Her eyes darted around, the red on her cheeks deepening as she surveyed the surrounding darkness. When her shoulders slumped, his followed, relief coursing through his body because he wouldn't have to ... what? Drag a strange woman to the community home? The whole town would know before he'd even get home. Keeping a secret out here was like trying to stop a sieve from leaking.

"Who are you again?" she asked.

"Owen. I live in Wattle Junction."

"You don't look like a local."

Owen glanced down. He'd left his tie on the passenger seat, and his navy suit and white business shirt were rumpled. Old habits died hard, and he still tended to wear his suits when working, even if his short, dark blond hair was no longer neatly combed and his jaw was covered in stubble, something he never would have allowed in his old life. Besides, she could hardly talk. Her outfit screamed big city, not country town.

"I've come from a meeting," he said.

Her gaze lingered on his face, and she sucked her

bottom lip into her mouth. Her eyes narrowed, and a rush of heat crept up his spine.

"I think it's the battery." She hitched one shoulder towards her car.

The problem-solving part of Owen roared to life. "I've got jumper leads."

She nodded. Added a small "thank you" like it was an afterthought.

Owen swiftly manoeuvred his 4WD, parking it nose to nose with hers. "What's your name?" he asked, lifting the hood prop into place and attaching the jumper leads.

She pushed a few strands of loose hair away from what he could now see were deep blue eyes framed with thick lashes. "It's, um, Marguerite."

He nodded, pausing when he realised her eyes weren't bruised but rather covered with streaked make-up. God, he thought she'd been ... Lulu was right. He needed to get a life.

"Where are you headed tonight?" He walked towards her car.

"Why?"

"The battery needs to charge once I get it going or it might not start the next time you need it."

"Hypothetically, if I was heading to Wattle Junction, how far away would it be?"

"Five minutes. It'll need longer."

Marguerite smoothed her hands over her skirt. "I'll take my chances."

"That's not how batteries work, especially one this old." There was white crust around the terminals. "You'd be better off replacing it."

Two minutes later, the Volvo's engine ticked a couple of

times before it caught. A small smile bloomed on Marguerite's face before disappearing.

"Thank you," she said stiffly as Owen wound the cables into a neat circle.

"You should still consider getting a new battery. There's an auto shop in Somers Gully about fifteen minutes that way." He pointed in the opposite direction. "Better to be safe than sorry so you don't find yourself stranded again. A woman like you ..."

Her eyes flashed, her posture straightening until her back was ramrod straight. "Like what?"

Walked right into that, hadn't he? "I only meant it's not safe to be out here on your own."

"Because I let my phone and car die? Because I'm a stupid woman?"

Owen's chest tightened. Great, now she thought he was a misogynistic ass. "I didn't say that."

When Marguerite rolled her eyes, it was like a lit match hitting a fuse, the last of his patience burning away to nothing. "No one should be out here at night," he said, "especially a wo ... *person* who's obviously not from here."

She threw her arms in the air, groaning at the starry sky before sending him a look of pure loathing. "Thank you again for the help. And the bonus mansplaining."

"Now, wait a second ..." he started, but Marguerite ignored him, slamming her bonnet shut and flinging herself into the driver's seat. She flicked on her headlights, yanked the door closed and roared away without so much as a wave. He watched until her rear-view lights disappeared.

You know who wouldn't have behaved like that?

Horse Face.

Shit. He meant Denise.

Owen needed to get some sleep.

When Alice woke, a flock of cockatoos were staring at her. She blinked. Twice. Pushed the heels of her palms into her eyes until everything went fuzzy, and then she remembered.

Phoenix.

The live stream.

Everyone knows my marriage is a sham.

Then finally, the weird Australiana wallpaper and décor at the Wattle Junction Hotel. Her hand slapped at the bedside table until she found her phone.

She forced herself to sit up, leaning against the heavy wooden headboard with gum trees carved into it. The whole room looked like Crocodile Dundee had been commissioned as the hotel's interior decorator.

Alice said a silent prayer to the universe and turned her mobile on. Notifications filled the screen.

> Dad: Answer your phone, please. If it's money you need, we'll sort something out.

Rico: Holy shizballs. Does Fuckface's penis really have a massive curve in it? Some of the stuff online is WILD. Don't look. Let's burn your wedding dress, eat tacos and drink margaritas. It'll be a fiesta of freedom! Chin up, gorgeous.

Dougie had sent a picture of his cat, Mr Whiskers, and a sweet message about being there for her whenever she was ready to talk. He'd also attached a list of paperwork for her to start getting together.

She scrolled through several texts from her manager, Chris, which ranged from confusion about where she was to optimism about how they could spin the scandal to their advantage by putting on a united front.

Alice dropped her phone like it was a bomb and stared up at the ceiling. *Was that* … The metal light fitting was made up of Australian birds—an emu, a galah and a kookaburra. Wattle Junction was weird.

Her stomach growled. Right, this was a problem Alice could solve. She showered and dressed quickly, wiping drops of condensation off the mirror. A stranger stared back at her. Alice's skin was dull with dark shadows under her eyes. No way could she go out in public like this. She dried her hair, her fingers moving deftly, twisting the strands into a crown braid.

If she was recognised, which was likely, she was going to look fabulous. People would wish they could look so refreshed and relaxed the day after their husband 'accidentally' broadcast to the world he was a two-pump chump who preferred brunettes. She brushed blush across her cheeks, tilting her face from side to side to make sure her winged eyeliner was even. A few drops of highlighter gave her skin the dewy, carefree look she adored, and she was ready to face the world.

Kind of.

ALICE WASN'T sure why she'd expected Wattle Junction's High Street to look like the Wild West, but she was still disappointed it didn't. Where she'd been imagining saloons with swinging doors were red brick shop fronts, some with second storeys, a handful of take away places, and at the very end, a sweet brick cottage painted a brilliant white with black shutters framing the front windows. At either end of the main block were two roundabouts, each with a massive wattle tree planted in the middle.

She kept her head down, skirting around the outdoor tables with long bench seats until several stands on wheels appeared in her peripheral vision. They were overflowing with shiny red apples, bananas, and zucchinis that were very similar to what Rico now knew Phoenix's penis looked like.

Alice squeezed her eyes shut as the opening refrain of 'We Saved Each Other' played from the speakers in the ceiling. Would she ever escape Phoenix? It was unlikely now his album had gone double platinum. The back of her neck itched, and she twisted around, catching two women pointing at her. She smiled brightly and grabbed some oranges, apples and blueberries—Alice wouldn't be adding scurvy to her list of problems—and she was almost ready to bunker down in her room until this whole nightmare was over. Pushing inside the store, a jar of organic peanut butter and two packets of corn thins completed her shopping.

The older woman behind the register grimaced as Alice

approached. She'd accessorised her green apron with a frown. "Got everything?" she asked, pushing gold-rimmed glasses up her nose.

Alice started to reply but was distracted by the stack of newspapers in front of the counter. It was a funny thing seeing herself on the front page. She'd never really gotten used to it. They'd used a photo from her wedding. *Take a Chance on Love's* logo was stamped in the bottom corner and a computer-generated tear had been placed between her and Phoenix's faces. *Who's really to blame?* was splashed across the top in big, bold letters.

Her basket thudded onto the counter.

Someone said something—in a deep, masculine voice—but it sounded like they were underwater.

The cashier waved her hands in front of her face. "Twenty-four fifty. Alice?"

Alice blinked, her vision clearing and face burning when she realised the cashier knew who she was. "Oh, um. Right." She rummaged through her oversized tote bag, searching for her purse.

"I'll be right with you, Owen," the older lady said.

Oh, God. Not the guy from last night. She'd been so rude to him. Alice's back stiffened, and she gritted her teeth before she reminded herself to smile. There were probably lots of Owens. Even in a town this small. It *was* a reasonably common name.

She tapped her card against the EFTPOS machine and reached for her groceries.

"Shame they don't sell car batteries here, Marguerite," Damn-It-Was-Definitely-Owen said. He smelt offensively good, like citrus and something musky. Sandalwood, maybe.

"Marguerite? Who's Marguerite?" the cashier asked.

Alice stared at her Doc Martens covered in painted

flowers before turning around to face him. Today's suit was dark grey and clung to his muscular frame. She'd noticed how hot he was last night but had hoped it was a trick of the darkness. Owen was clearly a guy who didn't skip any day at the gym—not legs, back or arms. He was muscular *every-where*. His dark blond hair was closely cropped and styled perfectly. He exuded the air of confidence she'd been trying to fake for years.

Meanwhile, here she was looking like a piñata that had been hit a few times but hadn't yet busted open in her cropped silver cardigan with glittery buttons and bright orange denim miniskirt. She was too bright ... too *look at me*. But this was what people expected from her. What she'd taught them to expect.

What did a girl have to do to get access to a time machine?

Owen tilted his head towards her, and she thrilled a little at the question in his eyes. He had no idea who she was. What a nice change.

"She is," he said.

"No, she's not. She's Alice Aspinall. From the TV. The reality show about falling in love with a stranger." The cashier held up the newspaper. "See. The one with the cheating husband."

Confusion crossed his annoyingly handsome face, and Alice was in the process of pasting another defensively large, toothy smile across hers when Owen spoke.

"That makes sense."

"Excuse me?" She imagined laser beams shooting out of her eyes, turning him into a pile of smoking ash. Hopefully, his undoubtedly expensive cologne was extra flammable. The headlines would be worth it. But then she remembered her media training and the disaster that was her life. That would only cause trouble, especially now all the other customers were shamelessly watching them. Alice bit the insides of her cheeks until she worried she might draw blood.

But you know what should be illegal? Smirking. And when Owen smirked at her, Alice decided her media training could go jump. "What makes sense? The fact I have a cheating husband?"

Owen's expression melted. Was that regret in his eyes? Whatever it was, it was gone as quickly as it appeared. "I was talking about the fact you gave me a fake name last night ..." He paused.

The whole freaking store was waiting with bated breath.

"... when I stopped to help you with your broken-down car."

Goddamn heart eyes shot out of every woman in the place. The wave of warmth and affection for him was so tangible Alice really didn't need her cardigan anymore.

What would it be like to have people be genuinely happy to see you? The last time Alice experienced that was when she volunteered at the children's hospital. No one there cared who she was married to. In a previous life, she'd been a children's party entertainer and her face-painting skills were still next level.

Alice was about to reply when the cashier frowned at the register. "Your card's been declined."

For God's sake.

She dug through her bag, almost groaning with relief when she found a few notes at the bottom. "Here." She thrust them towards the register. "Have a good day," she said stiffly, then walked out with her head held high.

Past the whispers.

Past the phones.

Past the pitying, intrigued looks.

She didn't crumple until she'd flicked the lock on her hotel room door.

OWEN JUMPED when the alarm on his phone for footy training buzzed. Truth be told, he didn't want to go. Footy had always been his brother Nate's thing. His brothers had brow-beaten him into agreeing, promising it would be a good way to show everyone he was serious about making a life here. Surely buying the old law office and a half-reno-vated property on the outskirts of town had sent the message that he was home for good, hadn't it? Nothing said commitment like several hundreds of thousands of dollars of debt.

Saving what he'd done for one of the women staying at Kathleen's Place, Owen made a note to review it in the morning. Jessica had tried contacting Legal Aid, and they would have done a good job for her, but time was of the essence. He flicked a quick look at his empty calendar. Time was something he had.

Owen headed to the bathroom to change, but voices in the reception area distracted him. His new secretary, Frankie, stopped laughing when she saw him. She smoothed her curly hair, one hand snagging in the huge gold hoops she wore.

"Owen, hey," she said, her voice infused with cheer and a bit too much familiarity, in his opinion. "Camille stopped by to say hello. I was just about to send her down to your office."

It had been years since he'd seen Camille Arturo, but Owen recognised her immediately. His ex's long dark hair was streaked with blonde and red. Everything about her looked expensive, from her chunky gold bracelets to the rings with colourful stones she wore on every finger. Her body was fuller, more voluptuous. All traces of the gangly girl he'd thought he loved many years ago were long gone.

He'd been expecting someone from the Arturos to make contact once his office was officially open. But given Camille had lived interstate ever since she'd walked out of his life without a backwards glance despite all their years together, he'd assumed one of her brothers would visit. No doubt they were all still unimpressed with his refusal to represent them at his previous law firm. The Arturos weren't used to hearing the word 'no'.

Camille raised her arms to hug him as he thrust his hand forward. A handshake was more than she deserved, but Owen wasn't stupid. Kicking a wasp's nest was never a good idea. Camille squeezed his palm lightly, her lips fixed in a mischievous grin like they still meant something to each other. As though their shared history was filled with warm, fuzzy memories.

"I heard you'd moved back out here. Thought I'd come and say hi while I was in town. Dad told me about the mix up at Malus, Mendax and Associates. We're always looking for good lawyers like you."

'Good' was the wrong way to describe the type of representation the Arturos wanted. Owen had no interest in being in their pocket. And it would undermine the police investigation his other brother Rafferty was leading into their family.

"Your needs would be better met with my old firm," Owen said coolly. "They have more scope and expertise at their disposal."

It wasn't a lie. Malus, Mendax and Associates was the

biggest law firm in Melbourne. A fact he'd prided himself on when he'd been hired. But over the years, as the founding partners retired, everything changed. The firm's staunch morals and ethics had been replaced with new managing partners who had rubber arms and elastic necks. For the right price, anyone could be a client.

When Owen had been tasked with representing Camille's brother, convicted drug dealer Adrian Arturo, the whispers from his conscience had become screams. He'd resigned immediately and been given fifteen minutes to pack up his desk, security guards watching his every move.

A phantom headache reminded him of the hangover he'd woken with the next day. The only thing stopping nausea from consuming him had been the realisation that he was finally free. To be his own boss, really make a change and be closer to his family.

To not just be Owen, the guy who had lost his way.

"Still, you never know. You might change your mind," Camille said, pulling him from his thoughts as she lifted a bottle of scotch out of her Louis Vuitton handbag and offered it to him. The honey-coloured liquid swished from side to side.

"I won't," Owen said.

The corners of Camille's mouth tipped down. "Keep it anyway. We should get a drink some time, too. I'm going to hang around while Mum recovers." Lulu had mentioned that Sofia Arturo had suffered a stroke recently. Sofia and Camille's fractured relationship had obviously been healed.

"I'd rather not, thanks all the same." Owen's tone was clipped.

He strode towards the plate glass door at the front of the office. He pulled it open, breathing in deeply. The fresh air carried a hint of the jasmine that grew along the fence, and his thumping heart slowed. Camille winked at Frankie and strutted over, chest thrust forward.

"Always so proper." Camille rolled her eyes as she pulled a packet of smokes out of her bag, the gold of her lighter glittering. "It's good to see you. I've thought about you a lot over the years."

Bullshit. When she'd been forced to choose between him and the opportunity to get even further away from her family, she hadn't hesitated. And Owen had been so busy with work and trying to build a stable future for them both that he hadn't realised what was going on. Pretending she still cared now was laughable.

Owen exaggerated checking his watch. *Shoot.* He was going to be late for footy training. "No, thanks. Have a pleasant evening."

Owen wanted to be clear from the beginning that James and Associates wasn't a law firm for everyone. It was for good, honest people who really needed help. If he helped enough of them, he'd be able to atone for all his mistakes. He might even finally get some proper sleep.

But if he was ever going to succeed, he'd better get his ass to the oval and remind everyone he was back for good.

3

Owen looked up when there was a soft knock on the door. Eloise, the social worker at Kathleen's Place, pushed back from her desk and smiled warmly as Jessica stepped into the room. Eloise often let Owen use her office when he conducted private meetings here. He stood, wincing when his knee spasmed. A ten-kilometre run the morning after footy training hadn't been his best idea.

"Hey, Jessica." Eloise ushered the younger woman into the office. Eloise's long dark hair was pulled into a ponytail and her T-shirt dress was covered in different coloured spots.

Jessica rubbed her toddler, Sam's, back as she rocked from one side to the other and the boy grabbed a fistful of her plain grey shirt. Her short brown hair stuck out in all directions, a sure sign she'd gotten little sleep. The poor woman had been through so much. She'd ended up homeless and living out of her car with Sam when her ex, Rob, had run off. With no income and several loans she hadn't known about, she'd struggled to get back on her feet.

"Two more teeth are coming through, but we're here now and I want to get this over with," she said.

"Why don't you guys come down to art class once you're done? I've got a play area set up if this little munchkin isn't feeling creative. He can even nap in there," Eloise said.

Jessica rubbed her face with her free hand. "Maybe."

"No pressure," Eloise said, squeezing Jessica's shoulder. "Let's make some time to catch up in the next few days, too." With a nod of farewell to Owen, Eloise left the room, pulling the door closed behind her.

"This won't take long." Owen gestured towards the chair covered in patchwork fabric in front of the desk. "Do you want to sit? Have a quick read of the changes. Once it's signed, I'll submit it and we can get started figuring out this mess."

"I better stand. I really hope Rob doesn't fight this."

It'd be much easier if her ex didn't.

Jessica sniffled loudly and blinked a few times. "You must think I'm an idiot," she said.

"I can assure you I don't." And he really didn't. Owen had lost count of how many people he'd met over the years who found themselves trapped in situations that had spiralled out of their control. Some were easy fixes, some more complex. But they were all important.

Jessica shifted Sam to her other hip, ignoring his squawk of displeasure, and tried to turn the top sheet of paper over. The little boy jerked against her, his small body flailing backwards. Owen reached forward and turned it over for her. He'd offer to hold Sam, but he didn't know the first thing about kids. He could handle a sleeping baby—maybe —but Sam was looking more alert, his big brown eyes scanning the room suspiciously. Owen stretched out his bad leg, some of the tightness around his knee easing.

"All I pay is the court costs? And they'll do a payment plan?"

Owen nodded, reaching for the schedule of fees he'd printed out for her.

"And you won't charge me? Like for real?"

Malus, Mendax and Associates had allowed employees to complete a certain amount of pro bono work each quarter as long as their billable hours didn't decrease. It wasn't widely encouraged, but they certainly didn't hesitate to rebadge it as a community engagement plan when they got bad press. Now he was paying his own wages, it didn't mean he planned to stop. "I'm donating my time."

"Why?"

He smiled at Sam when a chubby hand swung out, reaching for his dark green tie. "I like to help where I can."

Sam lurched forward, and Owen caught the little boy before he fell out of Jessica's arms.

"Buddy, come on," she groaned.

Owen spied a box of toys in the corner of the room. A plastic dump truck was perched on top. He skirted around Jessica and Sam, picking up the toy. He snagged a few plastic blocks as well, perfect for loading into the tray.

"Can I?" he asked, gesturing towards Sam and holding out his arms. He wasn't qualified to hold Sam, but he could sit next to him while he played with a toy.

"That'd be great, thanks." Jessica passed Sam over, and Owen readjusted his grip, hefting him closer to his body. Sam was heavier than expected. He crouched down, kneeling on the shaggy rug. "Do you like dump trucks, Sam?"

The young boy flailed his arms and said something that was clearly meant to be 'dump truck' but unfortunately sounded a lot like 'dumb fuck'.

"How long will this take to process?" Jessica asked, dragging Owen's attention away from Sam.

"Hopefully, he agrees to our terms. If not, we'll get a date for mediation within a few weeks."

Jessica sighed and picked up the pen he'd left next to the papers. Her eyes closed when she was done. "I really appreciate all your help," Jessica said.

"It's no problem."

No one realised how much this work helped Owen, too.

ALICE WAS PAINTING her toenails when her phone rang.

Chris didn't bother with a hello. "I would've never believed you were hiding in some shithole small town if I hadn't seen the shots myself."

In the online pictures from Swift's General Store, Alice's face was partially hidden by Owen's strong back, but it was obviously her.

"You need to get your ass back here so we can sort out this mess."

A glob of polish slid down the side of the bottle, and Alice wiped it away with her finger.

"Phoenix says you're dodging his calls."

"I wonder why. Would you like me to list all the reasons?" All their money was gone. Phoenix had been siphoning it out of their joint account for months. Alice's hands trembled as she shoved the brush into the nail polish bottle.

"It's not an ideal situation, but—"

"Chris!" Alice leapt off the bed, hopping awkwardly to stop her wet nails from making a mess of the carpet. She yanked the heavy, mossy green curtains completely closed.

The walls pressed in on her, the air heavier without the breeze rolling through her window. She lowered her voice. "Have you seen the papers? She wasn't the first."

Of course, he'd have seen the papers. That was Chris's job. Alice had known about the partying, but she'd never realised how out of control Phoenix had gotten.

"Nothing we can't fix, doll. It's all a big misunderstanding."

She rubbed her hand across her face and felt the sticky nail polish smear across her forehead. Hard to *misunderstand* a bank statement with a zero balance or pictures of women lying next to a sleeping Phoenix. Alice took a deep breath, sucking the air all the way into her diaphragm and releasing it in a long whoosh.

She couldn't keep living a lie.

This morning when she'd been up before the sun, she'd gone out for a jog and seen a group of men running together, their feet moving in unison as they joked and chatted with each other. By the time she got back to the hotel, store owners were greeting each other, and the local café was delivering coffee to everyone. Life was simpler here. It felt safer. She could finally breathe properly again. Maybe Alice could stay awhile, get back on her feet.

In a quiet, firm voice, she vocalised what she'd been thinking for over a year. "I want a divorce."

"I know things have been difficult lately, but ..."

Alice flopped on the bed, the springs groaning in a thoroughly unfair way, given her rigorous workout regimen. "Things aren't difficult, Chris. They're horrible. We don't speak unless we have a camera pointed at us or are out in public. He spends his nights God knows where—well, I guess we all know now." She laughed bitterly, ignoring the sting of tears behind her eyes. She wasn't even sad about Phoenix taking his stupid curved penis elsewhere. Not one single tear was from heartbreak. How pathetic was that? Their marriage had been over six months after they'd said their vows, when she realised how cataclysmically dumb she'd been.

"Let's give everyone a chance to cool off." Chris's voice was low, placating ... *infuriating*. "Phoenix will apologise publicly. No marriage is perfect. The comeback's always better than the original, doll. You wait. This might be the ticket to your own reality show."

The thought of inviting even more criticism into her life made Alice woozy. She pulled her shirt away from her body and used it to fan herself.

"You guys are tied up contractually with lots of endorsements, too, so there's plenty to think about."

Says the man who gets fifteen percent of everything.

"I want a div—"

"I'm getting another call," Chris interjected. "Don't say anything else or you'll mess this up for everyone." He hung up, and she stared at the home screen.

It was one thing for her parents to speak to her like she was a child ... at least she'd been *their* child once upon a time, but this ... this was too much.

No more standing still. No more pretending.

She tapped 'divorce lawyer + wattle junction' into Google.

Thankfully, there was one. James and Associates was only a few doors down. *Score another one for small towns.* As soon as she finished her nails, she'd set up an appointment. It'd do her good to get out of the room. Maybe she'd even brave dinner in the pub downstairs.

There was a knock on her door. A strange, gruff voice called her name before heavy footsteps faded away. *Damn.* The paps were already getting antsy.

Maybe she'd wait a little bit longer.

4

Owen hit enter.

Hit it again.

For the ninth time, nothing happened.

How was it possible for someone to be the dux of an undergraduate law program but not be able to work the supposedly simple—according to the reviews—invoicing and accounting program he'd bought for the office?

He cursed loudly, grateful Frankie was finished for the day. She'd shown him this morning, but he'd been distracted by Alice walking past the office followed by a group of cameras. He'd politely rebuffed Frankie's offer to show him again before she'd left because she seemed keen to hang around. There'd been a casual offer to 'grab an early dinner', and Owen wanted to be clear from the start that he didn't mix business with pleasure. Any dalliances would be kept strictly away from his professional life. And his mother's knowledge.

Thumbing through the instruction manual, he tried to figure out what he was doing wrong. He tossed it back onto his desk and undid his tie.

The program was defective. After last week's conversation with Lulu and the heavy-handed hints she'd dropped at trivia on Monday night, he didn't want to ask her for accounting help, even though she'd recommended this program. Owen rubbed his face, remembering the phones still weren't working properly either. All the calls were now going to voicemail and he had no clue why. They'd been working perfectly well two days ago and bam. Starting his own law firm had been full of challenges, mostly administrative, he hadn't anticipated. He should send his old secretary a bunch of flowers for all his gruffness and impatience when she was obviously dealing with technology created by Satan.

He was about to try again when the bell over the front door chimed.

Strange. It was well after five.

Pushing back from the oak desk he inherited from his predecessor, Owen stood and fixed his tie. The thick, cream carpet in the short hallway muffled his steps. He was pleased to note any lingering smell from the pale grey paint he'd chosen had disappeared. He shook his head—really, his mum had chosen the paint and most of the other décor except for the art hanging on the walls. He'd picked the bluey-grey Rothko print for the reception area, and the picture Nate had painted him for Christmas hung behind his desk. It was a swirling mixture of soft greens and blue watercolours, calming and tranquil.

He stepped into the reception area.

"Really?" Alice looked around the room, her hand opening and closing around the strap of the leather bag slung across her body. "You're the lawyer? Huh. The suit makes sense now."

Owen looked down at his navy suit. It was one of his favourites. "Plenty of people dress like this," he said.

Alice rummaged through her bag, scraps of paper falling to the floor as she fished her phone out. "Not here. Not from what I've seen."

He put his hands in his pockets and watched her closely. "From what I hear, you haven't seen much of Wattle Junction. Rumour is you've been bunkered down in your room at the pub."

She pursed her bright red lips and smoothed her hair. It was arranged in that strange twisty style around her head again. She looked like someone from *Game of Thrones* had gotten lost on their way to wardrobe and been attacked with feathers and sequins. If she was trying to hide, why did she always dress to stand out?

"I'm here for some legal advice."

He raised his eyebrows and gestured around the room. "Luckily, that's what we do. I'm sure we can fit you in tomorrow."

Alice's face paled, and she glanced over her shoulder. Late afternoon sunlight sliced through the gaps in the blind, bits of dust dancing lackadaisically in the air. "I tried to get here without anyone following me."

Protectiveness thumped in his chest, and Owen moved out from behind the counter, crossed the floor and peered out the front door. "There are two men with cameras near Swift's and a few sitting outside the pub."

"I want a divorce," Alice blurted out, her shoulders slumping for a second before her perfect posture returned.

He'd handled enough high-profile cases at his old firm to know there'd be a media shitstorm when this got out. The paparazzi would triple within hours. "From Phoenix Storm?"

Signs from the universe weren't his thing, but Owen had always believed in opportunities and standing in front of him—admittedly, in a skirt that looked like a distant relative of Big Bird's had met an untimely demise—was one too big to pass up. A case like this could put his fledgling business on the map.

"Let's go to my office." He gestured towards the hallway. "I'll lock up, so no one interrupts us."

Alice nodded stiffly, the sleek line of her jaw jerking twice before she stalked past him. He caught a whiff of her perfume. It was light and subtle, with a hint of something flowery—a total juxtaposition to her outlandish outfit. He flipped the deadbolt and closed the blinds before following her.

When Owen entered his office, Alice was sitting in the chair in front of his desk, hands folded primly in front of her handbag, her face impressively blank. Owen would've believed the façade if her pulse wasn't noticeably thrumming in her neck.

He rested his elbows on his desk, his gaze catching on the flagged emails in his inbox. There was a new one from his builder with the subject line, *Delayed materials + new quote*. Bad news, no doubt. When Alice didn't say anything and avoided his gaze, Owen broke the silence.

"I looked you up," he said. "People are really invested in your life and marriage."

Her blue eyes snapped up. A small flush bloomed on her neck, skating towards her cleavage. "Which is why I need this divorce to happen quickly. How can we make that happen?"

He pushed back into his chair, the leather moulding to his frame. "It depends."

Alice huffed out a dry laugh, the muted light from his

office window sliding across her face as she shook her head. "On?"

"Did you have a pre-nup? How many assets do you have? Do you have children ..." There hadn't been any mentioned in the articles he'd read, but he had to ask.

Alice's mouth fell open, but she clamped it shut before spitting, "You think I'm the kind of person who'd leave her children behind? With a cheating ex?"

Years of listening to depositions without reacting usually allowed Owen to keep his voice devoid of colour and depth, but her anger made him uneasy. "I don't think anything," he said, the edges of his words harder than normal. He softened his tone—because really, he needed her more than she needed him right now. "I'm trying to establish the facts. That's all."

Alice fiddled with her hair. "There is something you should know."

The wooden desk was hard under Owen's arms as he leant forward.

She took a deep breath, her face pinching, shoulders rounding. It was like looking behind a stage curtain, seeing something he shouldn't. Gone was the brash, fiery Alice he'd always encountered before. A pit opened in his stomach. His years at Malus, Mendax and Associates had reinforced that things were never what they seemed, especially when any sort of fame was involved. "Alice?"

She tugged at her skirt, trying to smooth the feathers so they lay flat. And then the weakness was gone. He imagined armour layering itself across her skin as she pursed her lips and straightened her chin so their gazes met.

"Cash flow is a minor issue at the moment."

She almost had him convinced of her indifference to her

current situation, but the flush staining her neck and chest had spread to her face, her cheeks like two red apples.

Owen opened his mouth to say they could sort out the money later because this was an opportunity too good to be missed. But Alice cut him off, one perfectly manicured hand lifting into the air, a slight sheen to her cheeks and forehead. "I'll figure something out," she said. "But I need a divorce. Fast."

She held his gaze for a beat, her pools of blue drawing him in. One of the things he'd always loved about his job was sorting through problems. The challenge of using the law to find solutions. Helping people.

That must be why he found her so intriguing.

He shook his head to clear it and picked up the leather, monogrammed folio his parents bought him when he graduated.

"Then we'd better get started then, hadn't we?"

EVEN THOUGH ALICE was sitting down, she was sure she was falling. She looked at her banking app again and adjusted her glasses like they were the problem. By her calculations —and she suppressed a shudder at having to trust her mathematical skills—her 'small cash flow issue' meant she'd be homeless by the weekend. Soon her parents would notice the charges she was sneaking on to their emergency credit card.

A text cut through the heavy silence in the room.

> Dougie: Alley Cat, consider this a friendly, casual welfare check from your fave brother. We miss you. When are you coming home?

Alice sighed.

> Alice: Not soon. I've hired a divorce lawyer.
> No offence. Tell Mum and Dad, please. Call
> later. Promise.

She flopped back on the bed. At least this would give her family something to talk about at their biannual 'How Do We Solve A Problem Like Alice' catch-up. It'd pair nicely with their favourite champagne and her mother's famous salmon puffs with dill dressing.

> Dougie: I could've done this for you. Also,
> you might want to tell your husband that it's
> over. Rico says his new video's blowing up
> online.

Panic curled in her stomach, climbing into her chest until it was hard to breathe. She hadn't looked at social media since last night, right after she'd been terminated from her three biggest online campaigns because her brand 'didn't align' with theirs anymore.

Alice snatched her laptop off the small table in the corner of the room, knocking her ring light and several cables to the floor.

It took two seconds to find the post. Phoenix's face was half in shadow, smoke twisting through the air from the incense burning in the bottom corner of the shot.

"I guess I deserve it." Phoenix dragged a hand across his face. "But, Alice, *sötnos*, you have to come back to me. I won't stop until we're together again."

Sötnos was another nickname she no longer cared for, even if it did mean sweetheart in Swedish. He'd only ever used it for show.

That manipulative ... She kicked the bed frame, crum-

pling to the floor when pain shot through her foot. "Ouchh-
hhh." She reached up, her hand slapping against the quilt
cover until her fingers wrapped around her emergency
bottle of rosé. She unscrewed it and took a long swig before
pulling her computer onto her lap. Reading the comments
was always a bad idea, but she couldn't resist.

What are people saying about me now?

And ... it wasn't good. Sure, plenty of people were
ripping Phoenix for cheating, but an equally large number
were blaming Alice. Saying she'd driven him to it? That
she'd be nothing without him? Her bank balance flashed in
front of her eyes again, the mango yoghurt she'd had for
lunch curdling in her stomach as it mixed with the citrus of
her wine.

Alice closed her computer slowly, slumping against the
bed frame and tipping her head back so it rested against the
mattress. She had two options, and both made her want to
cry. She could actually ask her parents for money instead of
charging things to their credit card and use it to find somewhere to live and pay Owen. Suffer through the accompa-
nying lecture punctuated with several 'we told you sos'. Or
she could go along with pretending there was a chance they
could reconcile until she had a proper escape plan ... She
slid down to the floor until the carpet itched against her
neck and arms.

> Phoenix: Stop being a drama queen & come
> fix this. You're behaving like a child.

Her gaze snagged on the box she'd hidden in the far
corner under her bed.

Good Lord. She was an idiot. The answer to her problems had been right in front of her ... well, technically under

her … this whole time. Alice slid under the bed and stretched out, her fingers wrapping around the small box.

She scuttled backwards, blowing out a long breath once she could sit up. Nestled inside on rich red velvet were her engagement ring and wedding band. She thought she'd feel something when she looked at her rings, but they may as well have belonged to someone else. Maybe because the four-carat pear-shaped diamond and chunky wedding band weren't what she would have chosen? Maybe it was because she realised mere months after Phoenix put them onto her finger that she'd made the biggest mistake of her life? *What was I thinking?* But she hadn't been thinking, had she? Instead, she'd gotten swept up in a manufactured love story, not realising she was interchangeable. Nothing more than a pawn in someone else's game.

None of that mattered now, though.

She had a plan. Unintentionally, Phoenix had given her exactly what she needed to get out of her current mess.

Alice grabbed her lights and tripod. Another long gulp of wine burnt down her throat.

There was no need to ask her parents to bail her out yet again. She had another way to get the money she needed to be free from him for good.

If Phoenix wanted to get her attention by posting videos online, she'd return the favour. Two could play at his game.

5

Alice ducked behind a wizened gum tree surrounded by dropped branches when she heard voices behind her. She crouched behind the thick trunk and rested her palms against the rough bark. She couldn't face people this early in the morning. The whole point of exploring the local running trails had been to clear her head and implement her plan for the deposits she'd received for her rings. The sound drew nearer, and she peered between the moss-covered branches.

A tall man breezed along the fire track, his dark curls moving in time with his cadence. Several others followed a few steps behind, the easy camaraderie of friendship palpable in the air around them as they chatted amongst themselves. Most of the group wore matching faded khaki-coloured running shirts and caps with a wallaby stitched in grey thread. She recognised the owner of the Wattle Junction Hotel by his chin-length dark brown hair and half sleeve of tattoos. Wyatt. That was his name.

And then she saw him. Her mouth dropped open. She

snapped it shut lest she swallow one of the bugs crawling all over her hiding spot.

Owen.

But not the suited-up Owen who always looked ready to dominate a court room. His sweat-darkened hair glowed in the bright morning sunlight. Alice leant forward to get a better look at the scruff covering his jaw and how his black singlet clung to his well-defined chest and broad shoulders. Based on his muscular physique, she'd pegged him as a gym junkie, not a runner. Sure, he was in the back half of the pack, his eyes fixed on the slightly overgrown trail, but he was moving quickly with the confidence of someone who ran these hills regularly. His quads bunched and flexed, the strength of his body on display with every step he took.

He was getting closer to her tree when a few drops of sweat slid down his neck, and she pressed her lips together, imagining how salty his skin would be. How warm his body would be ... If she'd been standing, she might've swayed a little on her feet. Skipping breakfast had been a mistake. Based on her body's reaction to his top half, she didn't trust herself to look too closely at his shorts.

But ... *woah*, Owen lifted the bottom of his singlet without breaking his stride, wiping the perspiration away. Alice's eyes betrayed her, drifting lower to his surprisingly tanned stomach. A dusting of hair pointed down to his ...

She shook her head, freezing when the leaves around her rustled loudly. She closed her eyes and breathed in deeply. Eucalyptus tickled her nose. When she looked back, he was gone.

It wasn't like she liked him or anything.

He wasn't her type. He thought she was useless. She had a husband.

All this tumbled around her mind, mocking her and the ache in her body.

So what. He was a good-looking guy. That wasn't news to her. Seeing him like this was just unexpected, which explained why she was so rattled by his appearance. And it'd been a long time since she'd had sex. God, it had been even longer since she'd been hugged. She was craving comfort, clearly. Nothing a bubble bath, some Netflix and a glass of wine couldn't fix.

Alice stayed hidden until the only thing she could hear was the occasional cockatoo squawking and the pounding of her heart. Checking her watch, she turned around and headed back towards the start of the trail. For the first time in a week, she had an appointment she couldn't miss. The privacy she craved was finally within reach.

ALICE WAS ALMOST at her car when she saw Chris.

Damn. She plastered a big smile on her face. God forbid she made him mad, although judging by the steely expression in his eyes, it was already too late.

"I figured if you wouldn't take my calls, I'd come to you." He was dressed in his usual uniform of an open-necked business shirt and pressed slacks. His salt and pepper hair was slicked back, the platinum of his watch a sharp contrast to his tanned skin.

Alice tucked a loose strand of hair behind her ear. Today's braid wasn't her usual standard because she'd stayed in the shower too long trying to avoid thinking about Owen's shoulders and chest and ... and now she was running late. If the showerhead had been one of those adjustable ones on a hose, she might never have gotten out or been able to look at her lawyer without blushing. She pressed her thighs together, silently chiding herself.

"Walk with me." Chris pointed towards the park across the road with his takeaway coffee cup. "Or better yet, let's just go back to the city."

"I've got an appointment, sorry." Alice's words were hollow, with no trace of her pretend apology. She'd have to do better to avoid a scene.

"I wasn't asking." Chris crossed his arms and blocked the driver's side door of her car. "Quite the stunt you pulled with your rings," said the man who had rebuffed every one of her attempts to stage an intervention for Phoenix's partying, maybe even organise a stint in rehab, citing the 'bad optics' of those suggestions and gaslighting Alice into thinking she was over-reacting.

Alice straightened. She didn't want to make a spectacle of herself, but she wouldn't be bullied. Not today. Not when her ticket to more freedom was within her reach. The other night had been a victory for her, and one she'd really needed. Selling her rings was going to solve a lot of her problems. And, *fine*. It had been fun. She'd gone live every time she'd hit a milestone bid, whipping her followers into a frenzy. Pissing Phoenix off was the cherry on top of her independence-flavoured sundae.

"What were you thinking? Now no one will believe you guys are getting back together. And what about Phoenix? He's trying to fix this, and you do this to him?"

Alice was suddenly very aware of how quiet the street was. A group of older women, including the grumpy cashier from Swift's General Store, were sitting at a table outside the pub, their coffees forgotten as they watched her. Wyatt was pretending to clear a table near the door, too.

"We can talk later," Alice said to Chris.

"No." Anger simmered in his tone.

When she'd first met Chris, he'd been all smiles and big promises. He'd pledged to help them transform their fifteen minutes of fame into an empire. But somewhere along the line, the focus had shifted to Phoenix and his music career. Alice had become nothing but a commodity.

"Could you move, please?" She spoke through gritted teeth.

"No."

Alice sucked in the cool air, kept her hands wrapped around the strap of her bag. She wouldn't give him the satisfaction of seeing her rattled. A painful silence extended between them until Chris pushed off her car and lumbered towards her. It took everything she had not to step backwards. The scent of cigarettes and extra minty gum washed over her. The thick sole on her Doc Martens added a few extra centimetres, but Chris still loomed over her.

She jumped when a hand touched her elbow.

"Everything okay here?" Owen asked. Where'd he come from? He was still in his workout gear, flanked by three other men also in running shorts and slouchy jumpers. Alice recognised them from the group she'd seen running earlier that morning. They all held steaming coffee cups and varying expressions of concern.

"Alice?" Owen asked again.

Like he'd flicked a switch, Chris smiled, his perfect teeth gleaming. "Christian Lamorne, pleased to meet you."

Owen ignored Chris's extended hand. He tilted his head towards Chris, but his eyes never left hers. "Friend of yours?"

"My manager." Alice tried to smile but imagined she looked like she'd eaten some bad fish. "He's leaving." She tried to inject some confidence into her tone, but Chris spoke over her.

"Alice always loves to meet a fan, but we're in the middle of a business meeting, so if you could excuse us ..."

Owen looked between them, his forehead wrinkling as he raised his eyebrows. "Sounds like you're done here, mate."

Chris's smile turned predatory, his friendly pretence discarded like one of the designer suit jackets he bought by the dozen. "And this doesn't concern you, *mate*," he said to Owen.

Owen slid a business card from the back of his phone case. "As Ms Aspinall's lawyer ..."

Chris whipped his gaze towards Alice. This time, she did step back. The heel of her boot caught in a crack in the pavement, and she stumbled. Owen grabbed her, the heat of his palms scorching through the long sleeves of her polka-dot blouse.

"Alice doesn't need a lawyer."

"That's not your decision."

The hard edge to Owen's words snapped Alice out of her shock. She ignored the itch at the back of her neck and inched away from him, breaking the physical contact between them. Something flickered across his face before disappearing, but she didn't have time to analyse it.

"It's fine," she murmured.

Chris's thin lips stretched into a saccharine smile. "I knew you'd come to your senses, doll. Now, let's get you out of this shithole," he said loudly, and the women watching shot open looks of derision at Chris ... and her.

"This place is great," she snapped, but it was too late. The damage was done.

"Listen—" Owen started, but Alice held up her hand.

"He's right." She nodded towards Chris. "This doesn't involve you."

"If this guy's harassing you ..." Owen lowered his voice and leant closer to her.

The men with Owen traded a look, and she was so done with this.

Done with everyone telling her what to do.

Done with people expecting her to behave a certain way.

She was supposed to be figuring out where she would sleep that night, for God's sake. Not dealing with a pissing contest and alienating the locals even more than she already had.

Owen and Chris stared at her.

Everyone stared at her.

Alice almost believed she had eaten bad fish for breakfast from the way her stomach roiled.

"Right. If neither of you will leave, I'll go. Problem solved." She brushed past them all, her head held high as she pushed back inside.

She didn't stop until she was in her room. Even the strange menagerie of animals decorating the walls and light fixtures watched her closely, judging her with their beady little eyes.

She couldn't keep going like this. Caring so much.

She tore her hair out of its stupid crown braid, her shoes thudding into the wall as she kicked them off and fell face forward onto her bed.

She groaned, burying her face in the floral quilt.

Her life was a disaster. Like always.

And now she'd missed her chance to inspect the only house available in her price range in Wattle Junction until the rest of her ring money cleared. With no active campaigns secured or even promotion opportunities on the horizon, she was determined not to make the same mistakes again.

But why did everything have to be so hard all the time?

~

"So that's Alice, huh?" Teddy rocked back on his chair, stretching his long legs out until his feet rested on the corner of the kitchen table. He twisted his shoulder-length dirty blond hair into a bun.

Owen shoved his brother's legs out of the way as he sat down. Maybe letting Teddy rent the small apartment above his new law office had been a mistake. "It is."

"Seems like she really enjoyed you butting in," his older brother Rafferty said without looking up from his phone.

"I especially liked the way she acted like you'd electrocuted her when you touched her. It's a unique skill to have." Teddy smirked, crossing his arms behind his head, exuding the casual confidence most twenty-four-year-olds had. "I always assumed you never brought anyone home from the city because you didn't want to excite Mum, but now I get it. You're bad with women. You've got no game."

That got a laugh out of Rafferty and Nate, who was rummaging through the fridge. Assholes.

"Shut up. She looked like she needed help."

Teddy stood and pushed Nate aside, grabbing a pizza box from the fridge. "Here's a novel concept: you don't have to help everyone." He pulled out a slice before offering the rest to his brothers. Rafferty helped himself, but Owen and Nate shook their heads.

"Come on." Owen looked at Rafferty and Nate for support. "It was obvious something wasn't right there."

"Exactly, but someone else could've stepped in." Teddy flopped back into his seat, his runners automatically returning to the top of the table. "It didn't have to be you. Wyatt was keeping an eye on her. You've got a saviour complex."

Owen pushed Teddy's feet off the table again and moved to refill his water bottle, anything to escape his brother's smug grin. "It's called being a decent human being, Ted. Maybe you should look it up. Besides, she's new in town and ..." He paused, and his brothers perked up, waiting expectantly for him to continue. "She's my client."

"So?" Teddy asked around a mouthful.

"It's literally my job to help her."

Teddy pushed a chunk of hair that had escaped his man bun behind his ear. "It's your job to get her a divorce, not be her bodyguard. Why'd she marry that idiot, anyway?"

That was the question Owen had been asking himself for the last few days. The background checks he'd run had all come up clear. Alice didn't seem like the type to idolise a rockstar. He shrugged.

"How's business going?" Nate pushed his shaggy brown hair away from his face and changed the topic. Owen shot his brother a small smile.

"Slow, but fine." He pulled his phone out of the front pouch of his hoodie, brushing away the errant fleecy fibres that clung to the back of it. It wasn't eight yet, but he was suddenly desperate for his own space. He needed to follow up on a few things for Jessica's case today. A lawyer representing Rob had left a message for him yesterday, which made him think the easy slam dunk case they'd been hoping for wasn't going to happen. "Speaking of which, I'd better get in the shower."

He grabbed his suit bag from the hook on the back of

the front door. The hot water system at his place was dying a slow death, so he usually showered here after his morning run. "Any luck with your roommate search?" he asked Teddy.

His brother stopped picking pineapple pieces off his slice, looking up as he licked his fingers. "Are you asking as my brother or as my landlord?"

The apartment had been included in the sale of the building, but Owen had never planned to live in it. The temptation to duck downstairs and keep working late into the night would've been too great. Instead, he'd chosen the little detached studio that was part of the land he'd purchased on the outskirts of Wattle Junction. Teddy's offer to move in here had been an ideal solution. And it was, mostly. But with his bills piling up, the extra rent from another tenant would ease some of the pressure.

"Either. Both." Owen toed off his runners while he waited for a response.

"Seeing as though you keep vetoing my mates and this town is the size of a thimble, I'm a bit stuck. And I don't want to live with a stranger."

Owen picked up his black leather toiletries bag. "Keep me posted, okay? The sooner, the better."

"Like you need the money," Teddy scoffed as he moved to the futon in the corner and picked up an Xbox controller.

When Owen turned around, he could practically see the wheels turning in Rafferty and Nate's heads. Between Rafferty's detective training and Nate's overflowing bank account, thanks to his years overseas in the NFL, it was obvious what was going to come next.

"Is everything—?" Nate asked.

The idea of his family knowing how much he'd overextended made Owen answer too quickly. "Just seems good business sense to have as much incoming cash as I can while I'm starting out."

He felt his brothers' eyes on him until the bathroom door closed.

He could only keep this ruse up for so long.

6

It was always horrible when a client cried. It didn't matter if they were angry or sad tears, big or small. Thank goodness Eloise had taken Sam for a walk so Owen and Jessica could talk in private. Big, gulping breaths shook her small frame. "I'm sorry. I'm wasting your time."

"Not at all." He nudged the tissue box closer to her. "When you're ready, we can go through the custody split they've proposed and the financial implications."

"But I don't want Rob to have Sam! I don't care about the money." Jessica buried her face in her hands.

Owen picked up his pen, eager to start working on a solution. "I know, but we need to comb through their proposal so we can refute it and argue that our suggestion is what's best for Sam."

Jessica sniffed. "I don't get it. He hasn't seen Sam for over a year and now he wants fifty-fifty custody? Suddenly he has money to support him? Since when? Why is he doing this?"

"If you were to agree to an equal split—"

Jessica shot to her feet. "I won't!"

"And I'm not suggesting you should. Just explaining that

it would have an impact on any child support. Possibly that's a motivator for Rob?"

Owen pulled the document up on his laptop as Jessica paced around the room. "Apparently, he's been trying to get money to you ever since he started working. They've attached phone receipts from when he called and sent messages. There's also a record of the bank account he's opened for Sam."

"I never got those messages. I had to sell everything to clear Rob's gambling debts, and then I ended up changing numbers to stop the loan sharks from harassing me."

Right. Owen could do this. Help Jessica get the best outcome for Sam and herself. "Is there anything else I should know about Rob? Now that we know he wants to fight for custody?"

"I guess there is something he might bring up ..."

Call him a cynic, but there was almost always something. Owen waited.

"I've got a criminal record."

He swallowed a sigh. Why hadn't she ever mentioned this before? And why hadn't he checked like he usually would? "What for?"

"I got done for public intoxication during O'Week at uni. Only once and it was years ago, but a conviction was recorded because there were so many of us and we got a bit gobby with the cops. I'm not proud of it."

"Okay." Owen made a few notes. This complicated things, but it wasn't the end of the world. They could still secure the outcome Jessica wanted.

"Does this change anything? For you, I mean. Do you not want to help anymore? Especially now this is going to drag on?" Jessica whispered and dabbed her red nose.

Owen was going to lose more billable hours than he'd

expected, but his determination to see it through to the end didn't waver. "I'm still happy to help."

Jessica slumped down in her chair. "How will I ever repay you?"

Owen shook his head. Chalking up another win for the good guys would help balance out the times he hadn't listened to his conscience at his old job.

"Oh my God!" Frankie's gasp echoed down the hallway, and Owen hurried out of his office. He would've waited in the reception area, but his secretary had been batting her eyelashes so dramatically at him he'd almost googled if it was possible to strain your eyelids.

Alice was frozen in the doorway, her delicate features arranged into a look of mild horror. Outside, cameras clicked, and people jostled to get a better shot of her. Her hair was different today, falling in loose curls that skimmed the top of her breasts. Owen told himself that he didn't know why he'd noticed that. He cleared his throat, his breath catching when her blue eyes locked on to his. She'd done something different with her make-up today too. Her lips were a soft pink.

Frankie jumped to her feet. "I'm so excited you're here. I can show you around town if you'd like. Or maybe you need a friend to talk to? With everything going on in your life now? Oh my God, did you see Phoenix's live serenade the other night? It was so sweet." She was looking at Alice the way a child looks at a new puppy.

"Frankie." Owen's voice was low, heavy with warning. She either didn't hear or chose to ignore him, rounding the counter so quickly Alice visibly recoiled, her back flush against the plate glass door.

"I loved *Take a Chance on Love!*" Frankie's wide grin reminded him of those arcade clowns you throw balls at. "I've watched your season so many times. It's the best one. When Phoenix proposed, it was so dreamy."

"Frankie!" Owen sidestepped his secretary. "Alice, come through." Her gaze snapped back to his face, her eyes widening for a second before returning to normal.

"Why'd you change your hair?" Frankie asked Alice. She pushed her frizzy brown hair behind her ears. "I've watched your crown braid YouTube tutorial a million times, but the twist is like ... my hair goes the wrong way or something? Maybe you could ..."

"Don't you have something to do?" Owen looked pointedly at Frankie's desk which was covered in scraps of paper and the rubbish from her lunchtime burrito. She'd offered to get him one when she'd ducked out for hers, but he'd declined.

"Could I just get a quick selfie ..." Frankie trailed off when Owen glared at her.

He reached towards Alice, who was pressed up against the door so tightly she should really buy it dinner. He hesitated, remembering how she'd flinched when he touched her earlier, and stuffed his hand in his pocket. "I'll meet you in my office," he said, nodding towards the hallway when she looked at him blankly.

Dazed, she swallowed before squaring her shoulders and walking quickly to his office.

He waited until Alice had disappeared, turning to face Frankie. "Remember the NDA you signed? Not one word, please. If they come inside, come get me."

Frankie nodded vigorously. "I was only trying to be friendly ..."

"I'M SORRY ABOUT THAT." Owen closed the door and unbuttoned his jacket.

"It's always nice to meet a fan." Alice grimaced, rolling her head from one side to the other. "That's a lie. It's still weird to me that people know who I am. And most people forget there's nothing real about social media and reality TV. She's probably texting everyone about what a cow I am."

When Alice looked back at him, her eyes were shiny. They were also extra blue today, like the deep water of the ocean. His gut told him the real Alice was nothing like who everyone thought she was. Owen straightened the papers he'd prepped on his desk and croaked out, "She won't."

What is wrong with my voice?

He cleared his throat and picked up his pen. "Right. Shall we dive right in? I've got your bank statements and contracts, but there's no lease or mortgage or title deed. Where were you living?"

A hint of colour appeared on Alice's cheeks as her spine straightened before she hurriedly explained that they'd been living rent-free in one of her parents' apartments.

They spent the next thirty minutes working through her financial and employment situation in greater detail. Everything was tied up together—bank accounts, promotional contracts they'd now defaulted on or had been cancelled, a loan for a car Phoenix had written off six months ago. He was thumbing through one of her contracts when she cursed quietly and tossed her phone into the handbag on her lap.

"Everything okay?" he asked. This time it wasn't the blueness of her eyes that took him by surprise. It was how glassy they were. All of Alice's bravado was gone.

"I need to find somewhere to live. There was a place on Peach Street I was going to inspect this morning, but that didn't happen and now it's gone."

Guilt made Owen shift in his seat. That must have been where she was going when he saw her with her manager. Inadvertently his gaze drifted to the apartment over their heads. Teddy's warning rang in his ears.

"The real estate lady said rentals can be hard to come by." Alice buried her face in her phone, one neon green fingernail scrolling so quickly he knew she needed a second to herself.

Sod Teddy's opinion.

"I might have a solution for you," Owen said.

"THE ACCESS IS AT THE BACK."

Alice watched Owen pull a set of keys from his pocket. When he opened the heavy door at the back of his store-room, sunlight spilt through, and she recognised his white Jeep. There was also an old grey hatchback and a battered silver ute with a missing side mirror.

He poked his head out before ushering her up the single set of stairs with chipped white railings. A gentle breeze ruffled Alice's hair, and she tucked it behind her ears. The jasmine flowers growing along the fence gave off a rich, sweet smell.

Owen knocked twice before inserting the key into the lock. "Ted? You home?"

When there was no reply, he opened the door. The

sound of running water and muffled heavy metal emanated from somewhere in the apartment. Alice focused on her breathing, trying to calm the nerves twisting around the base of her spine. A roommate wasn't ideal, but sharing the cost of a place would help her conserve her money for as long as possible.

Please be okay. Please be nice.

Her sneakers squeaked on the linoleum floor, her grip tightening around her cross-body bag.

The apartment was cosy, with large arch-shaped windows on either side of the front balcony. A navy and white striped hammock stretched from one end to the other. The interior was neat and mostly clean, with a few takeaway pizza boxes stacked next to the bin. Dark green subway tiles, probably from the first time they were fashionable, made up the splashback and matched the pale green paint. The oven looked like it was from the last century and the range hood over the cooktop had seen better days. A new-ish-looking fridge had been placed at the end of the counter. Two magnetic bulldog clips held a roster and footy fixture.

Owen scratched the back of his neck, then turned to face her. "It's not much, but everything works. Teddy will be at uni or work most of the time."

Alice spun in a slow circle. It was kitschy, kind of cute. Most importantly, it was cheap, and Owen had said she could pay the bond and the first two months when the rest of her money cleared.

She put her handbag on the small wooden table with four dining chairs that sat on top of a braided grey rug. Instead of a couch, there was a denim-covered futon with sports-themed cushions. A flat-screen TV was mounted on the opposite wall, and the entertainment unit was covered in gaming consoles. The three empty beer bottles next to the Xbox made her pause.

"Spare room's this way," Owen said, leading her down the hall past another arched window.

She looked around his shoulder, pleasantly surprised by the size of the room. A queen bed would fit, but a double would be better. It was empty except for a mattress propped against the far wall and an old wooden wardrobe. The doors had mirrors attached, reflecting the light streaming through the big window. The curtains matched the beige-coloured carpet; vacuum cleaner tracks were still visible in it.

It was nothing like her old apartment.

Which was perfect, really.

And with a few small touches like an ivy plant in a cute pot on the window and maybe some new curtains, if she could be bothered, it'd be nice and homey. She'd set up her ring lights, camera gear and computer in the far corner. Storing her clothes would be a challenge, but that wasn't a new problem. It was time for another wardrobe cull, anyway, and she could donate the profits to the children's hospital again.

Alice walked to the window. The blue water of the Wattle Junction community pool peeked out from behind the small hall. She was only a few blocks away from her room at the pub, but everything seemed different from here. Quieter. Nicer.

The mountains she'd run through this morning glowed in the afternoon sunshine. Now everyone knew where she was, she couldn't wait to use them in promo shoots. And there'd be a lot of those in her future now she had to support herself. It wasn't like she had any other marketable skills. If she could convince brands to give her another chance. She promised herself this time it would be different, though; she'd only work with companies she really trusted. It still stung that everyone had dropped her.

Alice looked over her shoulder when Owen spoke. "I'll go make sure Teddy knows we're here."

She slid down the wall until her fingers were twisted in the soft carpet and looked at the blank canvas in front of her.

This could work.

ALICE PAUSED IN THE HALL.

"Wait, what? A roommate? Since when?" a deep voice asked. Teddy, obviously.

"Shhhhhh," Owen hissed. "Alice's in her room."

"She's already here? And what do you mean 'her room'?"

She crept backwards when she heard footsteps, pretending to inspect the wardrobe. Damn thing shrank every time she looked at it.

"First, you scare the shit out of me by waiting outside the bathroom—"

"I said 'hey' when you opened the door."

"—and then you tell me a stranger's moving in with me."

"Alice needs somewhere to live, and I don't want to hear it, okay? I know what you're going to say."

Maybe this wasn't such a good idea. She was letting someone else solve her problems for her. Again.

"Fine," Teddy grumbled. "But you have a problem."

Owen's heavy sigh seeped through the apartment, and Alice snuck outside, her curiosity piqued by the mention of his mysterious problem.

"Just don't let on that she's living here, okay? Frankie almost wet her pants with excitement."

Teddy sniggered. "Sure she wasn't looking at you? You should've heard her at trivia. Banging on about how she'd like to play boss and naughty secretary. Although, from what Mum said, she'll have to get in line. When is dinner with ..." Teddy's voice faded, but it sounded an awful lot like he said, 'Horse Face'. Alice's stomach twisted, and she was abnormally disappointed to learn Owen was like every other guy out there.

She stomped down the hallway.

The brothers spun around in unison. Aside from their brown eyes, there really weren't any similarities between them. Owen was the picture of professionalism in his grey suit and navy tie. His brother, however, was wearing light blue jeans and a sage shirt with 'Wattle Junction Hotel' printed on the front. He had a deep tan and a beard her brother and Rico would write poetry about.

"Alice, great. This is Teddy. Teddy, Alice," Owen said.

"It's nice to meet you," she said, shaking his hand. "I think I've seen you at the pub?" It was hard not to notice the mega-tall bartender who looked like a Viking.

Teddy smiled. "Likewise. And speaking of the pub, I'd better get going. My shift starts in ten. When are you moving in?"

"As soon as possible? But what's with the mattress in the room?" She'd have to figure out how to get her stuff from Melbourne.

"That's Owen's old one. He'll get rid of it for you."

"Would you mind if I borrowed it? Until I can get my stuff here?"

"That's fine," Owen said at the same time Teddy said, "It's practically brand new. Never saw any action, did it, little fella?"

Owen mostly ignored his brother's jibe, an exasperated

expression anyone with a sibling would recognise settling on his face. She'd never seen him look so … normal. How could a smile so small change the entire structure of his face? Light shone from his eyes, and his lips curled softly. A desire to make him laugh struck her. A big belly laugh that made tears spring to his eyes and his cheeks hurt. She'd bet he didn't give those away often. He'd make people work for them, but oh boy, it'd be worth it if she could make it happen.

"Maybe Alice will get to live here alone," Owen said.

And what? A joke? The teasing lilt to his voice was so charming it should be illegal.

She ducked her head, her long blonde hair falling across her face like a curtain, her lips pulling into a grin. Her chest tightened. Also, God, she missed Dougie and Rico. Moving out of the pub would mean they could visit her.

"Please. He's all talk. I'm his favourite brother. Make yourself at home," Teddy said, slipping his phone into his pocket and grabbing a set of keys off a little hook next to the door.

His heavy footsteps clattered down the stairs.

"Teddy seems fun," she said once they were alone again.

Owen filled a glass with water and leant against the counter. "He goes alright."

Alice picked up her bag and slung it over her shoulder. Before she agreed to this, she had to know one thing. Teddy didn't seem like the type to take pictures of her while she was sleeping, but this wasn't going to work if he had people over all the time. "Seems like he'd be a popular guy. Does he have a girlfriend?"

Owen drained his glass before putting it in the dishwasher. "Teddy doesn't do girlfriends. He likes variety, and he doesn't usually get involved with women from around here if that's what you're asking." The dishwasher door thumped shut.

Heat rushed to her face. "God. No. I didn't mean it like *that*. Not for me. I was checking if there'd be people here all the time. That's all. My long-haired, charismatic men phase is well and truly over. I'm not looking for a date. From anyone. Probably ever. What's your policy on cats because there are at least fifty in my future? Maybe more." Alice snapped her mouth closed, willed herself to stop speaking. The only person she'd thought about in *that way* was standing in front of her. Thinking she was keen on his brother.

God.

Owen's eyes were confused, but his mouth quirked up into a shadow of a smile. His tongue peeked out, sweeping across the plush, full pad of his bottom lip.

It was adorable.

He was adorable.

Like he found her inability to control her mouth despite weeks of media training was cute. And there was no way he thought she was cute. Was there?

Owen picked up his phone. "A pet would be fine if it didn't make a mess. I'll text you Teddy's number and organise some keys this afternoon."

"Great. And it will only be for a few months, tops."

As she followed Owen down the stairs, not looking at his ass in those gorgeous tailored pants, Alice promised herself she'd only stay until she was back on her feet and had paid off all her debts. Then she'd get her own place in Melbourne.

Be responsible for herself.

Live in the real world.

Finally.

7

"I like it," Dougie said, stepping into Alice's apartment for the first time three weeks after she'd moved in. He passed her a bottle of whiskey and her favourite rosé.

Rico gave her a kiss on the cheek. He was carrying a suspiciously large box.

"Was anyone outside?" Alice peered out into the car park. Owen had put up several 'No Trespassing' signs after finding cameramen and fans in the rear car park throughout the last week. He'd also called in a favour from his police officer brother—Owen seemed to have an endless supply of both: brothers and favours—and a few extra police patrols had helped deter people.

"Nope, it's very quiet out there." Rico put the box and a pair of scissors on the kitchen table. "Except at the pub. It's rammed."

"It's trivia night. Teddy invited me, but I'm still keeping a low profile."

Things had been full-on ever since news of her meetings with Owen broke. She'd ignored several calls from Phoenix and Chris before letting Owen take over all communication. He'd gone through their bank statements and contracts and sent a letter of intent to Phoenix. So far, he hadn't replied. Shocker.

"Can you make the cocktails, babe, while I give Alice her present?" Dougie batted his eyelashes at Rico, who was already pulling sugar cubes, bitters and oranges out of a bag.

"We wanted to get you something to celebrate this new stage of life." Dougie tapped his fingers against the big box.

"I suggested a vibrator," Rico called from the kitchen. "But Mr Fun Police"—he tilted his chin towards Dougie— "wouldn't have it."

Dougie groaned, adjusting his glasses before running his hands through his sandy blond hair. As usual, it was a mess. "Let's not revisit this topic of discussion, please. I'm still traumatised."

"No one should be ashamed about meeting their own needs, babe."

Alice tried to smile, to give them the level of excitement they deserved, but she was still flat after Owen's call a few hours ago. He'd renegotiated her biggest contract so she could appear solo, but they were paying her less—a lot less —and if her brand engagement decreased further, they'd probably cancel the whole thing again. She'd spent her afternoon prepping three content shoots to show them she was serious.

The scissors sliced through the tape, and she pulled the flaps of the box open, digging through a mountain of bubble wrap before her hands closed around something heavy. It was a bag of wax. Five bags, actually.

Did they think she wanted to be a beautician?

That wouldn't work—there was already a hair and

beauty place on High Street. She'd never win over the locals if she tried to steal business from them. Most still threw her a healthy serve of side eye when she went out.

"Um, thanks?"

"It's a candle making kit!"

Oh. But what was she going to do with a candle making kit? Aside from making candles. But why would she do that?

"We figured you must have a bit of spare time now. And you've always been so creative and good at working with your hands."

"Which is why the vibrator would've been a good idea," Rico teased as he set three Old Fashioned cocktails on the table.

Dougie nudged her in the side. "It's okay if you hate it. Honest. We won't be offended."

"I don't know how to make candles."

"There are instructions." Dougie rifled through the box. "Here." He thrust a glossy booklet at her. Alice blinked as the words swam in front of her eyes. She'd have to add going to the optometrist for a check-up to her never-ending list of jobs.

"How about we let Alice have a look at this later," Rico said, picking up cocktails and passing them around. "Let's christen this place with a proper toast and then dig into the sushi we brought."

Alice had always loved Rico but never more so than in these moments when he picked up on her panic, something her family had never properly mastered. Whenever the conversation turned too academic, he was always there to ask her what she thought of the latest episode of *RuPaul's Drag Race*.

"To Alice for starting over again!" Dougie raised his glass.

Okay, it was a backhanded compliment, but Dougie never meant to upset her.

"For such a smart person, you sure say dumb stuff," Rico mumbled. "To Alice, who we love and adore. For being brave enough to take chances and always saying yes to adventure. May we all be more like you."

"Isn't that what I said?" Dougie muttered.

Oh yes, this place was starting to feel like home.

"WHAT ARE THE LOCALS LIKE? Are they nice?" Dougie picked up the last piece of California roll.

Alice tried to smile, but her face wouldn't cooperate. "I've mostly been keeping to myself."

"And what about hot guys in flannel?" Rico sighed as he played with the metal straw in his cocktail. "Who get up early to feed orphaned lambs? That happens here, right? This is a Hallmark movie, yes?"

Owen came to mind immediately. Despite the fact she'd never seen him in anything other than a suit or his running gear, she had no trouble picturing him with a tiny lamb curled up against his plaid-covered chest, bicep popping as he bottle-fed it. She took a too-big gulp of her cocktail, the bitters and spices burning her throat. Her eyes watered, and Rico passed her a serviette.

"Okay, spill," he said. "Who'd you imagine? It's Tom Hardy for me."

Alice coughed, then wiped her mouth. "I didn't ... no lumberjacks for me."

The memory of how earnest Owen had been when he asked if she'd mind him using the shower in the apartment after his morning runs ran through her mind. The thought of him in her shower made her blush. She always left for her run half an hour before he was due to get here.

"Look at her face! There so is!" Rico crowed, and Alice ducked her head, prising open an edamame bean. "Who is it? Oh my God! Is it your flatmate? Because I stalked him on TikTok, and if he's half as hot in real life, that gene pool would be a very welcome addition to our family. Is he a doctor? He was wearing scrubs in one and wow."

"Because our family needs another doctor in it? The dean of medicine at Melbourne's biggest university and chief of surgery at St Clementine's Hospital isn't enough?" Alice tried to keep the snark out of her voice when she mentioned her parents.

Rico put his glass down, waggled his eyebrows suggestively and ignored her groan. "Not if he looks like that in scrubs."

"He's studying to be a dentist. And there's no one," she mumbled. "Even if there was, and I'm not saying there is, it's not like it could go anywhere. My life's a dumpster fire, remember?"

Dougie reached for a slice of pickled ginger. "But once everything settles down, you should have some fun. And don't get mad, but it's been ages since you were happy."

Alice pushed an edamame bean around her plate. "I've been happy." The lie slipped off her tongue easily which was no surprise. She'd tried to convince herself that things would get better for so long, that Phoenix had actually cared for her. Instead, he'd disappeared on tour as much as possible, leaving her isolated and alone. She'd thrown herself into charity work and done her best to keep up appearances because everyone had been so happy for them. Alice had hidden behind her fear of disappointing their fans for way too long because she didn't want to admit how wrong she'd been. About Phoenix. His 'harmless' little parties. The lifestyle he'd totally hidden from her.

Rico's hand settled on top of hers, stilling her chopsticks. "Really?"

She pulled her hand away gently, smiling softly at him. She didn't want him to think she was upset. "Things were different, and there were still good days. Now, can we please stop talking about me? What's new with you guys?"

"We have some news," Rico said, lacing his fingers through Dougie's.

"Now's not the best time," Dougie said. "It's not a big deal."

"What's going on?" Alice asked, reaching for another piece of tuna sashimi.

Dougie and Rico looked at each other with so much love in their eyes that she had to drop her gaze to the empty gluten-free soy sauce fish littered across the table. *Hang on.* They were wearing matching rings on their ring fingers. The sushi fell to her plate.

"We've decided to get married." Dougie's gaze never left Rico's. Lost in their own world, Rico pulled Dougie in for a quick kiss. They broke apart, and Dougie offered her a guilty smile. "I'm sorry, Alley Cat," he said. "The timing's terrible ..."

"Nonsense!" *Nonsense?* Who the hell said that? Had she suddenly morphed into an old woman? "This is the best news ever!" she screeched, and they all winced. *Okay, dial it down, fruit loop.* But it was great news. Dougie and Rico had always been perfect for each other. She was thrilled for them, so why was her heart thumping so hard? Alice pushed back from the table, needing to burn off the sudden energy racing through her body. She yanked the hair tie off her wrist, twisted her hair into a bun. "Right, we need some champagne. Prosecco. Whatever it's called."

"We can toast with these drinks." Dougie pointed at the three empty glasses on the table.

Alice took a deep breath. She wasn't going to ruin their big moment with her own baggage. "I'll run to the pub. Grab a bottle of something nice."

She could do this.

OWEN PICKED up the tray of drinks and was turning back towards his table when someone charged into him. The black plastic slipped, liquid sloshing over the rims of the glasses. He hissed as three beers and two red wines soaked through his white business shirt.

"Damn it," a familiar voice said.

Alice.

The sound of glass shattering reverberated throughout the room, mixing with the buzz Owen suspected still followed Alice most places. Her milky skin was paler than normal, and she worried her bottom lip between her teeth. A few strands of hair had escaped her bun, giving her a sexy, messy look. Everyone shifted their attention back towards the stage when the microphone squawked, signalling the next round was about to start. Trivia was serious business in Wattle Junction.

"Sorry." Alice grabbed a stack of serviettes, her hands hovering in front of him like she didn't know if she should touch him or not. He shouldn't have wanted her to, but he did.

"Here." She thrust the paper towels towards him. "I wasn't watching where I was going."

"It's fine." Owen took the napkins, wiping futilely, clumps of sodden crepe paper sticking to his shirt. This was the cherry on top of his shitty day. It started with a local farmer baulking at his prices, not understanding that 'mate's rates' didn't mean 'free'. Then a call from his builder letting him know there were even more delays to his house renovation, but the worst bit? Telling Jessica that Rob was set on a fifty-fifty custody split for Sam. "Can I get another round, Ted?"

"On it," Teddy said, passing him a dustpan and brush for the broken glass at his feet.

"Please." Alice reached for the cleaning stuff, her cheeks flaming. Owen didn't fight her, pulling his shirt out of his pants and wringing the excess liquid into a handful of fresh serviettes. When he looked up, Alice hadn't moved, her gaze firmly fixed on his torso, where his wet shirt had moulded to his abs. He cleared his throat, and her blush spread to her chest. Ah, he wasn't the only one who felt the chemistry between them, then.

She busied herself sweeping up the broken glass. "If you leave your shirt at the apartment tomorrow, I'll get it dry-cleaned for you. And your ..." Was he imagining the way her breath hitched? "... pants."

"It's fine," he repeated, grimacing at the reddish-brown stain but really, he had ten other white business shirts.

"Maybe this will stop him from dressing like a tosser all the time." Teddy winked at Alice as he put two very full wine glasses up on the bar. Something like jealousy roared in Owen's belly when Alice smiled gratefully at his brother, the easy friendship Teddy had mentioned appearing like they'd known each other for years, not weeks.

"It's called being professional," Owen said. "I came from the office."

"That might be the problem, bro," Teddy said.

"What?" Owen pulled the sticky material away from his chest, indignation bubbling inside him. He was in no mood for ribbing, friendly or not.

"Why were you still at the office at almost eight? Skip out early next week and come for dinner beforehand. There's always a crew from footy here before trivia."

Nice of Teddy to mention that before. "I'll try."

"And ..." Teddy looked Owen up and down.

Owen gave up on his shirt, leaning over the bar. He dropped the mountain of sodden, crumpled paper towels into the bin. "I won't wear the suit."

"Bingo." Teddy winked and headed for the other end of the bar.

Alice looked around the packed dining room. "This is trivia, huh?"

Teams were well and truly into the third round now; heads huddled together over tables covered in plates of parmigiana and burgers with chunky, golden chips. "Folks take it pretty seriously."

"Owen, darling, aren't you going to introduce me to your friend?" His mother plonked her purse on the bar next to him. Her curly black hair was streaked with grey and arranged like a porcupine was sitting on her head.

He picked up his schooner. "Mum, meet Alice Aspinall. Alice, this is Lulu Hampshire-James. She owns Lulu's Boutique."

"Hello," Alice said politely. "I think I've seen you having coffee each morning? Outside with the other ladies?"

Lulu's face shone, her bright red lips parting in a wide grin. "Ah, yes. This guy and his brothers call us the Old Girls Gossip Brigade and think we don't know."

"I can assure you, there's nothing we think you ladies

don't know," Owen said dryly, sipping his pale ale. It was hoppy and cool. Finally, an antidote to his nightmare day. It definitely wasn't seeing Alice unexpectedly.

Lulu smacked his shoulder before turning back to Alice. "I think we're going to be brilliant friends."

Alice tilted her head to the side. "You do?"

"Any woman who dresses outside the box is a friend of mine," she said. "Knowing you've engaged the services of the best lawyer in the area helps too."

"Thanks?"

Owen tipped his head towards his mother, trying to ignore the itch where his damp shirt was stuck to his stomach. "Mum's not known for keeping her opinions to herself. Fashion or otherwise."

"You should come and see my shop," Lulu said. "Unless you want to join us for trivia. This one's only good for random sports, legal stuff and scouting facts."

"Scouts like Boy Scouts?" The amusement in Alice's eyes stirred something deep in his belly. This was a first for them. A conversation not about her or her divorce. How long had it been since he'd spoken to an attractive woman like this? And, *hell*. There was no denying how attractive he found her now as she stood before him in a short, fitted navy dress. He'd been avoiding admitting it to himself ever since he'd met her. Unwilling to consider Alice as anything other than a client. But he could do this. Be friendlier without it meaning anything. He was off the clock at his local pub, starting a new life. "I was a Venturer Scout. I'm not ashamed to admit it."

A cold hand snaked around his shoulders. "That's funny. You used to keep it pretty quiet."

Camille. He had been hoping she'd left town.

"Looks like you need a new drink," his ex said. "My shout."

The Paul Kelly song playing in the background finished, and the bar should've been filled with conversation between rounds, but it was so quiet Owen could hear the sharp hiss of the industrial dishwasher in the kitchen. He didn't need to look around to know it wasn't Alice who was the main attraction this time. The Arturos always commanded this reaction from the locals.

Add his and Camille's history in on top of that, and well, it was a train wreck.

"It's almost time for the next round," Lulu cut in. "I'll see you back at the table, Owen. Alice, it was lovely to meet you properly. Please come by my shop so we can chat more." Her long skirt swished around her legs as she walked away, not acknowledging Camille.

"Since when do you like trivia?" Camille scoffed, resting her hand on Owen's arm. He didn't miss the way the corners of Alice's mouth tipped down or how he wanted to push Camille away, which was exactly what he did, stepping away from her. He ignored the way his ex laughed lightly like this was all a big joke.

"I'm so sorry, I'm being rude," Camille said. Pivoting on her high heels, she thrust her free hand towards Alice. God forbid she let go of him. She'd always been territorial; he'd just been too in love to notice when he was younger. Back when he'd thought he could save her from her family.

"I'm Camille Arturo. We go way back." She winked conspiratorially at Owen, and he gently prised her fingers from his sleeve.

"I should go. Sorry again about your clothes," Alice murmured.

"It was nice to meet you," Camille sing-songed dismissively, which earned her a stiff nod from Alice. Owen wanted to say something. Make it clear there was nothing between him and Camille, regardless of Alice's status as his client.

He'd have understood a lingering fondness for his ex. Despite their messy end, Camille had been the first and last person he'd given his heart to. That should've counted for something, right? But instead, he was hollow, disinterested. Just like Camille had obviously been every time he'd talked about their future together. Would've been nice for her to give him a heads-up. But she'd made her choice and, in hindsight, it had been the best one for them both. He never would've been able to reconcile the things her family did once he properly understood them, and after seeing her now, it was clear Camille still toed the party line.

For so long after she'd left, Owen had closed himself off to the possibility of something more with another woman. He'd done the same with his friendships. No wonder no one had told him about the pre-trivia dinner group. He'd spent years telling himself he was too busy; it wasn't fair to start something when work was his number one priority. And what did he have to show for it now? A fledgling business, a handful of fractured friendships and an empty house at the end of the day.

"About that drink ..." Camille murmured. "I've got some time before I have to get home to Mum. We've reconnected these last few years, and it's made me realise all the things ... and people I've been missing."

Ahhh. Sledgehammer subtlety. His favourite.

"No, thanks," was all Owen said. He didn't owe her anything, and a weight he hadn't acknowledged for far too long lifted off his shoulders.

Camille's mouth dropped open before she snapped it shut. Her eyes narrowed.

In his peripheral vision, he noticed Alice standing next to the door.

Camille followed his gaze. "Lights are on and no one's home with that one," she said.

Owen ignored her and picked up the tray of drinks. She was looking for a reaction, and he wasn't interested in giving her one.

"No surprise that guy left her. Hard to believe she didn't know her husband was screwing everyone in sight."

Realisation dawned on him like the waterfall of spilt wine and beer. This was the kind of crap Alice put up with every day. People weren't cruel to her face, but they said stuff about her. All the time. In person. Online, where they thought their anonymity protected them. How she managed to ever leave the house bamboozled him.

"You don't know the first thing about her," he said quietly.

"Oh, who cares? She's just some girl who wanted to be famous."

Without replying, Owen walked back to his table. As he handed his father his favourite red, he looked back across the room.

And shit. He shouldn't like it that Alice was still standing at the door, watching him. Would she care if he had a drink with Camille? He sipped his beer and tried to ignore the gnawing in his stomach that appeared whenever he thought of Alice. Entertaining those thoughts would only lead to trouble.

8

Alice was dozing in the hammock when feedback cut through the air.

"Testing, testing, one, two, three."

She scrambled up, her denim skirt twisting around her legs. The domestic thriller she'd been trying, and failing, to read fell to the floor along with the blanket she'd draped around her shoulders.

"Hello, Wattle Junction!"

Oh, no.

Years ago, the velvety smoothness of Phoenix's voice would've made her weak at the knees. He was everything she'd always thought she'd wanted. Rugged. Artistic. Not afraid to disappoint his family by turning his back on their dreams of him being a doctor to pursue his own. He'd been so different from anyone she'd ever met before. He seemed to embody music. It was layered into the way he moved his body, how he spoke. His soft vowels and lilting voice had made her shiver when they first met on the show. It was like the universe had gift wrapped the perfect man and hand delivered him to her.

But like all things that seemed too good to be true, Phoenix wasn't real. He was a character created by a man whose real name was Pieter Skoglund to sell records. Like the rest of the country, she'd fallen for the fairytale.

Phoenix strummed his guitar, his most famous song, 'We Saved Each Other', blanketing the usual afternoon noises of High Street. The piano kicked in, followed by the drums. For God's sake, he'd brought the whole band.

His skinny jeans hung halfway down his ass while still being so tightly fitted it was unlikely he'd ever father children. She'd have bet money she really couldn't afford to risk that his 'lucky', beaten-up black boots would complete his onstage look. But his bare feet were curled in the grass. Phoenix was a germaphobe ... except for when he was using. Alice resisted the urge to bang her head against the wall.

Now everything made sense.

"My wife won't speak to me. And I know what you're all thinking."

She eyed the sliding door. Remembered the tomatoes she'd bought earlier in the week. She could wing a few at him, but he'd have her arrested for assault after he made her pose for a happy reunion photo.

The drums and piano faded out. All that was left was his tortured voice, another well-rehearsed apology that made Alice want to hurl. Phoenix turned his head in her direction, and she refused to hide. It was no secret where she was living in Wattle Junction.

"Alice, each day without you is like a song without words. Please help me fix this."

The music swelled, and he stretched his hand out towards where she stood on her balcony. Anger threatened, but there was no way she'd cry in front of him.

"I wrote this song for us. Remember?"

She remembered Oskar, the keyboardist, writing this song for his ex-girlfriend, but hey, *whatever*. Some things got lost in translation.

"*Sötnos*, if you let me, I'll spend the rest of my life making this up to you."

He began to sing again as he crossed the street and headed towards her apartment. A crowd was forming behind him, sunlight hitting the phone screens held aloft.

Alice stood her ground until he disappeared. She'd heard all the excuses before. Her mind whirred as she tried to remember how many times she'd confronted Phoenix about the drugs at his afterparties. How every time he'd told her they weren't his, that he didn't do that stuff. She never should have believed him, but it was easier to think he was telling the truth rather than blow up their life and admit how foolish she'd been.

She was pulling the curtains closed when the front door burst open. Alice's hands flew to her chest. She'd locked that, hadn't she?

"Hey," Owen said. He wasn't wearing his jacket; his sleeves were rolled to his elbows. How was it possible for forearms to be so muscular? "I've been calling," he said.

"Hi." She walked into the kitchen, yanked the fridge open and pulled out one of Teddy's soft drinks. She'd replace it later, but right now, she needed a drink and that was all they had.

Owen stayed in the doorway, hands stuffed into his charcoal suit pants. "Ah, so, Phoenix ..."

"Yep." She downed half the can in one go, the bubbles fizzing in her throat. Covering her mouth with one hand, she swallowed a burp, feeling the burn behind her nostrils.

"I wanted to make sure you knew he was here."

"Pretty hard to miss that."

"Yeah." Owen grimaced. "But I have some good news. I finally heard from his lawyer, and they want to move forward with mediation. Next week. Chris has been calling too."

Alice breathed deeply, an attempt to release some of the tension simmering in her body. This impromptu concert was all for show. Nothing more than Phoenix trying to repair his reputation and paint her as the villain. The unforgiving wife who wouldn't talk to him. Chris probably put him up to it, sick of her ignoring his calls.

"Listen, there's something you should know about Phoenix's lawyer—"

She crossed her arms. "Can you draw up paperwork to terminate my agreement with Chris?"

Owen leant against the door. "Sure."

She'd found two new contracts in the last week, and it pissed her off knowing she'd be forking over a percentage of her earnings when Chris had nothing to do with the deal. She tossed the empty can into the tub they used for recycling. "What was the other thing you had to tell me?"

"Phoenix has hired Malus, Mendax and Associates to represent him."

The name was vaguely familiar.

"I used to work for them. I didn't leave on good terms."

Alice slid onto one of the fake leather barstools at the counter. "What's that mean for me?"

Owen frowned. "Nothing changes. We keep going. This is all white noise."

She pointed towards the park. "This is murdering cats. Calling it anything else isn't fair."

Owen laughed softly, and the sound was so unusual; she paused. His face was softer, less guarded. She had a vision of what he must've looked like as a boy. She'd bet he was everyone's friend, the one who stood up to all the bullies.

"If you're okay, I'd better get back to work," Owen said.

"Thanks for checking in, Boy Scout."

Another gentle laugh from Owen lit up her insides.

"You're not going to let me forget that, are you?"

She smiled, something she would've thought was impossible even five minutes ago. "It's unlikely. Besides, you said you were proud."

Owen's business shirt pulled tight across his chest as he crossed his arms. "It's a quiet type of pride."

Then she remembered the woman from the other night. The one who'd thrown her past relationship with Owen in Alice's face.

She dragged her foot across the linoleum, through the dirt and mud she'd tracked in after her morning run. "Your friend seemed to have a strong opinion about it."

"She's wrong about a lot of things. And we're not friends. We're not anything to each other."

The air in the apartment changed, becoming heavier, reflecting the tone of their conversation, and she wanted to ask more questions. Camille was obviously an ex of some sort. *Warning, warning,* chirped the voice of reason in her mind.

But her mouth didn't listen. "You know, I was thinking of watching a movie. You could hang around, too, if you wanted?"

Owen's phone rang, and he looked at the screen before whispering that he'd have to take a raincheck. Heat rushed to Alice's cheeks, and she gripped the kitchen counter so she didn't drop to the floor and hide behind it.

What am I doing? Why did I ask that?

Owen nodded farewell and opened the door as he answered his call. "Can you give me a second, Jessica?"

Mortification seeped through Alice's body.

He was probably doing more than watching movies with Jessica.

"You can't come up here," Alice heard Owen say. "This is private property. I'll call the police."

"I want to see my wife," Phoenix said.

"No," Owen said firmly. "Now get lost."

Two seconds later, Alice's phone buzzed.

> Owen: Sit tight. I'll get rid of him. Might take a while.

Great. She was stuck inside for the rest of the night. She huffed out a big sigh, resting her elbows on the bench and staring at the takeaway menu for Tino's Italian on the fridge. Twice a week they offered a different cuisine and tonight was Mexican. Teddy swore the rotating menu was part of the small town charm or something? When she looked up, her gaze snagged on the present from Dougie and Rico.

Tacos and candle making sounded pretty good. Besides, it wasn't like she had anything better to do.

OWEN SHIFTED IN HIS SEAT, trying to focus on the agenda for the committee meeting instead of the woman he couldn't stop thinking about.

He could've stayed. Watched a movie.

He scribbled a note in the margin to change all the lights in the driveway and car park to motion detector ones. At least then Alice would know if there was someone outside. He was going to install an alarm with cameras, too.

"We didn't get the full council grant," Lulu said, and a sigh rolled around the table. Most of the Old Girls Gossip Brigade pulled double duty as committee members for Kathleen's Place.

"Real shame considering our waitlist is getting longer by the day," Mrs Mandrill, one of his old primary school teachers, said, fiddling with the tea bag in her mug. "We'll have to shelve the renovation plans for the old shearers' shed."

The community house had grown significantly over the years and was now able to house up to ten families in the main house, refurbished stables and old servants' quarters. Renovating the original shearers' shed would increase their capacity even more. Most of their funding came from the trust his great-grandmother Kathleen had established, and each year, a swag of grants were secured to help with the upkeep and programs they offered.

His stomach rumbled. His mum's chocolate chip cookies sat atop a mosaic platter made from bits of old china. Learning how to mosaic was one of Eloise's most popular art therapy classes. All the broken pieces on the tray formed a rainbow, stark white glue visible in the gaps. The reds, greens and blues shone under the trio of pendant lights above. Owen's thoughts returned to Alice. At first glance, she was bright and glittery—often literally —but the truth lurked below the surface. Signs she'd patched herself up time and time again and covered herself in shimmery armour so no one would look too closely.

The problem was Owen wanted to know all her secrets.

"Darling?" Lulu stirred her black coffee. "Any ideas?"

He sat up straight. "Hmmm?"

"Even without the reno, we're struggling to keep up with operational costs. We need more money, and we can't always ask Nate. He donates so much already and runs all the sports programs for the kids here."

Owen knew all about drowning in costs. Business was picking up—finally. He'd written three wills this week and two old clients had reached out to ask for help with estate planning after seeing his name connected to Alice's. But this wasn't about him. The rest of the committee stared back at him.

He looked around the wooden table with its mismatched chairs. Like everything else here, all the furniture had been donated. The oversized teak table had come from Somers Gully's old council chambers. Nate had stripped all the lacquer and sanded it back, exposing the notches and imperfections. Its natural honey colour was much more suited to the rest of the homey kitchen with its ruffled green and white checked curtains and laminate benchtops. The commercial oven and cooktop they had installed recently stuck out like sore thumbs, all shiny newness and energy rating stickers.

Owen toyed with his pen. There was another option to raise a significant amount of money, but it would involve a lot more effort from him. He hadn't asked Nate yet, either.

"What did Eloise mention? Something about puppies? The animal shelter?" Lulu asked Mrs Mandrill.

Owen cleared his throat. This he knew about. Eloise had told him about it when he'd called and asked to use her office last week. "They're looking for somewhere to shoot the annual calendar fundraiser for the Somers Gully Animal Shelter. If we let them use our grounds and split production costs, they'd share the profits with us."

With its sweeping fields, orchards and rustic charm, Kathleen's Place would be a spectacular setting.

"But aren't calendars a little outdated? Everything's

online these days," Mrs Mandrill said. He'd never be able to call her Joan, even if she did insist on it and have hot pink hair now.

"We could ask Alice to help promote them," his mum said.

Owen coughed, the mention of Alice catching him unaware.

Lulu tapped on the table. "Owen will ask her, won't you, darling?"

He leant forward, his palms flat on the table, keen to change the topic. He'd apologise to Nate later, but this might be the push his brother needed to commit. "Nate and I have been toying with the idea of doing the Wattle Valley Adventure Race in August."

"The one you did with Raff years ago? The charity one?" Lulu asked.

Owen nodded. They'd been lucky and came away with second place ten years ago, but since then, the competition had grown significantly. "There are cash prizes for the top three teams, ranging from ten to thirty thousand dollars. There's no guarantee we'd place because it's become a lot more popular, but you can attract a fair bit of corporate sponsorship as well. We raised forty grand, remember? With Nate's profile, we'd probably raise a lot more than that."

"It certainly wouldn't hurt," Lulu said. "Everyone in favour?"

Everyone nodded.

"Now, onto the next matter of business ..." Mrs Mandrill directed everyone to the second page of the agenda.

"Owen ..." Lulu elbowed him.

"What?"

"You should bring Alice to trivia. Help her meet folks.

People will be more accepting if they see her trying to fit in. I'm sure she could use a friend here."

He picked up a biscuit and stared at where the chocolate oozed out. His conversation with Alice at trivia flashed to the front of his mind. Followed by her gentle teasing yesterday. "Maybe."

"What's with the hesitation? Is it Camille? Because you were always far too good for her."

"What?" The wooden back of his chair pressed between his shoulders as he slouched backwards. His ex was so far from his thoughts she might as well be in the North Pole. "No."

This had everything to do with his interest in Alice, not that he'd be telling his mother that.

Interest that couldn't go anywhere because she was his client.

He shoved the biscuit in his mouth, vowing to call Nate and organise their training schedule. He'd ignore his silly crush and focus on what was important: helping the people who needed him.

When the elevator doors opened, Alice froze. *Busted.* Standing in the middle of her old penthouse apartment foyer were her parents. They wore matching tortoiseshell glasses—green for her mother, brown for her father—and expressions of resignation.

She'd been so busy worrying about a sneak ambush from Phoenix that she'd forgotten it was one of her parents' signature moves. Alice raised her eyebrows. "Weren't we meeting at the restaurant?"

There went her plan to cancel at the last minute.

"We thought it'd be easier to talk here," Marguerite said, smoothing her neat blonde bob. "More private." Which was code for: *we knew you were going to bail on us.*

"We brought take away from Madame Fu's." Her father, Douglas, lifted a brown paper bag stamped with a dragon logo off the glass-topped table behind him. All Alice had inherited from him was his copper-coloured hair, which she'd been dyeing blonde for years.

"Great."

"Where's Phoenix?" her mother asked.

"Sydney." He'd been tagged in several posts at a trendy café in Bondi less than an hour ago.

Probably best to get this over with. Taking a deep breath and releasing it to a four-count like she'd been taught in yoga, Alice slipped her key into the lock and pushed open the door to her old home.

A putrid smell forced her backwards.

Twisting around, she tried to push her parents towards the lift, but it was too late. They might not be overly emotionally aware, but their sense of smell was just fine.

"Really? Alice?" Douglas stalked past her. He put his hands on his lean hips, the takeaway bag hanging limply at his side. "Explain yourself."

"Oh my." Marguerite's blue eyes were wide behind her glasses, her expression mimicking Alice's.

Alice clamped her jaws together and allowed herself a second to sink into the indignation racing up her spine. Of course, her parents would immediately think the worst of her. Then, as calmly as she could, she said, "I haven't been here for weeks now. It was never like this when I lived here."

Focusing on breathing through only her mouth, Alice catalogued the damage. A dining chair with three legs missing was upturned, and takeaway containers littered the concrete-topped table. Against a dazzling crisp blue-sky backdrop, bugs flew around the half-eaten burgers and nuggets mashed into the crystal centrepiece that had promised to bring calmness and peace to her home. Several blunts and joints were strewn across the soil of her giant snake plant, which explained the large scorch mark in the middle of the tan leather couch they'd been gifted in January.

"I don't even know what to say." Douglas shook his head.

Alice's vision blurred as she blinked back tears, her initial anger replaced with the numbness that came from disappointing her parents. Again. "I'll clean it up and I'll speak to Phoenix. Tell him to find somewhere else to live."

Douglas stalked past her, wrenching the balcony doors open. The cool, fresh air did nothing to temper the tension in the room. Saying anything now would be pointless. The rigidness of her father's shoulders and the way his jaw clenched and unclenched made it clear he wasn't done.

Alice followed slowly, bracing herself for the inevitable lecture.

"Let's all take a breath," Marguerite said once they were seated at the long metal table on the apartment's biggest balcony. "The divorce is an unfortunate but necessary step. You're being given a chance to start again. To finally do something meaningful. It's a good thing. Do you have any idea what you'd like to do?"

"I'm still figuring it out," Alice said.

"You've been figuring it out for the last twenty-four years. First, you defer uni on a whim, then you dropped out of that overpriced hair and make-up course you were desperate to do, and don't get me started on that ridiculous TV show." Douglas set bowls of pho in front of himself and Marguerite.

Her parents had never understood the appeal of *Take a Chance on Love*. But Alice had seen it as a chance to be validated, be chosen. If she could convince strangers that she wasn't a total idiot, maybe her family would finally take her seriously. But it had blown up in her face, hadn't it? Just like her mum and dad had always said it would. The shame that came from admitting her mistake was a huge part of why Alice had stayed with Phoenix.

Alice blinked and looked at her father.

"Hmm?" Douglas's raised eyebrows shattered Alice's resolve to stay calm.

"Look, I'm sorry I'm not a brainiac like you lot who can do whatever you want and be perfect at it, okay?" She regretted the words as soon as they were out of her mouth.

"That's not what your father meant." Marguerite passed Alice a container of grilled chicken and steamed vegetables. "You've got so much potential. You shouldn't be wasting it taking silly photos and telling people which vitamins to buy."

"Especially without the correct medical knowledge—" Douglas winced when Marguerite elbowed him.

In a perfect world, she'd tell them about her candle making business idea. For the last week, she'd been honing her skills, and while she still had a lot to learn, the process had been calming, almost meditative. It was easily the best part of her days and a very welcome respite from the roller coaster that was still her real life. But what did she know about running a business? They'd think this was a worse idea than being an influencer. At least she'd made money from that. The rest of her ring money had been deposited into her account, but that was everything she had. After giving Owen his retainer and the rent and bond she owed him, and paying her parents everything she owed their emergency credit card, her account had already taken a hit. She was determined to manage her money properly this time.

In the end, she went with: "I'll make it work."

"In this Wattle Junction?" Douglas arched an eyebrow at her. He said it like it was a dirty word.

"Wattle Junction's great. I need a new start. Mum just said the same thing, like, two seconds ago, remember? You guys never think I can take care of myself." Alice's hands shook; she shoved them into the pockets of her pink overalls.

"Then you'll have no problem giving back the emergency credit card you've been using to fund this new start."

"What? Why? I paid everything back." That card was her safety net. Couldn't they see how hard she was trying?

"Douglas ..."

"No. We've always made things too easy for her, Margie. She got herself into this mess and says she can get herself out of it. Tell Phoenix to get his stuff out of here by the end of the week. Then I'm having the locks changed. This ends now."

Alice felt about as big as an ant. Not trusting her voice, she nodded.

"The card, please."

Fingers like butterknives, Alice dug through her bag, trying to find her purse. She pulled out the card and handed it over.

"It's time for you to grow up, Alice," he said.

He wasn't wrong.

If only she knew what she wanted to do with her life.

10

Owen and Jessica were in the middle of a meeting when his office door burst open. Phoenix Storm fell into the room.

"Can I help you?" Owen put his pen down calmly.

"Where is she?" Phoenix demanded. His eyes were red, his beard scraggly and unkempt. He looked like he hadn't slept in days and smelt like a few of the uni parties Camille had dragged Owen to. What had Alice ever seen in this guy?

Frankie peered around Phoenix's shoulder before squeezing past him, fluffing her hair. The top two buttons on her blouse were undone. "Phoenix Storm is here to see you."

Owen bristled. "Yes, thank you, Frankie. I'm with a client right now."

"He said it's urgent."

Owen didn't for a second think her flushed cheeks were from embarrassment, but he had bigger problems to focus on.

Phoenix paced from one side of the room to the other, muttering to himself.

"I think I've got everything I need for today, Jessica. We'll reconvene next week. I'm sorry for this interruption." He stood and buttoned his jacket, turning his attention to the furious Swede. "Let's discuss this somewhere else." He shooed Phoenix out into the hallway.

"Where is she? You won't believe what she did!" Phoenix growled.

Owen pasted a bored expression on his face, determined not to let on that he had no idea what Phoenix was talking about. "If it's in regard to your estranged wife, you should discuss it with your lawyer, not me."

Phoenix wiped a dirty hand underneath his nose. "She kicked me out!"

Well. That was one way to send a message. Owen fired off a text to Alice, warning her Phoenix was in Wattle Junction, while Frankie fussed around the musician.

"That must have been a big shock. Maybe you'd like to have a seat? A glass of water?" she cooed.

"Nope. Time to go. Take this up with your lawyers, Mr Storm." Owen pointed towards the front door.

"I want to see Alice." Phoenix scratched his arm. A long, angry red welt bloomed underneath the Norse tattoos covering his pale skin. Owen had a sneaking suspicion he knew what was causing those sores and Phoenix's erratic behaviour.

"She's not here," Owen said calmly. Hopefully, she wasn't home. Or if she was, she'd see his message and wait until the coast was clear.

"Ring her then. Get her here. Tell her I'll only play nicely for so long. She knows I can bury her."

Owen rocked back on his heels and kept his expression neutral even though his mind scrambled, trying to decode

Phoenix's threat. Alice hadn't mentioned anything that he might try to blackmail her with. "No."

"I'll knock on every fucking door if I have to."

Owen moved closer, noticing the stale scent of alcohol. This was going to end badly. "Fine. Let's go out the front and I'll call her. Reception's better out there."

Phoenix stumbled sideways before drawing himself up to his full height. Owen hated that Phoenix was looking down at him.

"She's not going to get away with this."

They were almost back in the foyer. A few more steps were all he needed. "Get away with what exactly?"

"Pretending she's a victim."

Almost there.

"Here we go." Owen pushed open the front door, and Phoenix missed the step, catapulting himself out onto the footpath.

A few locals stopped to watch, whispering amongst themselves. A group of tourists were seated outside the pub. Bags from Lulu's Boutique and Swift's were scattered around them, the table dotted with mimosas and pastries.

"Why is it so fucking bright out here?" Phoenix moaned, shoving a pair of oversized aviators onto his face. "That's all her fault too. Alice!" he yelled and headed towards the café. "Come out, come out, wherever you are!"

Owen watched from the doorway, dialling the Somers Gully police station. It was the biggest one in the area, servicing several of the surrounding districts. As luck would have it, his brother answered.

"Raff, it's me."

"Let me guess," Rafferty said. "Mum put you up to this."

"Uh, no? You know I don't get involved in Mum's

schemes. This is a police thing—Phoenix Storm is drunk and causing a scene on High Street. He might be on something too. He's headed towards the pub, looking for his ex."

The weariness usually present in his older brother's voice these days was heavier, probably because he was at work. "Alright, we'll send a car over. Where's Alice? Any ideas?"

"I'm trying to find her."

Owen watched as Phoenix changed directions, heading for the park next to the school. Where the hell was she?

ALICE BENT over next to the drinking fountain, chest heaving as she tried to catch her breath. The easy five kilometres she'd set out for had quickly morphed into a hard fifteen on the trails. But still, the noise in her mind lingered.

In the distance, a man called, "Aliiiiiiiiiiiiice!"

Huh. That sounded an awful lot like—*oh, no.*

She straightened and brushed sweaty flyaways off her forehead. Phoenix ambled towards her, loping across the park like a toddler still learning to walk. A brown paper bag was clutched in one hand; the paper moulded to the bottle inside it.

Fight or flight kicked in, and she spun around. People were scattered around the park, relaxing on benches or in the shade of the big wattle trees. A group of mothers sat in a circle to her left, their babies resting on a patchwork of blankets in the middle.

She spied Owen hanging back. It was annoying how the sight of him calmed her.

Phoenix was a mess and not in the carefully arranged

state of dishevelment he'd made his signature look. His dirty flannelette shirt was buttoned incorrectly, and he was wearing two different boots. Both were black, but only one had laces. He pushed his sleeve to his elbow, scratching his forearm. Alice frowned at the sores covering his skin. She was looking for needle marks when he yanked the fabric down and glowered at her. This was the man she'd married?

"Think you're pretty clever, don't you?" he snapped.

Alice looked over her shoulder, smiling in what she hoped was a friendly way at the mothers' group. Like this was normal. "Lower your voice," she hissed through her teeth.

Owen edged closer to where they were, but she held her hand up, stopping him in his tracks. She might be able to calm Phoenix down enough to get him to leave, but there was no way he'd listen to Owen. Not like this.

"Now you're worried about what people might think?" Phoenix threw his arms wide, slipping in the grass as he lurched forward. "No one cares about you, Alice. That might change after I show them what I've got, though ..."

Alcohol fumes and the tang of lemon made her stomach twist, but that was nothing compared to the fury that burnt through her body. How dare he bring up the stupid pictures he'd convinced her to take right after they were married? Saying he needed something to take with him on the road while he was touring. Alice wasn't naked in them, but they were still more revealing than she'd been comfortable with. She could blame youth and naivety, but it was just another example of when Alice should have known better.

She clenched her fists to stop her hands from shaking.

"My tour's been cancelled! Are you happy? The least you can do is give me the keys to my fucking house."

She cleared her throat. Reminded herself she was in control, not her fear. Her skin heated, despite the dappled shade of the big trees. "It's not your house. It never was."

"Says who?" he spat, and Alice flinched, reaching for where she'd tucked her phone into her running tights. It was pointless to try and reason with him. When she tried to step around him, he mimicked her movements, blocking the sun, his tall build looming over her. The park was silent; not even the leaves were moving in the light breeze rolling through. She faked left before darting to the right. If she could get away from Phoenix, she'd call Chris to come and get him.

But her ex grabbed for her, his sweaty hands yanking at the straps of her running crop.

The smell of Owen's cologne surrounded her. He thrust himself forward, his body shielding hers. "You need to step back, Mr Storm," he said.

Something fluttered in Alice's chest. She'd never heard Owen sound so authoritative. So ... ice cold. *So sexy.*

"This is between me and my wife." Phoenix's hands dropped to his side. The two men were practically chest to chest.

"Phoenix, people are looking." A trio of cameramen were watching; they must have followed Phoenix. The rest had given up and gone back to the city earlier in the week.

Phoenix sighed loudly, finally stepping back. Alice's breathing relaxed, and she rubbed her face. "Please go," she whispered loud enough for him to hear. "You're making things worse for everyone."

"If you're so worried about what people think, maybe you should cover up. Let yourself go, haven't you?" Phoenix hissed at her, his gaze lingering on her bright yellow running crop top.

Her weight had long been an issue between them because she wasn't a twig and never would be, so this wasn't the first time he'd said something nasty about it. So much for loving her curves when they'd first met. She ducked her head, willing herself not to cry. Alice hated he could still control her this way, even after all this time.

"Enough," Owen said.

"Don't tell me what to—" Phoenix snarled at Owen.

This asshole. Seriously. "Would you shut up? Everyone's watching. If you're so concerned about your career and cancelled tour, you'd leave," she hissed, her fingernails biting into her palms. "I'm trying to help you. Like I have a million times beforehand!"

A police car pulled up to the curb, two men climbing out.

"Really?" Phoenix glared at Alice.

"I didn't call them," she whisper-shrieked. "You're the one swearing and stumbling all over the place!"

"This isn't over," he sneered.

The tall man with curly black hair reached them first. "Morning," he said, introducing himself as Detective James. His partner, a tall Māori man with a crew cut and polarised Ray Bans, followed.

"What seems to be the problem here?" Detective James asked. It took Alice a minute to connect the dots. This was Owen's older brother Rafferty. He was taller and leaner than Owen, more like Teddy. His clothes were creased, and the dark circles under his eyes matched his hair. Alice was struck by how beaten down he looked.

Phoenix tipped his chin towards Alice, the threat clear in his eyes. "Nothing," he muttered.

She quickly retied her ponytail, trying to look calm. "Phoenix was just leaving." She sent a pointed stare his way, and he glared back at her, tossing his greasy hair defiantly.

"Okay, you stay here," Rafferty directed Alice. "And you come with me, please, Mr Storm. We're going to have a little chat."

"You should apply for a restraining order," Owen said as soon as they were out of earshot.

The headlines flashed before her eyes.

"I don't think that's necessary," Alice replied, ignoring Owen's scoff. "This isn't the first time he's"—she flicked her ponytail over her shoulder—"had too much to drink a bit early in the day. He's harmless."

"This is more than a bit too much to drink. Does he have a history of drug use? As your lawyer—"

She cut him off. "Look, I don't want to add fuel to the fire, okay? Nothing happened. He'll leave."

Owen sighed. He seemed to do that a lot in her presence. "You kicked him out of the apartment in town?"

"My parents wanted him gone."

He nodded, his mouth a flat line. "There was probably a better way to go about it. An official way."

"I thought I was clear." She propped her hands on her hips. "I don't want a big drawn-out battle over the pathetic marriage we had. This"—she gestured towards the park and where Rafferty and his partner were standing with Phoenix —"is only going to make everything worse. A police report and restraining order will set this clusterfuck on fire."

"There's a difference between standing up for yourself and not making things worse," Owen replied flatly. "A big difference."

"Obviously." She rolled her eyes. God, Owen must think she was such a moron for getting into this mess. "But it's my decision. Not yours. Not anyone else's. And I want this to go away."

He watched her closely. The weight of his gaze and midmorning sunshine made her squirm.

"Fine." His tone was heavy with resignation.

Owen didn't understand. No one did.

But this was the way it had to be.

11

W hen Alice woke up, hours after silencing her running alarm, the light filtering through the gaps in her curtains was muted, sombre. She reached for her phone automatically, her heart thumping at the notification-filled screen. Ignoring the ones from the usual suspects (TikTok, Instagram, her mother), her finger hovered over the Google Alerts icon. Tucking the covers tightly under her arms, she took a deep breath and opened the app.

There they were. In the park. There was no audio, but it was clear from her rigid posture and Phoenix's waving arms that they were fighting. Her fingers twisted in her hair on the video, and she had to physically stop herself from doing the same thing.

Cops Called to Domestic Dispute Between Estranged Stars.

It was all her nightmares come true. Alice scrolled through the first article, words jumping off the screen like grenades. Phoenix had always been so much better at playing the media game than she was.

"I never thought she'd give up on us so easily. She won't even try to fix this," Phoenix said.

Anger raced through her veins. What about all the times she covered for him? Made excuses about where he was, what he was doing. Alice was all out of tries because Phoenix had bled her dry.

A comment caught Alice's eye. She pushed back on her pillows, brushed her hair off her face, and sat up, the hard wall behind her shoulder blades reminding her this wasn't fan fiction.

@ShutUpPhoenix: '*He even went so far as to wipe a lone tear away, struggling to compose himself.' Are you f*cking serious? He cheated on her & now he's playing the victim? #nodeal #jogonmate If UR reading this, Alice, RUN. Don't stop. Don't look back. U deserve better. We all deserve better. Can't wait to see what U do next. My days as #PhoenixPhanatic are officially over. #TeamAlice*

It wasn't the only comment of support; there were more than she could've ever imagined. Alice threw the covers back so quickly her phone fell to the floor, landing in an Ugg boot. Her feet barely touched the carpet before she yanked her cupboard open, reaching for her favourite soft, fluffy cardigan.

No more standing still.

She recited her sales pitch for Lulu all throughout her shower and as she blasted her hair and put on her make-up. When she swiped her liquid eyeliner on, curling it at the end into the perfect cat's eye, she was invincible.

Alice nodded at her reflection.

She could do this.

≈

THE BELL above the door jingled, and Alice wiped her feet on the doormat, her lips stretching into a grin. 'Buy yourself something pretty' was written in blocky, black letters on the brown coir. Hidden speakers piped out soft jazz, the music drifting down from above like the leaves slipping off the trees outside. Her sample candles clinked against each other in her oversized tan shoulder bag.

Lulu waved enthusiastically from the counter a few metres away, mouthing an apology as she pointed to the cordless phone held to her ear. She was wearing a gorgeous blush-coloured cropped velvet jacket and an intricately beaded headband. Alice smiled at the older woman before turning and looking at the store properly. Some of the tables were covered with delicate lace tablecloths, others with velvet or fake grass. Miniature pewter birds were lined up next to leftover Easter stock, bright yellow sale stickers stuck to their ears. Rows of necklaces dangled from a tiered hanging stand attached to the ceiling and a crystal display glittered next to the counter.

Alice walked past shelves of bath bombs and face masks, her shoulders relaxing when she realised there weren't any candles. She'd checked the website, but it was a little outdated, so she hadn't been sure.

She was so lost in reading the ingredients list for a bath bomb that smelt like heaven that she didn't hear Lulu's sandals slapping across the hardwood floors.

"Alice!"

She jumped, almost dropping the raspberry and vanilla bath fizzer as her hands flew to her chest.

"Sorry! How lovely to see you." Lulu beamed at Alice, her bright red lipstick bleeding a little into the fine lines around her mouth.

"Your store is so ... I don't even know how to describe it."

Alice couldn't keep the awe out of her voice. Why had she waited so long to come in here? She'd been skirting around the sweet white painted brick cottage with its picket fence covered in climbing roses ever since she arrived. She spied a gorgeous pastel pink leather jacket hanging behind Lulu and added it to her mental wish list. If Lulu agreed to stock her candles, maybe she *would* buy herself something pretty.

"I've been here twenty years next month. I needed an escape from all the testosterone at home." Lulu's eyes twinkled as she placed her hands on her face. The delicate stack of bracelets on her wrist tinkled with the movement. "I still can't believe it's all mine some days."

There was a pang in Alice's chest. This is what she wanted. Not necessarily a store, that was quite the leap from the small candle start-up she was planning, but something she built with her own two hands. Something that was hers, that she created. That no one could take away from her.

Alice took a deep breath, gathering her courage. "There's something I was hoping to talk to you about."

"Perfect." Lulu linked her arm through Alice's. "Me too —unless Owen's beaten me to it."

OWEN STOWED his umbrella under his arm, balancing the bag of food and tray of drinks as he pushed open the heavy door to his mum's boutique. A few raindrops snuck through the black canvas awning. They slid down the door, dripping off the chin of the lion's head door knocker.

He wiped his feet, shivering until the blast from the heater hit him.

"Excellent timing!" Lulu called once he'd closed the door.

Alice's cheeks reddened as their gazes met, her lips falling into a flat line. *Great.* She was still annoyed about yesterday. He wasn't exactly happy about it, either.

"Help me convince Alice to have lunch with us," Lulu said, smiling at them both. She turned to Alice, half dragging her over to the counter and nodding towards one of the shaggy grey stools behind it. "There's always too much. Do you like corned beef?"

Alice paled. Owen didn't blame her. He felt the same way about boiled meat. Always had, but it had been a staple in the James household when he was growing up. Alice's hands fluttered around the handle of her bag. "I don't want to intrude."

Lulu scoffed, knocking shoulders with her affectionately as she placed a candle back on the counter. "Rubbish. Look at the super cute candles Alice has been making, Owen!" She threw a pointed stare at him, tilting her head towards the stool next to Alice. She'd never get any points for subtlety. "I'll go get my chair from my office. Better for these old bones anyway."

Owen made a show of checking his watch. He had a phone meeting with Jessica in forty-five minutes to go over their plan for tomorrow's mediation session one last time. "Why don't we catch up another time, Mum?"

"Don't be silly. You're here now with the food. Sit down."

He readjusted his grip on the bag, weaving between the tables of trinkets and curios until he was on the other side of the counter. "I'll get the chair."

When he returned, Lulu was trying to convince Alice to take half her sandwich.

"No, no, it's really okay. I had breakfast not long ago," Alice said, smoothing her hands over her hair. It was braided again, but not in the funny crown style, instead in a long golden rope down her back. Her hands fell to her side when her stomach growled.

"There's extra gravy." Lulu pointed towards the takeaway container with her half of the sandwich. "And Owen gets himself a coffee, but my drink's always a fun surprise. What is it today, darling?"

"Mulled wine."

"I'd better not," Alice said.

A light bulb went off in Owen's mind. "Is this about what Phoenix said yesterday?"

Alice scratched her neck, a red line marring her milky skin. Shit. He wasn't supposed to notice things like this about her. But it was hard when she kept visiting his dreams.

"Was this when he called you fat?" Lulu asked as she peeled the top off her drink.

The red line on Alice's neck extended towards her chest. "Does everyone know?" she mumbled.

Lulu tipped half of her drink into an empty water glass, smiling apologetically as she pushed the keep cup towards Alice. "You know what they say about small towns."

Owen picked up one of the candles in front of him, reading the label. The tropical, fruity scent reminded him of a Piña Colada. "*The Banana Hammock*?"

"Aren't the names great? Look at this one." Lulu thrust another candle towards him. *Clean as a Whistle* made him think of fresh sheets and lavender. Which made him think of Alice in bed, hair rumpled, lips swollen from kisses. His kisses.

He cleared his throat and dropped his gaze to the counter where more candles were arranged in a straight line.

Centred in the middle of each label in a reddish sparkly print was her company name: The Emancipation of Alice.

"Interesting business name." He unpacked the knife and fork he'd brought from the office.

"We're going to do a trial run of stocking the range here once Alice has finished her website."

Owen mixed his salad together. "You're going to sell candles?"

Alice sipped her drink slowly, her tongue darting out to catch a drop that escaped. Owen stabbed at a piece of chicken and missed, a cherry tomato ricocheting over the side of the takeaway container.

"I've been making them to keep myself busy. Figured I may as well try selling some." Alice frowned at her drink, worrying her bottom lip between her teeth. "If they take off, I'll have to find somewhere else to make them, though. The kitchen at home isn't ideal."

"You've been making them in the apartment?" This was no good. Her determination was dangerously sexy. "How many do you have?"

Alice cleared her throat. "Five hundred."

"Five hundred is a ..." He paused, gobsmacked. Teddy hadn't said anything about candles, and he hadn't noticed them during his visits to borrow the shower. They must be in her room. "It's a lot."

"Anyway," Lulu cut in, offering Alice the sandwich again. "Eat up while we tell you about a very exciting opportunity."

Alice leant back, away from the soggy mess of corned beef, bread and gravy. "I can't eat that, actually. I'm gluten free."

Her stomach rumbled, the flush on her skin deepening. What Owen wouldn't give to know if she blushed all the way to her toes.

"Are you coeliac or gluten free by choice?" Owen's tone was gruffer than he intended as he tried to banish the image of her naked body from his mind.

"Coeliac."

"My salad's gluten free. You have it."

"But what about you?" Alice asked.

Lulu nudged the sandwich of doom towards him. It was everything he didn't want to eat on a plate.

"Eat the salad," he said. "Please?"

Lulu wiped her mouth with a serviette, leaving a red smear of lipstick on the crepe paper. "Now, Alice, you know about Kathleen's Place, right?"

Oh, crap. He'd forgotten to ask her about the calendar.

Alice speared a snow pea. "I've seen the signs around town."

Owen watched as realisation dawned on Alice's face as his mother explained about the calendar.

"You could pick your puppy and month. Outfit, too. Whatever you want, really. Think of it as a great way to meet a few more locals!"

Owen shoved a too-big bite of sandwich in his mouth when Alice bit her lip, probably searching for a polite way to say no.

"Come on. It'll be great fun. My boys are posing too."

Wait, what?

"Uh." Owen wiped his mouth. "No, we're not."

"Yes, you are. The Old Girls and I decided. Didn't we tell you? Oops." Lulu saluted him with her wine.

"Mum," he groaned. This must have been what Raff was talking about yesterday.

Lulu smiled widely. "Just agree, darling. Or we'll dress you all up as firemen."

Alice tried to cover up her shocked laugh with a cough,

but there was no hiding the sparkle in her eyes. Not that he was noticing things like that about her anymore. Nope. No, sir.

"Don't you think Owen would look good in a fireman's uniform?" If Lulu smirked anymore, her face would split in half. "Shirtless, of course. Joan thinks we should oil them up, too. See if we can break the internet or something."

Alice choked on a sip of water, her eyes wide.

Lulu squeezed her shoulder, winking at Owen. "I'm sorry. I didn't mean to shock you. Although, it's not the most dramatic reaction we've ever had to someone seeing Owen without his top on. His first girlfriend fell in the pool the first time he brought her home for a swim."

"Mum," he groaned again. "Please stop."

"I'm serious," Lulu said to Alice. "He took his top off, and of course, he did all the sports. All my boys did. The poor girl never stood a chance. She was so busy staring, she ..." Lulu mimed faceplanting into the pool. "She was an idiot, though. Left him without even a goodbye."

Owen shook his head slowly. Camille was the last thing he felt like talking about right now. "She slipped."

"Whatever you say, dear. He's back at footy too, you know. Always been keen to keep fit, our Owen." Lulu twisted towards him when he sighed. She batted her eyelashes at him innocently. "What? I'm making conversation. A skill you might like to work on, darling. Great, you'll both take part. I'll tell the committee. Goodness, I'm going to be popular."

And with that, she bustled off into the back room, her footsteps drowned out by the music and the rain outside.

"What just happened?" Alice asked Owen.

"You just became a local," he said, dropping his gaze to

the counter when Alice smiled shyly, because there was no point hoping she'd stick around. Was there?

12

Owen tapped his fingers against his leg in time with the loud ticking of the clock on the opposite wall.

"I should've been expecting this." Jessica crossed her arms over her chest, her gaze shifting to the floor-to-ceiling windows in the conference room. "For a second, I thought he might've changed, but ..."

The court-appointed mediator, a tall guy with sideburns Elvis would've approved of, started packing up his notepad and laptop.

Rob's lawyer pushed back into the conference room, a harried look on his face, gaze firmly fixed on his phone. "I still can't get through to him."

They'd officially been stood up.

Wannabe Elvis snapped his briefcase closed, the sound echoing in the large room and headed for the door.

"This is totally out of character. Something must've happened. I'll be in touch once I've spoken with Rob." His lawyer hurried after the mediator.

Owen waited until it was just him and Jessica. "You

doing okay?" He regretted the question the second it was out of his mouth. Asking something so obvious was a rookie mistake.

Jessica shook her head. "This is how it started. He'd miss dinner once or twice. Then not come home at all."

"I know it's frustrating, but this is going to work in our favour. Missing mediation is a big deal. This only strengthens our argument that he's unfit to have Sam as much as he wants him."

Something about the way Jessica avoided his gaze made Owen pause. That was the plan, right? He'd already started drafting his opening remarks for the court case.

"Do you know what keeps running through my mind?" Jessica whispered. "Sam's not even three. If I have to share custody for another fifteen years ..." She drew in a long, shuddery breath, but when she looked up, her eyes were clear, no trace of angry tears on her face today.

Owen had a bad feeling he knew what she was going to say before she even opened her mouth.

"I want full custody with no visitation."

"So, no contact for Sam with his dad at all?"

Fire flashed across her face. "Please don't judge me."

Owen sank into the chair next to her. "I'm not, I promise. I just want to make sure you understand that we'll almost definitely end up going to court over this. It's unlikely Rob will back down from fifty-fifty to nothing, even with a black mark against him for skipping today's session."

Jessica bit her lip.

"And it will probably get ugly. These things almost always do. I don't say that to scare you but to prepare you. They'll dig through your past and try to make you look bad." Jessica's criminal record would definitely be coming back to haunt them.

"But it's what's best for Sam, and there's nothing I won't do to protect him."

Owen kept his face blank, but the irony of the moment wasn't lost on him. Here was Jessica, who was prepared to go to war for her future, while Alice was desperate to make her troubles go away by not reacting at all. How was he going to balance each client's expectations within the realities of the law?

"Then that's what we'll do," he said.

Life was about to get very messy.

～

In hindsight, firefighter costumes would've been the lesser evil.

"How'd they managed to rope us into this anyway?" Raff asked, frowning at the hanging rack that held his suit. Lulu had wanted him to wear his police blues, but he'd refused, explaining it was against uniform policy. Owen's suit and Nate's NFL uniform were hanging next to them. Teddy would be wearing scrubs despite the fact he was studying to be a dentist, not a doctor. "Mum said it was your idea."

Owen raised his eyebrows, the whisper of a headache starting to pound behind his eyes. "Because this seems like something I'd suggest?"

"She trapped him," Nate piped up from the corner where he was fixing a chair with a loose leg. "He was trying to impress Alice. Didn't even put up a fight, apparently."

Brothers. They were the worst.

"That's not true," Owen huffed.

Each time the glass door slid open, barks and yips from the rescue dogs lined up in crates outside drifted in. Owen had walked past a few residents, including Jessica and Sam, cuddling puppies when he arrived.

"What's going on with the two of you?" Raff asked. "Teddy said you're always at their place."

Owen's grip on his mug tightened. "I'm not *always there*. Some mornings I shower there after my run. I always have. Nothing's changed."

"Because that's not weird," Raff mumbled as he looked out the window above the sink.

A mental image of Alice stumbling out of her bedroom, her little sleep shorts and long-sleeved pyjama shirt made from the material that made him think of waffles, all twisted around her body earlier in the week, sprang to mind. He cleared his throat. "The hot water system at my place is crap."

"So replace it?" Nate suggested.

With what extra money? Things had picked up, but there wasn't any fat in his budget. It was easy to say things like that when you had a bank account stuffed with earnings from a professional sporting career.

"Doesn't make sense when my place will be ready soon." The small lie slipped out easily. Impulsively buying a house as well as the business had been out of character for him. He didn't want to admit it had been a mistake.

He was about to make a crack about living with Teddy when the kitchen door banged open.

"Who's ready for their close-up?" Teddy's long hair fanned around his face, and his thongs slapped against the slate floor. "C'mon, Raff. Smile. No one likes a grumpy cop."

Raff rinsed out his coffee cup, put it in the dishwasher and checked his watch. "I'm going to see how long this is going to take." The door closed with a click behind him.

"What crawled up his ass?" Teddy asked.

Owen shrugged, happy to no longer be the focal point of the conversation. "Work's giving him grief. Dad said it looks like the guy they arrested in the Arturo investigation will be released."

Nate righted the chair and tested it for wobbles. "Sounds like you're seeing a lot of this clown these days," he said to Teddy, hooking his thumb towards Owen.

Teddy slung his arm around Owen's shoulder. "Oh yeah, he likes to come and flirt with Alice. Shows up all sweaty and red. Probably does some crunches in the car park to get his pump on before he comes up."

Owen elbowed his brother and shook his head. "I'll increase your rent if you don't shut up."

"He pretends he doesn't like her, but I think we all know the truth." Teddy held his hands together, so they formed a love heart and made smoochy noises.

Forget getting a social life; Owen might need a whole new family soon. At least he'd made inroads with the guys on the footy team after attending the last three pre-trivia dinners. "You guys are the worst. And you"—he pointed at Teddy—"are full of shit."

"You think? Nate, watch this." Teddy waited until Nate had packed away all his tools before turning to face Owen. "Sometimes she walks around without her bra on and ..."

Teddy stumbled to the left when Owen shoved him. "Don't be a dick," he said.

"What?" Teddy was all smirky, wide-eyed innocence. "We know you're a boob guy. Not as much as Nate, but still ..."

"I'm going to hit him properly this time," Owen said to Nate.

"Just not the face. Mum will be pissed if it shows up in the pictures."

"Language, Nathaniel," Lulu said as she stepped into the kitchen with Raff. "And why would I be 'pissed' as you stated so elegantly?"

"Because Owen—" Teddy yelped when Owen kicked him in the shins.

"Trust me. He deserved that," Owen said to his mother who ignored them all, used to their antics.

"They're almost ready for you all. Time to change." She pointed to the office off to the side of the kitchen.

They changed in silence, and Owen was pleased when Teddy winced, rubbing his hand over his shin as he held the exterior door open. "Let's go say hi to Owen's girlfriend."

If Teddy wasn't wearing pale blue scrubs, Owen would've pushed him sideways into the garden bed filled with agapanthus.

"Shut up," he growled, regretting it immediately when his brothers grinned. Anyone with siblings knew reacting was the worst thing he could've done.

"So, uh, where do you think you guys will get married?" Nate's lips twitched.

Owen breathed in deeply.

"Somewhere traditional, definitely," Raff added, a tinge of uncertainty in his tone like he'd forgotten how to tell a joke.

"He could wear a kilt!" Teddy slapped Owen on the back. "You've got the legs for it."

Nate laughed. "But we're not Scottish."

"Minor detail," Raff teased, his voice lighter. If Owen wasn't the target, he'd have been happy to hear his brother behaving like he used to.

"How's he going to pick a best man out of the three of us?" Teddy wanted to know.

"There'll be a pros and cons list. Or a roster. D'uh." As

Nate exaggerated the last word, the barn came into view. "Excel will be involved."

Owen tossed his hands in the air and then straightened his tie again, even though it was already perfectly straight. "You can all shut up. The hot water system at my place is dying. And work is closer to the trails."

"And he thinks Alice is super-hot," Teddy stage-whispered as they approached the barn.

"I don't think she's hot. She's not my type at all." Owen stared straight ahead, refusing to make eye contact with any of his brothers as he stepped through the open door. "Alice's my client. Nothing else."

"That's good to know," someone said from behind him.

Fuck. He'd know her voice anywhere.

At least Owen had the good grace to face her when he turned around. He was clean-shaven and in her favourite navy suit. *Since when do I have a favourite suit of his?* His maroon tie matched his pocket square, which matched the embarrassment on his face.

"Alice." Owen stuffed his hands in his pockets, but one immediately snaked towards his neck, pulling at his tie. "Hello."

She bit the inside of her cheek. Fine. If she was just a client, then he was just a lawyer. She could play this game. She tried to wave her hand, remembering too late it was full of dog leads. A handle whipped up, missing her face. *Smooth.*

"Here," Nate said, stepping forward, breaking the bubble of awkwardness they were trapped in. "Let me help."

Murphy, a gorgeous puppy with paws the size of dinner

plates, rubbed his nose against her yoga pant-clad leg, leaving behind a smear of dog snot and slobber. But it was impossible to stay mad at the pup with his chocolate eyes and sweet disposition.

"That'd be great, thanks." The shrillness of her voice bounced off the big beams in the barn, echoing in the cavernous space. Damn Owen for making her so off balance with his words.

"Awesome, everyone's here. You guys look fantastic," Eloise said.

Alice waited patiently while Eloise got all the brothers situated. Once they were ready, Alice tried to pass a border collie to Rafferty, but Owen leapt forward, claiming the dog for himself. The chatter in the barn dipped for a second before everyone kept talking, pretending it wasn't weird at all. Wattle Junction was starting to feel like home, but moments like this reminded Alice she was still an outsider.

"Here," she said, leading Murphy over to Rafferty. "You can have this love sponge instead."

"Perfect," Eloise said, and Alice hurried out of the shot. Murphy whined. He'd been stuck to her side ever since she'd arrived early to help—Lulu's suggestion so she could check out the old kitchen in the shearing shed. The 'kitchen'—and she used that word loosely—was nothing more than an old electric oven and cooktop paired with an equally decrepit fridge, but the space itself was so much bigger than what she had access to at home. Most importantly, everything worked. She'd be able to store all her supplies and the bags of clothes she still hadn't found time to sort through and sell in there. Once Owen was finished, she would ask him to draw up a lease for the space. She brushed at the clumps of dog hair stuck to her olive leggings, watching him from below her lashes.

"That boy over there can't stop looking at you," Eloise murmured, adjusting the dials on the top of her camera. "Maybe you should take him home with you."

Alice tore her gaze away from Owen and smiled at Murphy. The black and caramel fluff ball grinned back at her. "I'm not ready for a dog. I can barely look after myself."

"I'm not talking about Murphy." Eloise winked at Alice.

She twisted her ponytail around her hand. "Who? Rafferty? No, no, no." He looked a lot more like Owen in his suit, dark curls neatly brushed, face focused.

"Not talking about him either."

Eloise was imagining things. Owen wasn't looking at her. He was looking at the camera. And she was standing next to the camera.

"He definitely isn't," she muttered. His words still stung. Yeah, she was super dressed down today, and a whiff of Eau de Canine lingered around her, but to be told so bluntly he didn't find her attractive? Not a moment she needed to relive.

"Tilt your chin up a bit, Nate. Great. Hold steady, guys," Eloise called. Lowering her voice, she whispered to Alice, "But you were right about Murphy, and he needs a home ..."

"I wish I could," Alice said. The last few weeks Dougie and Rico hadn't been able to come to see her, and the pang of loneliness in her chest almost physically hurt. Murphy's tongue lolled out, and he gave the camera a huge, cheesy grin.

Maybe Eloise was on to something?

Besides, how hard could it be having a dog?

She went out running each morning, and dogs loved to run. If she got the shearers' shed, he could come to work with her. She tried to imagine the look on Phoenix's face if she'd had Murphy with her when he'd accosted her in the park. Phoenix *hated* dogs.

"You know what? I'm going to do it."

"Really?" Eloise grinned.

"Yep. I could use a friend out here."

Eloise looked up from her camera, eyes softening before she looked through the viewfinder again. "You should come to trivia next week with us. It's part of life out here. I should've reached out earlier, but I was trying to give you some space to settle in."

"Oh, I wasn't hinting or anything. The space has been good. I've needed it." She was a candle making pro because of it. Alice brushed at her legs again.

"You guys are done." The brothers stood and stretched. Eloise turned back towards Alice. "But you really should come. Everyone's dying to meet you properly."

"Maybe." Alice stepped forward, and Murphy broke away from Rafferty, bounding towards her.

"Hello, gorgeous," she said, burying her face into the soft fur of his neck. How anyone could not want this ball of love was beyond her.

"Guess what," Eloise said. "Alice's going to adopt Murphy!"

"Really? Is that a good idea?" Ahh, yes. Right on time. Someone to rain on her parade. The fact it was Owen hurt even more after his confession earlier. She'd thought ... well, it didn't matter what she thought.

Alice's head snapped up, and Murphy licked her neck like he knew she needed help to stay calm. She arched an unattractive eyebrow at Owen. "Why wouldn't it be?"

"A dog's a big responsibility, and you live in an apartment. A small apartment filled with boxes of candles," Owen said. He'd commented on the number of boxes that had spilt out of her bedroom and into the lounge room two days ago when he used the shower.

"Plenty of people have dogs and live in apartments. Besides, I've got a plan for my candle business." The old stove in the shearers' shed suddenly looked very good.

Owen shrugged, unbothered or oblivious to the bite to her tone. "Maybe a smaller dog, then. Less food, vet bills. He looks like a Bernese mountain dog."

Alice couldn't have cared less about what type of dog Murphy was. He was a sweetheart. And an orphan! Surely a Bernese mountain dog would enjoy running in the mountains. If it was in his name, it'd be in his blood. This would be better than fine.

She wrapped her arms around Murphy's neck, her decision made. "You hear that, buddy. You're going to be all mine."

"Oh, shoot, the light's going. We need to hustle, Alice," Eloise said, and Alice looked over her shoulder. The sky had changed while they'd been in the barn, the fingers of burnt orange sinking closer to the horizon.

"Give me ten minutes to fix my hair and face," Alice said.

Eloise folded up her tripod, attached it to her camera backpack. "Let's go with a natural look. You brought jeans, yeah? Pop them on with a nice white shirt, I've got a spare in the kitchen if you want, bare feet, and leave your hair out. I promise I'll make you look great—not that you need any help. You're gorgeous."

Nice someone thought so.

13

"Come on, big guy," Alice said fifteen minutes later. Murphy leapt up onto the bench, his paws resting on her thighs. She settled one hand on his back, the other arranging the ruffled skirt of her one-shouldered coral dress so it sat perfectly. Eloise's outfit suggestion would've been simpler, but Alice had wanted something bolder, more polished. An outfit that said she was doing just fine on her own, thanks very much. She wished she'd gotten a pedicure, but this wasn't *Vogue*.

"Owen, can you move the big light closer to me? Yep. Yep. There. That's as good as it's going to get."

Of course, he'd volunteered to help Eloise.

Alice tilted her chin and remembered to smile with her eyes as well. She shivered when a breeze rolled through, the scent of lavender following it like a wave at the beach. Murphy's nose twitched, and he sat up, looking away from the camera out towards the field of lavender behind them. "This way," Alice whispered, pointing, but he didn't turn around.

"Murphy." Eloise waved a hand above the camera.

A shrill whistle cut through the air, and everyone looked at Owen. "Murphy," he crooned, his voice unnaturally soft and velvety. And *holy moly*, Murphy wasn't the only one caught in a trance. God, the number of women Owen must have bedded with that tone. Obviously, this would be the only time Alice ever heard it seeing as though he thought she was a cave troll.

"Murphy." There it was again. It reminded her of the moment a spoon pushed into a chocolate pudding and all the melty deliciousness oozed out. Alice shivered again, and this time it had nothing to do with the wind.

"Okay, I think we're done." The glow from the LCD screen on the back of Eloise's camera cast shadows across her face.

"Good boy!" Alice nuzzled Murphy, and he responded by licking her face before leaping off the bench, cocking his leg. Alice was so pleased he didn't pee when he was on her lap that she didn't notice his lead falling. She was busy making a mental list of everything she needed to get for him.

"Murphy!" Owen called, his normal tone shattering her daydream.

Alice looked down. The puppy was gone.

She whipped her head around until she saw him barrelling through the lavender field in the fading light.

Oh God. This was a disaster, like everything else she tried to do.

"Come on." Owen's hand clasped hers, and he pulled her up off the seat. "We better catch him before he finds the dam."

"The dam?"

Sweet mercy. She was already a failure as a pet owner. This had to be a new record.

OWEN SHUCKED his jacket and passed it to Alice. The tall, thin reeds around the southern edge of the dam rustled in the wind.

"I'm fine." Her icy tone matched the temperature. "We should split up. We'd cover more ground."

He didn't blame her for being brusque. If the situation had been reversed, his feathers would've been ruffled as well. Of course, he wouldn't have been wearing actual feathers like she was. But the ombre pink feathered necklace she wore worked for her. Everything she wore worked for her, which was why he'd snapped at his brothers, worried his rapidly growing attraction to her was becoming too obvious. Owen swallowed. "It'll be dark soon. You could get lost."

"*You* could get lost," she volleyed back, wrapping her arms around her chest.

"Sure." He sighed. "I could."

Even if he hadn't been on thin ice, Owen wasn't about to point out he'd grown up running all over this place. He'd know it blindfolded. He held his jacket out again, trying to make amends. "Please?"

"Fine," she mumbled, shrugging it over her shoulders. The jacket was so big she could've wrapped it around her body twice. He definitely didn't notice how good she looked in his clothes either. Nope. Not him.

An excited yip cut through the air and Owen froze, trying to pinpoint where the sound had come from.

"Murphy," Alice called tentatively, reaching around Owen to point her phone towards the northern end of the dam where the jetty was. The wooden structure was a popular spot in summer when locals would don their life-jackets—no one was allowed to swim without one—and jump off it until they tired themselves out.

"Is that ..."

Owen ground his jaws together. Murphy was at the end of the jetty, his eyes glittering in the beam of light. Alice pushed past him, hiking her long skirt up around her knees. He grabbed her arm. "We don't want to spook him."

She looked down at his hand, and he let her go. Right, he wasn't supposed to touch her. Or notice how soft her skin was. Alice gestured for him to go ahead of her. He'd only taken one step when she grabbed his arm. Their gazes met. Her mascara was smudged like the night he'd met her. He liked her best when she was a bit messy. It was like he was seeing the real Alice, the one not many people got to see.

"Do you think he can swim? I mean, all dogs can, right? Like how birds can fly? Can baby birds fly?"

"Uhhh, I think so." Owen helped Alice over a mossy rock, his hands lingering against her soft palms before he let her go. He'd imagined kissing her for weeks now, and under different circumstances, the blossoming moonlight would've been the perfect backdrop. You know, if he hadn't lied about how gorgeous he thought she was, had her over-hear it and think he was an asshole and she wasn't his client.

All minor details.

The puppy barked again.

It only took two minutes to get to the jetty, climbing carefully over more rocks and navigating mud, but it felt like forever. "Murphy," Owen called, and the puppy dropped to the wooden planks, rolled over onto his back and begged for a tummy rub.

"Couldn't have made it easy and done what he was told, could he?" Alice whispered.

Owen swallowed a smile.

"I saw that." She nudged him in his side, her anger from before nowhere to be seen. "You were going to make a crack about him being like his owner, weren't you?"

"I don't know what you're talking about," Owen said softly. But yeah, he was going to, even though it would've been throwing fuel on the fire that sprung up whenever they were together. The thing was, he couldn't help it. It was like his brain and his mouth weren't connected when she was around. Alice made him feel out of control in the best way.

The plank under his foot creaked, and Alice lunged towards him, the warmth of her body pressing against his. "Oh my God." Her shaky laugh caressed his face. "That scared me."

They edged forward quietly; the only sound was the thumping of Murphy's tail against the wooden planks.

"He thinks it's a game." Owen shook his head. When Alice dropped to her knees, Murphy tried to jump up, his muddy paws skittering across the planks. There was a pause that felt like forever before the puppy fell sideways off the jetty.

"Murphy!" Alice cried.

Without another thought, Owen jumped into the freezing water. He coughed as he broke the surface, wiping his face. He'd guessed when he said all dogs could swim.

What if Murphy couldn't?

"He's over there. Can you see him?"

Owen squinted, finally seeing the dog-like blob amongst the small splashes near the support post on the other side. The poor thing was doing an improvised doggy paddle which was more like a crocodile's death roll. *Instincts, my ass.*

Owen swam in his direction, trying to ignore the way the icy fingers of the water seeped all the way down to his bones. The pup collapsed against him, his snout burrowing into Owen's neck. "Come here, troublemaker."

"Is he okay?" Alice called, her voice shrill.

Owen followed the light slicing through the gaps between the planks until the metal ladder brushed against his hand. "He's fine. We're coming up," he called, tucking Murphy against his chest.

All his afternoons at the rock-climbing gym in Somers Gully hadn't prepared him for climbing sopping wet with a wriggling puppy in his arms, but after a few tense moments, they got there.

"Murphy!" Alice cried, when he passed her the pup. She clutched him to her chest. "That was very naughty!"

She twisted awkwardly, shrugging her shoulders as Murphy's front legs dangled over her arm. Too late, Owen realised she was trying to take off his jacket. She held it out towards him. "God, you must be freezing."

He'd been warmer. And he'd never looked forward to his shower more, even if it would only be a few degrees warmer than the dam.

"I'm okay," he said, rubbing his arms. Goosebumps pricked his skin. His arms and legs were like logs as adrenaline flowed out of his body like the rivers of water pooling around his feet.

Alice rocked Murphy from side to side, a relieved smile on her face ... and, *worth it*. When their eyes met, there was no trace of the usual defensiveness on her features. Instead, her lips widened, her tongue darting out to wet the bottom one. "Thank you. I don't know what I would've done without your help." She seemed to sag, like a balloon that had lost all its air. The funny plait wrapped around her head had fallen out, wet strands of hair sticking to her neck and chest. "He could've drowned, and it would've been all my fault."

"But he didn't." Owen dipped his head so he could see her properly. Mascara snaked down her cheeks, and the top of her dress clung to her breasts where she was holding Murphy.

"Come on," he said. His hand hovered near the small of her back. Maybe he was imagining it, but he swore she swayed towards him. Touching her now would be a terrible idea.

"Let's get somewhere warmer." His car wasn't far, parked near the lavender field. He was still debating touching her when Alice placed Murphy on the ground, leant forward and hugged him.

His arms automatically wrapped around her, and he couldn't help but notice how perfectly she fit, tucked up against his chest, the top of her head resting under his chin. She sucked in a deep breath, her chest pressing against his. Turns out the cold water had been a blessing after all.

Because stirrings ... *so many stirrings.*

Alice released her breath slowly, the puff of warm air skating across his neck.

"I'm sorry about what you heard before," he said quietly, just loud enough to be heard over the rustling reeds.

She stiffened in his arms, creating space between them before she stepped away. The temperature dropped, and so did his stomach. He didn't like how weary she looked, like there was no fight left in her.

She offered him a tight smile. "You don't need to apologise. I'm not for everyone."

"No, that's not what I meant ..." *Shit.* Owen squeezed his toes, his socks squelching in his shoes.

She laughed, dry and brittle. "Someone like you would

never be attracted to someone like me. It's fine. I don't walk around thinking everyone finds me attractive. I know I'm flawed."

How had he made this even worse?

"That's not what I meant." Owen planted his hands on his hips. How could he convince her without seeming like he was cracking on to her, which would be inappropriate? He hated being inappropriate. He was practically allergic to it. "You're not ..."

"Wrong?" Alice's laugh was even more mirthless than before. "We should get out of here before you both catch a cold. You should use the shower at my place tonight."

He couldn't take another step until he'd cleared this up. He just couldn't. "I don't think you're unattractive. You weren't meant to hear that before. Teddy was being an ass, and I was trying to shut him up. I think you're very—"

"Owen," Alice snapped, raking a hand across her face. "Please stop. It's fine."

He was trying to figure out what to say when she climbed into his Jeep and closed the door on their conversation.

14

"Let's cut to the chase," Dean Malus, Owen's old boss, said. "There are very few assets to divide. All the business contracts have already been taken care of." He opened his leather briefcase and passed a document to Owen and the mediator, a pleasant woman in a floral blouse and pearls.

It took Owen a second to understand what he was looking at.

That asshole.

"There are only a few personal effects and the matter of the joint bank account to settle," Dean continued, adjusting his frameless glasses. Phoenix picked up his phone and started scrolling.

"Personal effects? He said he didn't want the furniture!" Alice hissed, shooting Owen an alarmed look. He resisted the urge to touch her hand—just enough to remind her she wasn't alone. But that would be inappropriate and unwelcome given how standoffish she'd been when she first arrived. If her outfit was an indicator of her mood, today's sequined skirt, black leggings and denim shirt sent a clear message. The warrior hair was back, too. Alice Aspinall, reality TV starlet, was in the building. Not the Alice he'd seen glimpses of over the last few weeks with her messy hair and the smattering of freckles across her nose and cheeks.

Phoenix snorted, mumbling something about remembering what else she'd done, a smarmy grin stretching across his face.

"Ms Aspinall damaged several of Mr Storm's guitars and other recording equipment when she cleaned out their old apartment. That's the estimate to have it all replaced."

"What?" Alice snatched the paper before Owen could remind her they were trying to bait her. "I didn't ... You want seventy thousand dollars? There weren't any instruments in the apartment!"

"There's another matter," Dean said, sliding another piece of paper across the oak table. "The rings."

Not this again.

"Any jewellery given on *Take a Chance of Love* remained the property of the production company for the two years after filming wrapped," Owen said. "Then they became the sole property of the recipient. Alice's rings were hers to sell. Phoenix can do whatever he likes with his."

Alice mumbled something that sounded a lot like "tiny cock ring for his tiny penis", which Owen chose to ignore.

"Hmmm." His old boss fixed him with a hard stare. It was one of his trademark moves, but Owen wouldn't bite. When he didn't reply, Dean continued, "That's your interpretation. Ours is different. Perhaps we could be persuaded to come around to your way of thinking and ignore the damaged equipment and instruments if Alice agreed to split the money from her rings. There's also the matter of my client's lost income from cancelled tours."

Owen slid a look towards Alice. Her hands gripped the armrest of her chair, her eyelashes fluttering around watery eyes. *Fuck it.* She had to know he was on her side. He touched her hand, felt the warmth of her skin. Alice's fingers wrapped around his, her breathing slowing. Her eyes flicked towards him, her cheekbones more pronounced than normal. Up so close to her, he could see the skin under her eyes was purple, her fatigue barely concealed by her make-up.

"No," Owen monotoned. "Where's the police report about all this damaged stuff? Insurance paperwork? If you're going to continue with these egregious claims, then we'll see you in court." He stood, and yeah, he knew it was a power move but fuck them. He'd had enough. This was a waste of everyone's time, and Alice was about to burst into tears.

Dean steepled his fingers together, shrugging. "I guess it all comes down to how quickly Ms Aspinall wants this divorce to happen. Mr Storm will only play nice for so long before he's forced to act in his best interests."

Owen used to tell himself he had to be competitive to win. He couldn't be blinking every time someone tossed a threat his way. But he'd been blinded by his desire to achieve for too long and ignored too many red flags.

"Let's pause here." The mediator looked around the table. "These are serious allegations, Mr Storm. Do you have any supporting evidence?"

Phoenix exhaled lazily, stretching his arms out wide. "Maybe Alice was high when she did it. She likes to pretend she's all innocent and virtuous, but that couldn't be further from the truth."

Owen's first instinct was to check in on Alice, make sure she was okay. His second was to smack the smug look off Phoenix's face.

"High?" Alice's hands gripped the table like it was a life raft.

"I would strongly advise you against making unfounded, slanderous accusations about my client. We're done here." Owen clenched his jaws.

Phoenix stood and sauntered towards the door, a satisfied smile on his face. "I think we all know the truth; maybe it's time everyone else did too."

Dean followed without a goodbye or backwards glance. His own version of a power move.

Owen waited until the mediator had also left to close the door. He'd barely turned towards Alice before she erupted.

ALICE TWISTED her hands in her hair, pulling out her braid. Her canary yellow sneakers were next to go, kicked across the room. "If Phoenix thinks ..."

What? That he'd get away with this. Why wouldn't he?

He always had.

She'd covered for him for so long. Her throat squeezed painfully. What was that saying? Something about the elephant in the room? Well, the one in here was sitting on her chest.

"I can't ... I can't ..."

If she didn't give in, Phoenix would show everyone those photos and tell them she'd been high when she stripped off and posed for those stupid, sexy pictures. The truth wouldn't matter. She slumped forward, crumpling like a house of cards.

This was it.

Rock bottom.

Alice blinked furiously, trying to clear her vision, but the carpet fibres blended into a big grey blob. Dizziness overwhelmed her.

"Here." Owen guided her to the nearest chair, his hand cupping her elbow. He knelt in front of her, tipping her chin up until their gazes met. His touch was featherlight, gentle ... so different from how firm she'd imagined he would be.

"It's okay. You're okay. Big, noisy breaths. Like me." He overexaggerated his breathing, the deep navy of his tie pushing towards her before pulling away in time with his breaths. She tried to mimic his movements, but all the neural pathways from her brain were broken.

"You can do it," he said. His calm demeanour smothered some of the clanging noises in her head. "Like me, Alice. In and out. In and out. That's it."

She slumped backwards, and he reached across the table for a glass of water.

"Someone once told me to focus on the things I could control when everything was spinning out of control."

"I can't control anything!" Great, halting breaths punctuated her words.

"Focus on the little details. One for each sense. What can you smell?"

She looked at him blankly. What the hell ...

"I can smell coffee." Owen nodded towards the cups on the table. "And I can feel my palms sweating."

She opened her mouth, but words were impossible.

"I can see a spot on the wall where I stuffed up the painting." He pointed to a section near the door. She squinted, her heart rate slowing marginally. There was a long smear in the brushwork above the skirting board.

"Do you want to try? What can you smell?"

She nodded, her throat bobbing as she swallowed. Her lashes fluttered closed, and she tried to block out all the noise in her mind. There was a hint of something crisp. Clean. "Citrus. Your cologne, maybe."

Owen smiled, the biggest one he'd ever given her. Alice wanted to put it in her pocket, keep it forever. His eyes had softened, his mouth relaxing like it was something he did all the time. And maybe he did, but she'd certainly never seen him like this before.

"What am I going to do?" she whispered.

"All divorces are a fight, Alice. Some are just nicer than others. But Phoenix is always going to steamroll you unless you try to burn his shit down."

When he swore, something inside Alice lit up.

"Figuratively. Promise me you won't burn anything."

She rubbed her face, a quiet laugh escaping as she reached for her water glass.

Owen cleared his throat, and she looked up warily.

"The best way I can defend you is with the truth. What Phoenix said about the drugs …"

"God! No. I'm stupid, but I'm not that stupid," she blurted, wanting—no, *needing*—to dispel any misconceptions he had about her. Would he still feel the same way if he knew about the photos? How quickly would the inevitable disappointment on his face send her spiralling again?

"Mum made us volunteer at drug rehabilitation programs when we were teenagers so we'd understand how dangerous they are. I've never touched the stuff. That's his thing, not mine."

"Then why would Phoenix say you might've been high? His threat made it sound like he had evidence of some sort?"

Alice paused. Here was the moment. Telling Owen

about the photos would be beyond mortifying, but it wasn't like she was the first woman to pose in her lingerie for their partner.

She bit her lip and looked up. The concern in Owen's gaze made her push away any thought of confessing. Hopefully, this would just go away. And she knew Phoenix. If she pushed back about the pictures now, this whole thing would drag on even more. Phoenix would get even nastier. Alice's chest squeezed again, a wave of fatigue sweeping through her body. When she spoke, she was quiet, defeated. "What do you think about their offer?"

Owen spun his chair towards her. She'd bet she looked as messy as she felt.

"Honestly, Phoenix wants to win. At any cost. He will destroy your reputation whether or not you pay him. And if he's using drugs, he'll be unpredictable and dangerous in a different way. The best thing we can do, in my opinion, is fight back. Legally, of course. Show him you won't let him get away with this. Sometimes things have to get worse before they get better."

She stared down at her chipped fingernail polish.

"I know it's a lot and there'd be more media interest, but ..." It was like he could read her mind.

Alice's head shook involuntarily. Taking a deep breath, she wiped her eyes.

Her face and name would be splashed across the papers again, social media filling with clickbait stories and God, if cancel culture caught up with her before her business was established, she'd be sunk. But a settlement would mean she was left with nothing again. All her ring money would evaporate, and she wouldn't have the capital to get The Emancipation of Alice off the ground.

"I need to think about this."

Owen leant away from her and zipped his folio shut. "Take a few days. Let me know if you have any questions."

Even though his voice was calm and even, Alice knew she'd disappointed him. She'd just add him to the long list.

15

A woman Alice hadn't seen in years stared back at her in the mirror. Her hair was now a short, textured bob with a sweeping side fringe. The coppery hue was so close to her natural colour; the hair stylist must've been part magician. Said magician was currently washing out Lulu's hair, the hum of their conversation mixing with the Taylor Swift song playing.

Alice twisted her head from side to side; the familiarity of this new-but-old look was exactly what she needed after yesterday's disastrous mediation meeting. She straightened her shoulders at the memory, refusing to let Phoenix and his threats destroy this tiny moment of joy that she'd carved out for herself. Instead, she remembered how earnest and sweet Owen had been helping her calm down and encouraging her to fight back. What would he think of her new look?

Things had changed between them since what she was now calling 'The Mr Darcy Incident' at the dam at Kathleen's Place. They were friendly ... not friends, but something more than lawyer and client or landlord and tenant. Whatever they were wasn't important now, though; she had to focus on figuring out what to do about Phoenix. The idea of giving him any money made her nauseous.

"I like it," Joan Mandrill, a friend of Lulu's and Eloise's grandmother, said from the station next to hers. Her pink hair was still processing, and she looked like a snow cone.

Lulu sat on the other side of Alice, a lavender towel around her shoulders, her short hair all spiky and wet. "Me too. And it's perfect timing, what with needing to reshoot your calendar pictures."

What had Owen called these women again? The Old Girls Gossip Brigade? They definitely knew everything that happened in this town. Eloise had only called to ask if they could redo the photos that morning.

"I love the idea of this being your public rebirth. Showing the world the new Alice," Joan said.

Alice's stomach twisted. Was there any point, though? Really?

Lulu snapped her fingers and pointed at Alice in her mirror. "This new Alice looks like she means business, too. I'm here for it."

Realisation hit her as Lulu and Joan argued over whether or not Lulu had used that phrase correctly—side note, she had. But this was what Owen had been trying to say yesterday.

It was time to stop caring about what could go wrong and fight for what she wanted for her future. Her business was taking shape at a rapid rate and now she had a new look, no one could deny she'd changed.

This was her chance to control the narrative.

Let people know she wasn't the silly pushover they'd always assumed she was.

Put her money—and her heart—where her mouth was and back herself. It was hypocritical to try and sell the idea of The Emancipation of Alice if she wasn't going to behave differently.

But a bad taste lingered in her mouth.

Fear.

Alice took a deep breath. Noticed the oversized birds of paradise on either side of the salon doors. The tumble of the dryer in the small back room. The French pear diffuser on the counter. She was bigger than her fear.

She had to be.

She pulled out her phone and found Owen's contact.

> Alice: Let's burn all of Phoenix's shit to the ground. It's time for the real emancipation of Alice.

She cleared her throat. Lulu and Joan looked up. "I've had an idea," she said.

A vision of Owen flashed before her, his brown eyes focused ... *encouraging.*

"I want to make special edition candles that benefit different charities. I'd donate all the profits, and I'd like to do one for Kathleen's Place. What do you think?"

The ladies exchanged a look, but it was Lulu who smiled first. "We're not in the habit of saying no to fundraisers. This will pair beautifully with the calendar and Owen's big race."

"What race?" Alice asked.

"Some adventure thing," Joan said.

"He's a good one." Lulu's smile widened. She looked almost predatory, which was weird, right? "Makes me proud all the time. All my boys do."

"I heard he rescued your puppy last week." Joan's eyebrows crept towards her fairy floss-coloured hair.

The intricately woven cane basket that stored the spare towels suddenly seemed very interesting. "He's a very good swimmer, which is lucky." Was Alice's face on fire? It felt like it was.

"Must be those big feet of his," Joan teased. "You know what they say about big feet ..."

Good God, the woman was a grandmother. And Owen's mother was sitting right there. Alice blushed.

Based on the way his pants had been glued to his body, despite the cold temperature, his foot size was ... *ahem* ... accurate. But Alice didn't say that.

"I wish someone would jump into a dam for me." Joan sighed. "So romantic."

An itch crawled across Alice's skin. "It was for Murphy."

It was quite impressive how Lulu and Joan snorted in unison.

"Owen isn't interested in me—he literally told me he finds me unattractive—"

"What? I raised him better than that!"

"—and even if he was, I'm in the middle of a divorce. A boyfriend is the absolute last thing I want right now."

"Who said anything about a boyfriend?" Joan asked. "Have some fun. I bet Owen could be fun. You could be friends with benefits!"

Lulu nodded. "Or ... what's the other name for it? Some type of buddies ..."

Alice blanched.

"We've got a book club, you know." Joan pursed her lips. "We read *Fifty Shades of Grey* last month. We're not *that* old. All those whips and contracts, though. So much effort."

Alice clapped her hands on her thighs. "Would you look at the time! I better get going. I have some candles to make before I meet up with Eloise."

Lulu picked up her coffee as the hairstylist reappeared.

"We'll meet you there and help you set up so you can finish making the candles for the launch."

"You don't have to do that."

"We look after our own out here, Alice. We're happy to help. And we'll bring gluten-free snacks." Joan winked.

A different kind of warmth spread throughout Alice's body, and she looked at her reflection again. This new version of Alice was already better than who she'd been pretending to be for the last few years.

OWEN WAS IN SERIOUS PAIN, and Nate and Teddy were about to wet their pants laughing at him. They giggled like children every time he ground his jaws together and groaned.

And he'd been groaning plenty.

"What's going on today, O? You normally lift more than this." Nate leant forward to spot him as Owen pushed the bar away from his chest.

Two more. Then he'd be done.

"But does he really?" Teddy quipped.

Even if a tsunami of sweat was sliding down Owen's forehead, he'd still be able to see Teddy's shit-eating grin.

"Have we considered that maybe he wears shoulder pads every day?"

Owen was this close to telling them to shut up, but a) that'd just make them happier and b) he might drop the bar on his chest. Really, his day had started brilliantly with a message from Alice telling him she was ready to light all of Phoenix's shit on fire. Once his heart rate had returned to normal and he'd had a second to translate her clumsy metaphor, he'd—embarrassingly—done a fist pump in his office. And then he'd reminded himself that she was his client because, *Jesus*, the breathy excitement in her tone made him forget he was her lawyer when he called her to confirm. He hadn't really needed to speak to her, but he'd wanted to ... which was a problem.

The residual energy and—*he huffed*—arousal had carried him through the morning with a spring in his step and a smile that made his cheeks hurt.

It had all come crashing down in this afternoon's mediation with Jessica. Rob had arrived early, both arms in plaster, courtesy of a car crash that had knocked him unconscious, which explained why he wasn't able to make the previous session. And then they'd presented all their supporting documentation. He'd spent the last year in a sober living facility and was a regular attendee at his local Gamblers Anonymous. He had a steady job and a small flat he'd toddler-proofed. There was even a swing set in the small courtyard. More evidence he'd tried to get in touch with Jessica and her family to give her child support. A thick binder full of character references and reports from his doctors. Through tears, Rob had apologised and stressed that all he wanted was a relationship with his son.

Owen had sat there, asking questions, taking notes, his expression perfectly blank, knowing Jessica's chances of getting full custody with no visitation for Rob were evaporating by the second. It was unlikely Rob would be given the fifty-fifty he was angling for, but ... Jessica was in for disappointment, and there wasn't anything he could do to stop it. He'd tried to talk to her about it gently, but she hadn't wanted to listen.

He pushed the bar up again, gritting his teeth and only letting go when it was safely on the rack.

Nate passed him a towel as he sat up. "I've got bad news."

This day just gets better and better.

Owen's arms ached as he wiped his face. "Hmm?"

"I can't do the race. I'm sorry, mate. My US trip dates have changed because of a scheduling clash with the main sponsor, and I can't really skip my own charity's gala. I won't get home until after the race has started now. But I'm still on board with being a sponsor, though. Or donating the money for the renovation. I'm always happy to support KPs."

Owen swallowed. Nate wasn't trying to throw it in his face that he could write a cheque with a bunch of zeroes on it. He'd always been generous, especially with his family. Hell, Nate had even offered to be Owen's silent partner, but he'd been too proud to accept. This was another reason he'd invited his brothers to his place for this weights session instead of the state-of-the-art fancy set-up Nate had at his house.

Owen was in a mood and needed to sweat it out before he did something reckless, like ask if Alice still wanted to watch a movie, dangerously blurring the line between their professional relationship and budding friendship.

"More like he's trying to get Eloise to notice him," Teddy muttered, and Nate threw his drink bottle at him.

"She notices me plenty, jackass."

"Then why are you stuck in the friend zone?"

Scratch the movie idea. Being relegated to friend status with Alice would be worse than wanting her from afar.

"You're not stuck if that's where you want to be."

"Please," Teddy scoffed. "No one believes that. You follow her around like a puppy. I should know, an actual puppy lives with me now."

"Eloise is my friend. And my best friend's sister."

"Let's not get distracted. It's not a big deal. These things come up," Owen said, but disappointment settled low in his belly. The race wasn't just for Kathleen's Place, either. It was another chance for him to reconnect with the community and keep spreading the word about his business. Owen guzzled half his water as he considered his options. Raff would absolutely beg off, saying he was too busy with work. He slid his gaze towards Teddy.

"Don't get any ideas. I'm going to Fiji with the boys to escape the crappy Victorian winter."

As Alice would say—something Owen found himself constantly thinking these days—that was 'on brand'.

"I'll figure something out. There's still plenty of time."

OWEN WAS LYING on the couch later, an empty beer in the crook of his elbow and a basketball game on the TV as he re-read his notes for Jessica's case when his phone rang. Next up on his list of exciting evening plans: prepping his opening argument for Alice's divorce trial. "How's my favourite brother?"

Rafferty laughed. "Teddy's already texted me. I can't do the race, sorry, mate. Work's bananas busy right now."

"It's not for a few months, though." And a shared goal would be good for them both.

"I'd love to do it ..."

Owen waited for the 'but'. Raff's voice was already heavy with apology. "It doesn't even matter if we don't place. We could focus on the sponsorships. I'll organise it all."

A long silence stretched between them, and Owen walked to his small fridge, pulling out another beer. He was searching for the bottle opener when Raff spoke.

"I just can't commit. There's all this *stuff* going on I can't talk about. You'll find out about it soon enough. It's, well, let's say, you'll be very aware of it. It's actually why I'm calling."

Wait, what? Owen put the unopened beer down. "Is there something I should know?"

Raff sighed. "Not exactly. But you'll be impacted, kind of. I can't tell you anything else. I shouldn't have even said that."

"What's that mean?"

"You should check on Alice," Raff said so quietly Owen wasn't sure he'd heard him right.

"Alice? My Alice?" How was she involved in the Arturo investigation? And if Raff noticed Owen's slip of the tongue, he didn't mention it.

"She could use some company tonight. Trust me. I gotta go." Raff hung up.

Owen grabbed his keys and wallet and rushed out the door. Dust swirled after his tyres like all the questions in his mind.

16

O wen balanced two pizza boxes and a Greek salad in one hand as he raised the other to knock on Alice's door. The bag at his feet held a bottle of mineral water and a DVD. Just in case. It would've been weird to bring wine. It was strange enough he was standing on her doorstep.

"Hi," Alice said as she opened the door. Murphy tried to dart past her legs, but she snagged him by the collar, scooping him into her arms.

"You changed your hair," Owen said. "And you're wearing jeans. And glasses." Thick black frames encircled her blue eyes. *Top of his class*, ladies and gentlemen, and *that's* what his brain had come up with.

Alice braced her hip against the doorframe, readjusting her grip on Murphy. "I did. And I normally wear contacts, but my eyes have been itchy today."

Christ. He'd thought she was hot before, but now she looked like a naughty librarian, he was done for. She would absolutely show up in his dreams tonight wearing those glasses and nothing else.

Her gaze dropped to the pizza boxes. "Teddy's gone out with mates."

Here goes nothing. "I was actually looking for you."

"Me?" Her eyes tracked up and down his body, over his jeans and long-sleeved navy Henley. Owen didn't blame her for looking surprised; he didn't really know why he was there either.

"Something strange happened. Can I come in?" he said.

Alice hesitated for a second as she chewed on her bottom lip. "Sure. Make yourself at home while I take this guy out." She snatched a dog lead off the hook next to the door and headed down the stairs.

The apartment looked different. The towering boxes of candle supplies were gone, replaced with several soft toys with the stuffing bursting out of them and a shredded blanket. All the cushions from the couch were gone, and three candles were burning on top of the fridge. Dining chairs were stacked against the far wall. Alice's laptop was set up on the table, surrounded by a collection of water glasses, coffee cups and a lone wine glass with rosé in it. There were other touches of her scattered around the room as well. A snake plant in a Buddha-shaped pot on the entertainment unit. The dusty pink blanket tossed over the side of the futon.

"Pretend you didn't see this mess." Alice reappeared, and Murphy pushed past her and wound himself around Owen's legs.

"Sure." Owen shrugged, leaning down to pat the dog. He straightened back up, rubbing the back of his neck. "I wasn't sure if you'd be hungry, but I brought pizza."

"Thanks, but I can't have—"

"It's gluten free. I called Tino's and asked for whatever you'd ordered last. Teddy mentioned you guys have had takeaway from there before. Mine's gluten free, too, in case you wanted some."

This time, her surprised look rankled a little. For God's sake, he was a nice guy.

"Thanks." She stepped around him, pulling a few plates out of the cupboard. Murphy tried to jump up, his front paws on the back of her denim-clad thighs. "No chance," she muttered.

Owen opened the boxes, steam wafting up, the smell of cheese and pepperoni filling the air.

"Why don't we eat outside?" Alice suggested, putting a few pieces of vegetarian pizza on her plate. "Murphy can chill inside. There's wine in the fridge if you want some."

"Do you want a refill?"

"Please."

And that's how Owen found himself sitting on the floor of Alice's balcony, drinking a rosé he'd never tried before, watching the sunset fade and stars begin to wink in the sky. Waves of warm air from the outdoor heater kept the chill of the night away.

"Hey, Owen," Alice said after a few minutes of silence, tossing her pizza crust back onto her plate. "This is nice and all, but why are you here?"

Owen set his drink down next to him, his thumb swiping at a drop of condensation on the side. "Raff called and said I should come and check in with you. That you might want some company."

"Me? Why?" Alice stretched out her legs, her glittery socks sparkling under the glow of the outdoor light above them.

"I don't know. He's working on this big investigation, and he had to go. So here I am."

She looked at him sideways from beneath her lashes.

"And here you are." Alice folded her pizza in half, taking a big bite as she pulled her phone out of the back pocket of her jeans. "No one's called me."

Owen shifted, trying to pretend the way his stomach squirmed was because he couldn't remember the last time he'd had pizza, let alone one loaded with processed meat, even if it was delicious. Raff wouldn't have said what he had without reason, but ... why did he? He wiped his hands on one of the serviettes and crumpled it up. Now he knew Alice was fine, he'd get out of her hair. Maybe sit in his car in the driveway for a bit to make sure she was really okay, but the last thing he wanted was for her to think he'd created an elaborate ruse to spend time with her. Shit, what if she thought he was hitting on her? He gulped the last of his wine, not even tasting it. He was about to stand when she spoke.

"I misjudged you originally, you know. Thought you were the stereotypical lawyer guy. All business, no fun."

His lips pulled into a relieved smile, and he relaxed back against the brick wall. What was the harm in staying a tiny bit longer? "I was. Still am a bit, really, but I'm working on it. You're not the only one trying to make changes."

"Maybe you should dye your hair," she teased, nudging him lightly with her elbow. "You could go super blond. Teddy would love it."

He rolled his eyes, her lilting laugh making his smile morph into a proper grin. "I don't think so."

"Imagine what the Old Girls would say, though. They were telling me about fuck buddies earlier."

Owen choked on a piece of pepperoni. "If my mother was there, I don't want to know. That information can't be unheard."

Alice snickered, reaching for a piece of his pizza with the lot. He pushed the box towards her.

"She has some *opinions*, shall we say?"

"Stop," he groaned, covering his ears. "Please. I beg you."

Alice pulled an olive off the pizza and popped it into her mouth, her eyes twinkling. When she looked at him like that, it wasn't hard to imagine all the other things he'd like to beg her for.

And even though he still didn't know what Raff had meant—it must have had something to do with Phoenix— this was the nicest night Owen had had in far too long.

Alice bit into the pizza and made a noise he'd imagined her making in the bedroom. He shifted in his seat, made sure his plate was on his lap.

"You don't know how lucky you are to have a place like Tino's, especially the gluten free. Usually they taste like cardboard." She picked up her wine, sipping it. She made the same floaty sound of happiness, tipped her head back against the brick wall and licked her lips.

This woman. She'd be the death of him.

Owen's gaze dropped to her mouth. Once again, he wished they were both someone else and their circumstances were different. Then he wouldn't have hesitated to kiss her. To pull her close, run his nose along the long column of her throat until his lips met her dusky pink ones. Find out if she tasted as sweet as he'd always imagined.

She sucked her bottom lip into her mouth and *shit,* it almost did him in. Owen shifted, trying to get comfortable on the concrete balcony. Closing his eyes didn't help. Visions of Alice tripped past his eyelids, her newly short hair all mussed, lips swollen from too many kisses. His kisses. He hadn't wanted someone like this so much ... well, ever.

He opened his eyes and was about to say something about her case when sirens cut through the night air, the loud wailing drawing closer.

They jumped to their feet, their makeshift picnic dinner forgotten. A white sedan sped down High Street with a police car on its tail. Strobes of blue and red lights flashed across the windows of the stores.

"What the hell ..." Alice said. The sedan did a sharp turn in front of Owen's office, tyres squealing. They shared an alarmed look before turning in unison and bolting to the back of the building where the apartment's front door was. Alice was quicker than he'd expected, but Owen beat her to the landing.

The sedan's driver's side door was thrown open, the car parked at an odd angle, blocking Owen's Jeep and Alice's Volvo.

By the time the police car had stopped, Phoenix was on the second step.

"GO BACK INSIDE, PLEASE." Owen nudged Alice towards the doorway. She refused to move, her breasts pressing into his muscular back, which was a super helpful thing to be noticing *right fucking now*.

"Alice!" Phoenix yelled, stumbling forward, dropping to a knee. His body was moving too quickly for his brain to keep up. His jeans were torn, and his knees were scraped and bloody. "I didn't do it! They're setting me up!" Phoenix white-knuckled the metal rail, pulling himself up another step.

"Go inside. Lock the door," Owen hissed, nudging Alice backwards.

"But—"

Alice couldn't move. Couldn't think. All her senses were heightened. Things she wouldn't register normally were amplified, echoing inside her mind. The crackle of the radio clipped to the police officer's vest. Her shaking inhales and exhales. How hard her heart was thumping against her ribs.

Up close, Phoenix was a wreck. All sweaty, pallid skin and wild eyes. He looked like he'd been on a bender for days ... weeks, maybe.

"If I'm going down, you're coming with me," Phoenix slurred. "We're a team, *sötnos!*"

Alice tore her gaze away from Phoenix when Owen grabbed her hands, their fingers linking together. Owen's voice was soft, but the urgency of his words snapped her out of her daze.

"You don't owe him anything."

If only she'd been honest, which was the story of her damn life. She opened her mouth to speak, but Owen beat her to it.

"And I'll never forgive myself if something happens to you. Please go inside?"

"Okay," she whispered, a chill creeping over her skin as the warmth of Owen's body disappeared. It took two tries to lock the screen door with her shaking hands. Alice crept onto her tippy-toes so she could still see what was happening.

"No," Phoenix yelled, lunging forward, arms outstretched. Owen's back slammed into the screen door, and Alice jumped. Her heart was about to beat out of her chest. "Owen!"

"Stay back," Owen snarled, and Alice didn't know if he was talking to her or Phoenix or both of them, but all the softness had disappeared from his tone.

She needed to get to Owen, but her hands weren't working. Her fingers fumbled around the lock. By the time she got the door open, the two police officers had Phoenix in handcuffs and were leading him towards the stairs.

"Are you okay?" She could barely get the words out; her teeth were chattering so badly.

Snatches of the rights they were reading Phoenix drifted towards Alice.

"... driving under the influence ... supplying a controlled drug to a child ..."

"I could ask you the same thing." Owen reached for her before stepping away when one of the police officers reappeared.

"What happens now?" she whispered.

There was a hard glint in Owen's eyes. "Now we wait."

17

"I don't understand," Alice said as Owen slipped his phone back into his jeans pocket.

"Raff's still not answering."

He reached for Murphy's lead, and she let him take it. It was properly dark now, the only light coming from the ones in the bottom of the fountain. Through the large windows, she could see Wyatt and his girlfriend, Billie, sitting at the pub bar, counting the till, all the chairs stacked on the tables. The rest of High Street was quiet; all the other businesses had closed for the night already. The small crowd that had gathered to watch Phoenix be driven away in the squad car had dispersed.

Alice swallowed thickly. The edges of the stars blurred as she rubbed her eyes, repositioning her glasses with a sigh. She'd been so unable to recognise who she'd become that she'd overlooked how much Phoenix had changed as well. "I didn't know he was dealing. If I had …"

"This isn't your fault." Owen's voice was firm.

"But if I'd …"

Rafferty's name flashed up on his device. "Hold on," he said.

The conversation was mostly one sided, punctuated occasionally with a "yeah" or "what?" from Owen. She knew it was bad when he swore. Even Murphy looked up from the pile of leaves he was sniffing. Alice's pulse spiked, blood thrumming throughout her body. Too tired to stand, she sank onto the grass, dewiness seeping through her jeans. She'd be itchy later, but she didn't care.

"Alice?"

She hadn't realised Owen was off the phone. He helped her up, his hands lingering around hers before he dropped them.

"A fourteen-year-old girl overdosed at Phoenix's party this afternoon."

The ground slipped out from underneath her, and Alice sagged against Owen. His strong arms held her steady.

"Come sit down." He led her carefully, gently, to the sandstone pavers that encircled the fountain. When they sat, Murphy followed, flopping down at their feet. Her shoulders curled in, head swimming as she tried to process what Owen had said.

"She's in a coma. They won't know if she has brain damage until she wakes up. If she does. Several witnesses saw Phoenix give her drugs, but he left before the ambulance arrived. The cops have been trying to track him down all afternoon."

"What if ..."

Owen turned towards her, his face bathed in the fountain's soft glow. "What if what? You'd confronted him? Put yourself in danger? You're not responsible for his actions, Alice."

She blinked furiously, trying to stop the tears from falling. It didn't matter what Owen said; if the girl died, she'd be partly at fault.

This is what happens when you lie.

A sob escaped before she could stop it.

"I should have tried harder to get Phoenix to go to rehab, but he wouldn't listen. Neither would Chris. And then the scandal it would cause if word got out ... and they'd both get so angry at me." Alice sniffed.

"Come here," Owen said, all the rough edges to his voice gone. He wrapped an arm around her and pushed her glasses up into her hair, which must've looked like a bird's nest now. But she couldn't bring herself to care. Instinctually, she nestled in, her head buried in the crook of his neck, palm flat against his chest. He smelt different, with no trace of his usual cologne. There was a hint of soap on his skin and something musky she suspected was his natural scent.

"Can I tell you a secret?" she whispered.

Owen brushed her fringe away from her eyes, tipped her chin up. "Of course."

She dropped her gaze, unable to look at him as she admitted this. The silence between them extended as she struggled to find the right words.

"It's super selfish. Especially now. With all this going on." She took a deep breath. "I'm worried everyone will always think of me as Phoenix Storm's wife ... ex-wife? Like no matter what I do, our lives will be tied together. And every time he does something terrible, I'll get dragged into it because that's my punishment for not stopping him. For not being honest."

Owen didn't speak for a moment, as was his way. By now, she knew he always chose his words carefully. "It might be like that for a while, especially in the media, but it won't last forever. Not if you don't let it. Think about all your business plans and the charity stuff. If you keep pushing that to the forefront, eventually, people will forget about this. Everyone's done things they wished they hadn't. It's human nature to have regrets."

She sniffed loudly, wiping her nose with the back of her hand. "But what if ..."

Owen's thumb tilted her chin up again, their eyes meeting. "What if what?"

Her heart thumped; her mouth was dry. Could she really tell him what kept her up at night? What had worried her for as long as she could remember?

After all, it wasn't so long ago he thought all she did was post silly pictures online and adopt a dog she had no idea how to care for. That she was someone who got married on a whim to be famous. Someone who would never be good enough for a guy like him.

"Alice?" His mouth wore a concerned frown, reminding her she hadn't answered his question.

But this was Owen, she realised.

The guy who jumped in a dam to save a puppy she wasn't ready to look after.

Who dropped what he was doing to come over when he thought she might need his help, even though he didn't know why.

Who didn't shove her inside her apartment and lock her up but instead asked her to go inside to keep herself safe.

She was so blinded by her preconceived opinion of Owen that she'd missed what was standing right in front of her.

He was her lawyer, but he was also her friend, really.

She liked him. A lot.

Her hand settled on his chest as she swallowed again, squeezed her eyes shut, gathered the shattered pieces of her courage. "What if no one likes me for me? What if I'm a disappointment? And they preferred the Alice everyone thinks they know?" Now she'd voiced her greatest fear, she wished she could snatch the words back and swallow them.

Owen's hand stilled. Had he realised he'd been drawing circles on her back? She'd noticed the second he touched her. Her skin had warmed instantly from the contact. His chest rose as he exhaled slowly.

Oh God. Here it comes. The gentle letdown. Or worse, the 'but you're awesome in your own way' speech. It had punctuated so many of the milestones throughout her life. It was always well intentioned … and painful to hear.

When Owen spoke, his voice was hoarse, dry. "I can't imagine anyone not thinking you're amazingly kind, clever and beautiful when they get to know the real you. Like I do."

Shut. The. Front. Door.

"Really?" she squeaked. In an artist's representation of this single, perfect moment, she'd be a cartoon mouse. Eyes the size of dinner plates, mouth agape.

She was caught, transfixed by the spell his words conjured. He shifted again, her hand slipping, a finger snagging in the unbuttoned neck of his Henley.

Alice was touching Owen's chest.

And he thought she was amazing.

And clever.

And beautiful.

Someone call a skywriter, *STAT*.

"Alice," he whispered, and all the sounds faded away. So many things—lust, need and wanting—were wrapped up in the way Owen said her name. Maybe they'd been there the whole time if she really thought about it. She curled her toes inside her sneakers, needing a tangible reminder this was really happening.

"Yes?" She inched closer, their faces almost touching. His breath moved across her cheeks like a caress, his big hand sliding into her hair.

"I don—"

She pressed herself up against him, her index finger on his lips, stopping him from saying "don't". Nothing good ever came after that word. For a split second, they stared at each other. When he didn't respond, didn't move, her stomach twisted. He reached for her glasses, carefully stowing them on the sandstone pavers they were sitting on.

"Please," she whispered.

His fingers twisted in her hair, tipping her head slightly to the side; the first press of his lips was so soft and gentle. It was exactly the kind of kiss she'd expected from him. The sort you'd share with someone at the end of a first date.

But then he changed tack, surprising her again.

The first tug on her hair sent a delicious spiral of pleasure racing down her spine. The second made her open for him, his tongue a soft swipe against her lips.

He tasted like spicy pepperoni and fruity wine. She wanted to feast on him. Their tongues moved against each other, his other hand gripping her hip, pulling her across his lap so she was straddling him.

"Okay?" he asked, the gravel in his voice making her thighs clench.

The movement made him groan, the sound vibrating against her chest and sending a bolt of heat right through her. Her hand slid through the hair curled at the nape of his neck.

She answered his question with another kiss, his hands kneading her ass as he shifted underneath her. *Oh, God.* He was hard. Hard for her. Alice was dizzy with desire. They broke apart when breathing became difficult, and Alice dropped her head to his shoulder. She bet he was like this in bed. Dominant but caring. Rough but tender. He'd make her beg for more, even when she was about to shatter into a million pieces.

Slowly she came back to her senses. The fountain bubbled. Leaves rustled. Owen's breathing slowed; his hands clasped possessively on the small of her back.

The hotel lights flicked off, leaving them with nothing but moonlight and the soft glow from the fountain.

She was trying to figure out what to say when Murphy jumped up, barking, surprising them both.

"Probably a possum," Owen murmured, his breath warm against her neck.

Alice reached for Murphy, and Owen's grip loosened, his hands falling slack to his side and the moment was broken. Murphy turned around briefly, his nose twitching, tail swishing against her leg.

"We should get out of here," Owen said after clearing his throat.

"Oh, yeah, of course." She stood, her body immediately missing his. She stumbled a little, fixing her jumper so it wasn't twisted around her body. A secret thrill raced through her when Owen discreetly adjusted his pants.

"Shall we?" He nodded towards his office and her apartment.

"Sure." Alice sucked on her bottom lip as they walked the short distance. It still smarted from his kisses. The security lights in the driveway were on, a few bugs lazily buzzing around. The tow truck was gone, and Phoenix's car was on its way to being impounded.

Damn it. That would've been the perfect excuse for asking him in. Asking for more of those kisses.

Owen's words from earlier floated to the front of her

mind. She was in charge of her own life. She could ask for what she wanted.

And she wanted him.

The words were on the tip of her tongue when Owen stopped suddenly, two steps from the landing. Alice looked up, her stomach falling to the ground below the stairs. Frustration was etched across his face.

"I don't think I can be your lawyer anymore."

18

Owen had barely finished speaking when Alice snatched Murphy's lead, her mouth clamping shut.

Shit. He should've pressed her up against the wall, kissed her like he wanted to and dealt with the consequences later. She tasted as sweet as he'd always imagined she would.

"It wouldn't be right." The words felt woolly in his mouth, and he had to force them out.

Alice stiffened, stepping past him, her face hidden by a curtain of golden reddish hair. Her shoulders shook, and a bolt of panic almost split Owen in two. Oh, *fuck*. He'd made her cry. Now he wouldn't only feel terrible because his balls were a shade of blue so dark, they were practically black, but because of the ache in his chest as well.

The universe was such a bitch. Here was the first woman he was interested in—*actually interested in*—in for-*fucking*-ever and she was the one he couldn't have.

Alice pushed her hair behind her ear, and Owen almost fell backwards down the stairs.

She was smiling.

The edges were a little frayed, her eyes a touch too watery for his liking, but her full, kiss-swollen lips curled upwards. Honestly. He'd never, ever understand women.

"Because we ... the kissing?" She pointed towards the park, failing miserably to keep the amusement out of her voice.

Owen jammed his hands into his pockets and bit the inside of his cheek. "I've got a personal policy against getting involved with clients."

Her eyes flashed, eyebrows disappearing behind her new fringe, which was a real achievement considering most of the strands of hair were sticking straight up after their make-out session. "You don't want to ..."

He followed her gaze to her front door.

"It'd be fun," Alice said.

Owen sent a silent apology to his painfully hard cock. "Is that what this would be? Two people"—there was that woolly sensation again—"having fun?"

Did he imagine the bitter tinge to her laugh? Alice put her key in the lock but didn't turn it. "I'm not exactly in the market for a boyfriend right now. I still have a husband."

"Hopefully not for too much longer," he muttered. Things might stall now that Phoenix had been arrested, though.

"Is it against the law?" she whispered like even talking about it could get him in trouble. As if he hadn't been in trouble ever since he met her. "Would it be a problem for your career?"

"Not exactly." It wouldn't look great, and it could be detrimental to her case, but he wouldn't be disbarred or anything over it.

"But?" she prompted.

"It's just..." He rubbed the back of his neck, squeezing the tight muscles. He paused, trying to find the right words. The corners of her mouth tipped into a grimace, and she crossed her arms, pushing her breasts together. Breasts he'd …

What was I saying? Owen shook his head, trying to clear it.

Alice pulled the security door open, her hand gripping it tightly. "It *is* me, then. I'm not good enough for you? What was all that in the park then? You said I was beautiful and kind and clever."

"No, no." The words burst forth violently. "I mean, not no. You are those things. It's complicated." No jury in the world would've believed him.

She snorted, stepping through the threshold and flicking the kitchen light on. "Let's forget this ever happened. Okay? We both know I'm excellent at pretending. I won't say anything to anyone." Then she frowned the saddest frown he'd ever seen and pulled the door closed so quickly that Owen felt the *whoosh* through the air as it moved.

The lock clicked, the wooden door closing with a heavy thump.

Shit.

Owen tipped his head forward, his forehead resting against the metal grill. He heard Alice moving around the apartment, talking to Murphy. The sound faded after a minute, replaced by the stillness of the night.

Owen flopped around. The bricks were rough behind him, all rumbled edges, all the warmth banked from the sunny day long gone.

The smart thing to do would be to go home.

Better for him, better for her. Keep their relationship

professional. If he made one of his trusted pros and cons list, there'd be no question.

But he'd spent his whole life doing what was right on paper.

He scrubbed his hands down his face, imagining her inside the apartment, all her bravado gone, believing he thought she wasn't good enough for him ...

He'd never forgive himself.

Owen raised his fist and pounded on the door.

ALICE WAS DRINKING wine straight from the bottle when she heard banging.

What now? Did Owen want to revel in her mortification some more?

She sucked in a deep breath, checked her pyjama shorts weren't on backwards and wiped her mouth. She balled up her clothes, tossing them towards her dirty washing basket. They hit the wall, thudding onto the carpet. Close enough. Murphy was already in his crate at the end of her bed, tucked up with his favourite headless tiger plushie. Before she opened the door, Alice gave herself a quick check-over. Her hair was a mess, but it was Owen's fault it looked like this, anyway. Same for her hard nipples which were still pebbled beneath the faded pink cotton shirt she wore to bed.

The pounding started again, making the air around her vibrate.

She steeled herself, squared her shoulders, ignored her tingling lips. "Did you forget some—"

She didn't get a chance to finish her question before Owen pulled her in his arms, his body pressed against hers.

Their gazes tangled. Neither managed a breathing rhythm that could be described as normal.

"Tell me if you want me to stop because I don't think I can."

His mouth was so close to hers that Alice didn't just hear his words, she felt them. Was it possible to want to shiver and burst into flames at the same time?

"I don't want to stop," she whispered, and he grinned—a real Owen smile that stretched across his face—guiding her backwards, his warm hands sliding under the back of her top. He kicked the door shut behind him and peppered kisses along her collarbone and neck. She thought she heard him flick the lock, but maybe it was her lady parts reporting for duty.

His stubble scraped against her skin, and she whimpered, her hips rolling forward. It was going to be so good between them. She could taste it. She'd spent weeks watching him move with purpose and practised ease, his commanding presence drawing the eye of everyone he passed.

Owen covered her mouth with his. This kiss was messier than before, fuelled by their lust for each other. His passion overwhelmed her, like water breaking through a dam wall, unable to be contained.

She felt his chest expand as he pulled away, his fingers grasping her hips, sliding beneath the elastic of her shorts. He nipped at her ear, biting gently before his tongue chased away the sting.

Gone was the urge to shiver; Alice was on fire.

She looped her arms around his neck, rose onto her tippy-toes and pressed her mouth against his, wanting more of his kisses, more of him. Owen moved her backwards again, the carpet disappearing under her feet, replaced with the kitchen linoleum, until her butt hit the edge of the countertop. He hoisted her up, her legs automatically wrapping around his waist, pushing himself against where she needed him most. It had never been like this with Phoenix, not even in the beginning when she'd thought he was the answer to all her problems.

Owen's kisses morphed from fast and frantic to long, slow ones that stole her breath and sent her pulse to the aching place between her thighs. Her fingers tangled in his hair as she slanted her mouth over his, taking what she wanted ... what she needed.

He slid his hands up her back, pulling away when he realised she wasn't wearing a bra.

"Are you trying to kill me?" he whispered against her skin, that authoritative inflection back in his voice. The one that always made her press her legs together and squirm.

He groaned, planting his hands on either side of her thighs, his fingers brushing against her bare skin. "You are. Aren't you?"

Alice bit her lip, trying to stop herself from smiling too big. Who knew Owen could be so fun? Or maybe she'd underestimated how much fun she'd have teasing him.

"Jesus," he said. "Don't look at me like that. Not when we're getting started. I'm going to bust out early like a chump."

Alice knew what to do—she figured it was how any self-respecting woman with the hottest man she'd ever seen between her legs would respond. She pitched her hips forward, pressing herself right against the hardness in his pants. Then she quirked an eyebrow at him, pulled her top off and leant back until she was on her elbows. If she laid all the way down, her head would be hanging over the other side of the island bench.

Owen dragged a hand across his face, his gaze roaming all over her body, lingering on her chest.

"The first time's going to be fast," he said, reaching up to cup her breasts, pushing them together, using just the right amount of pressure.

She arched her back, not missing the way he'd said "first time".

"But I'll make it worth your while." He winked, dropping his head to her chest, and she had to close her eyes, give herself over to the sensations he was stoking within her. He moved from one nipple to the other, and she hooked her ankles behind his butt, pulling him closer, grinding against him. His hand trailed down her side, a line of goosebumps following it.

She clenched involuntarily when his finger slipped inside her shorts.

The sound he made when he realised she wasn't wearing panties had her pushing upwards, off her elbows, until she was sitting up on the bench again, her fingers fumbling, pulling, snatching at the bottom of his shirt as she yanked it over his head.

He had the perfect amount of chest hair because, *of course,* and the tanned, golden skin of someone who loved to be outdoors. How had she never realised how sexy well-defined pectorals were? Because, *hello*, sign her up for a support group.

Owen dropped another slow, toe-curling kiss on her as she ran her hands through the soft, springy hair on his chest.

"Do you want to go to the bedroom?" His eyes were dark, hands gripping the waist of her shorts.

No way was she getting cock-blocked by a puppy, regardless of how cute Murphy was. "I'm good here." She lifted her hips so he could pull her shorts away.

"You're damn right, you are." Owen sank to his knees, pulling her to the very edge of the countertop. His ragged breath left a trail of fire across her thighs.

"Christ, what do you smell like?" he muttered, pressing his face against her sensitive skin, breathing deeply.

His words cut through the fog of her arousal. What *did* she smell like? Worse, *did she smell bad? Down there?* Was this why Phoenix had always refused to go to Taco Town?

She tilted her hips away, a shy reflex hitting her like a bucket of cold water. Here it was. She'd been waiting for the awkwardness that was inevitable the first time she was naked with someone new. But Owen didn't miss a beat, the flush from her embarrassment barely hitting her skin before he pulled her close again.

"No," he growled, pressing his nose against her. "You smell like heaven."

He started slowly. A few sweeping licks, a small kiss before he began to suck. The fire inside her body started to burn again. When he pushed a finger inside, Alice moaned, long and loud.

"Like this?" he asked, pumping his finger. "Or this?" He moved more slowly, drawing lazy circles with his tongue. It was so like Owen to quiz her while she was in the middle of the best oral sex of her life. Her hips started to move, and she swore she felt his smile against her skin. His free hand snaked up, across her body, plucking at her breasts, squeezing, and rolling her nipples until she'd almost lost her mind, a clanging noise building between her ears.

"Owen," she gasped, hips jerking against his face, but he sucked hard, moved faster, pushed her higher.

She squeezed her eyes shut, colours exploding behind them. The sound he made, positively dripping with pleasure, had her arching her back, burying her fingers in his hair.

He licked her softly until she'd stopped pulsing. When he stood and reached for her, it took her two tries to sit up properly. Her bones had been replaced with wet noodles. Owen wiped his face with his shirt, her eyes drinking in his torso, the dips and ridges he earned with all his time at the gym. His skin had a sheen of sweat, a few beads sliding down the mountain range that was his abs. She wanted to chase them with her tongue.

Alice scooted off the counter, stumbling as she stood and pressed her naked body against him. The fabric of his jeans rubbed against her stomach, and she undid them. They got stuck around his thighs, and he kicked them off.

When she reached for him, wrapping her hand around his hard length, he sucked in a breath, his hand stilling hers. He chuckled a little, dropping his head to her shoulder. He smelt even muskier now, a tantalising mixture of him and her. "I need a minute," he mumbled against her collarbone.

She pinched his side or rather, tried to pinch. He was so built there wasn't any excess skin to grab. "I thought you said this would be fast?" she teased.

Owen's chuckle deepened, the sound zapping around her body like a wayward current. "I also said I'd make it worth your while, which I'm pretty sure I did." He gripped her hips, nudging against where she was softest, and wettest. She squeezed his cock gently, revelling in the way skin so soft could conceal such hardness.

She lifted one shoulder, arranged her face into a bland smile. God, she was desperate to hear his chuckle again. She wanted more of everything with him, especially the side he didn't show most people. "It was okay, I guess."

Her hand moved once, twice. Firm strokes that made Owen clench his jaw tightly, hiss out a sharp breath. He tipped Alice's head towards his, capturing her lips in a scorching kiss that stole her breath, made it hard to think properly. Someone moaned loudly. It might've been her.

Smugness rolled across his face, his lips twitching. Playful Owen was more dangerous than she'd ever imagined. "Just okay?"

"Slightly better than okay."

His smile turned predatory. He reached for his pants, twisting his body away from her slightly as he fished his wallet out of one of the pockets.

She stepped forward, splaying her hands across the back of his shoulder. "You've got a tattoo!" she cried, looking at the tree inked there. The design was simple: a black tree outline underneath a full moon.

"Did you think I was too much of a rule follower?" he asked, kissing her neck. Alice shifted in his arms, one of her hands pressing against his chest, the *thump thump thump* of his heart vibrating underneath it. When she pushed him away, Owen released her immediately, watching her with eyes filled with longing.

She scattered kisses across his chest, licked those delicious abs and was about to drop to her knees when he shook his head, nudging her backwards. "Next time," he said. "I'm going to lose my mind if I don't get inside you now."

It was Alice's turn to growl as he pulled a condom out of his wallet.

"There you are, Boy Scout," she teased as she took it from him, tearing open the foil. They both watched as she rolled it down his thick length, groaning in unison as he pushed a finger inside her.

"You're sure?" he asked.

She'd never realised his eyes weren't just brown. There were little flecks of gold, a band of green around his iris. This man was always surprising her.

She leant forward, capturing his mouth, sucking his bottom lip into hers. "Would you please just take me, now?"

"Alice. *God.*" He gripped her hips tightly, his breathing ragged. She shuddered when he nudged inside her.

Oh, *wow.*

He pushed all the way in, and Alice grabbed the edge of the countertop, spreading her legs wider. Then he began to move. Slow, shallow thrusts that made her bite her lip, wonder how no one else had ever made her feel this way. With one hand, he hitched her leg over his hip, driving into her faster and faster, the kitchen filling with the sound of their bodies moving against each other.

"Do you think you can come again?" Owen ground out, his rhythm never wavering.

Alice tipped her head back, his mouth immediately sucking on her neck. "Maybe," she whimpered, letting go of the counter. She wrapped her arms around his shoulders, the muscles in his back flexing and contracting. He ground into her, his hand tightening around her thigh so he could go deeper, make her wilder.

"What do you need?"

You was all she thought. A low moan slipped from her mouth.

Alice buried her hands in his hair, pulling his mouth towards hers. He pushed his tongue into her mouth, licking and stroking in time with his thrusts. Each time he rocked forward, she pushed down to meet him. A realisation hit her square in the chest: in this moment, she'd follow him anywhere, trust he wouldn't lead her down the wrong path.

"So good," Owen hissed between kisses, snaking his hand between her thighs, pressing down where she needed him most.

Her eyes closed automatically.

"No," he ordered, his voice rough, strangled, cherishing. Oh, God, that voice did things to her. It was nothing like the professional tone she was used to hearing from him. "Let me see you, honey."

Her eyes snapped open as she crested the wave, everything around them blurring into the background. All she could see was Owen's face, pulled tight with determination ... *with pleasure*. She squeezed around him, felt him tense underneath her hands.

She'd never forget the sound he made. It was a magical gusting-groan-sigh she wanted to record and listen to on loop.

He sagged against her, his hands dropping from her hips to the counter. Beads of sweat slipped down her chest, skating over her sensitive skin. She tried to suppress a shiver but failed. Owen raised his head, leaning in to kiss her as he pulled out. She twisted her fingers in his damp hair, shifting forward so their chests touched.

"That was ..." He trailed off, his lips still resting against hers.

Should she ask him to stay? Make good on her promise to take care of him? Was it wholly inappropriate to throw a sheet over Murphy's crate and take Owen to her bed?

The screen door creaked, and Alice froze. Wind? Maybe?

Owen pulled away from her, a blast of cool air replacing where his body had been.

There was a bang, and then Teddy swore, something like keys dropping to the ground, a heavy thud. A woman laughed.

"Shit!" Alice leapt off the counter and grabbed her glasses, her heart thumping for a different reason. "He's supposed to be crashing at a mate's place in Melbourne!"

Owen grabbed her hand, swept their clothes off the floor and dragged her into the closest room, which was the bathroom. He slammed the door and flopped back against it.

Hurriedly, Alice pulled on her clothes. Talk about a mood killer.

Another door closed with a bang, the bass of Teddy's stereo reverberating through the apartment walls.

Alice brushed past Owen, opening the bathroom door a crack.

"Hey," he mumbled, his hand coasting along the side of her hip.

She wanted to lean into his touch even though she knew she shouldn't. What had they just done? She fiddled with her glasses, cleaning the smudges off the lenses with the bottom of her shirt. "You should probably go."

His brow furrowed, a line appearing between them. "Wait a second. We should—"

"You better get out of here before Teddy realises," she said.

Owen planted his hands on his hips. "I don't care if Ted—"

She swallowed. Owen wouldn't ever lead her astray, but could she offer him the same thing? There was no way Teddy would be able to keep his trap shut about this. And Owen didn't deserve to get dragged into all her bullshit when word inevitably got out. *What was I thinking?* "Well, I do. Would you go? Please?"

Owen's chest expanded as he sucked in a deep breath, and she forced the memory of how his body had felt beneath her hands out of her mind.

"If this is about—"

She cut him off again. Threw the word at him that he always used to convince her of things. "Please."

"Fine," he huffed, stalking through the living room with his shoes in one hand.

She almost called out when he opened the door. To tell him to stay and they'd figure it all out later. But she didn't. Honesty and vulnerability had never been her M-O.

And even though Alice was expecting it, she still flinched when the door clicked shut behind him.

19

"Owen?"

He jerked his head away from the table in the corner where Alice was sitting with Eloise and a few others, including a guy he'd bet was her brother based on the family resemblance. She was ignoring him like she'd been doing for the past two weeks. The guys from footy were at the table next to Alice's, which was why he was sitting with his family.

"What years did Michael Jordan and the Bulls win the championship? I can never remember when the second run started."

Wilbur was watching him over the top of his glasses, a knowing look on his face. Busted. Once a detective, always a detective.

Owen picked up his beer. "'96 to '98."

Wilbur filled in the answer and asked, "Have you managed to convince Raff about the race?"

"He's too busy with work." Owen wasn't going to push it, especially not when Raff had warned him about Phoenix. If he'd had managed to get to Alice ... His fingers gripped his pint glass tightly. He flicked a glance at the corner table, swallowing when his gaze met Alice's. She twisted to look at the specials board, tucking her hair behind her ear. Her skin was flushed … *Is she embarrassed about what happened?*

Christ. Here he was, reliving every tantalising second of their time together multiple times a day. He'd even locked his office door and taken matters into his own hands, *literally*, this morning before the office was open when he'd remembered the way she'd laid out across the bench, offering herself to him. There was no way he would have been able to focus if he hadn't.

But ever since that night, she'd pretended he didn't exist.

He didn't know what to do and hated not knowing what to do.

He'd left her another message that morning outlining the implications Phoenix's drug charges would have on her divorce. He sagged back in his chair and sipped his beer. The hoppy flavour was soapy, unpleasant.

Owen's gaze drifted back to her table. Alice's head was bowed towards Eloise, a glass of rosé in one hand, her profile covered by her newly short hair.

He'd stopped by the apartment twice in the last fortnight, waiting until he knew Teddy was out, but she hadn't answered the door. He'd heard Murphy inside the second time and what he thought were footsteps, but still nothing.

Nate dropped into the empty seat next to Owen. "Sorry I'm late. My meeting ran over."

Lulu pushed a plate of garlic bread towards him and signalled to Teddy behind the bar to order Nate's meal.

"Where have you been all week? Haven't seen you at footy training." Nate tore a piece of bread in half, scooping out the soft, buttery middle.

Owen didn't blink. No way was he admitting he'd been running the trails hoping to bump into Alice.

"Is your knee giving you trouble? I thought it was all better now?" It was no surprise his mother's mind immediately went to his old injury.

"It's fine. Raff's not the only one snowed under at work." He drummed his fingers against the table. Jessica had rejected two other custody split options from Rob, determined to go for sole custody and nothing else. Trying to find a way to secure the outcome she wanted was getting harder and harder. Their court date had been set for the week before the race. Add in whatever was going on with Alice and Owen hadn't been able to face training, pretending everything was fine.

"Got a partner yet?" Nate swiped another piece of bread.

Owen's gaze slipped towards Alice again before he snapped it back to the empty plate in front of him. "Nope."

Lulu tapped her chin. "What about Alice? She dropped off stock yesterday, and she was all out of sorts. I bet she could use something to keep her busy that isn't making candles."

Considering she'd been giving him the cold shoulder since they'd had sex, Owen highly doubted she'd want to sign up for a weekend in the bush together. And even though Alice had changed her hair and was dressed quite casually by her standards—tonight's jumper was an oversize pastel rainbow number paired with sparkly navy leggings that moulded to her ass perfectly—he was confident she thought camping was a dirty word.

Owen tried to look unfazed. "I don't think this is her thing."

"Why not? I see her running every morning, and she's

looking for ways to promote her new business," Lulu said. "She was a huge help with sponsors for the calendar."

He wasn't about to tell anyone the real reason, let alone his mother. Owen picked up his drink. "There's still a few days until the cut-off for team changes. I'll sort something out."

HALF AN HOUR LATER, the conversation had moved on to the bathroom renovation Lulu wanted to do, and Owen was listening half-heartedly, grunting when appropriate.

Teddy waved a hand in front of his face. Owen batted it away automatically. When had he sat down? He must be on his break. "What?"

"Has something happened with Alice?"

God, Teddy was a shit. Everyone's heads swivelled towards Owen. "No, nothing's happened ..." He coughed. Unless he counted her making him come so hard his ears had been ringing for a solid hour afterwards. He picked up his beer again. "You know I can't talk about cases."

Teddy shrugged, shoving a spoonful of brownie and ice cream into his mouth. Typical Teddy skipping dinner and going straight for dessert.

"Why haven't you been coming round to use the shower after your runs?"

Owen smiled tightly. "Fixed the hot water system at my place." He should've done it ages ago.

"How is your place going? The new one," his dad asked.

"The kitchen's in and the bathrooms are almost done. There's been a delay on the tiles I chose so we're at a bit of a standstill. Hopefully, I'll be able to move in soon."

"What will you do with the studio once you've moved

into the big house?" Lulu asked, looking up from where she'd been sketching a floor plan on a napkin.

"Probably rent it out," he said as casually as he could manage.

"Really?" His parents exchanged a look. Not so casual, then.

"No sense turning down extra cash while I'm still getting established here. Besides, this guy"—he pointed at Teddy—"pays me peanuts for the flat above the office."

Teddy flipped him off, earning himself a shoulder smack and a "Theodore!" from Lulu before she said, "You've taken on a lot lately, Owen, and you can always come to us if you need anything."

A bit of beer sloshed over the side of his glass as he set it down. "I know. Things are good. Business is picking up—besides, it was always going to take a while to get settled. It makes sense to recoup as much cash as I can."

With its rendered grey exterior, concrete floor covered in paint splatters and cream walls, his little studio was totally different from the super-modern apartment in Melbourne he'd lived in for years, but it had finally started to feel like home. He'd figured out most of the flat's foibles, like how he had to press his body as close as he could to the tiles on the far side of the shower while he waited for the water to warm up. It was that or he'd end up wrapped in the stage five clinger shower curtain. Owen might even be a little bit sad to leave it behind when his new place was finished.

The idea of having a stranger living there made his stomach clench.

At least it was far enough from the main house that he wouldn't ever cross paths with whoever was living there.

A bit of feedback echoed through the room.

"We've got a tie tonight, folks," the quiz master said.

"Can I have a representative from Get Fact"—Alice's table whooped, his chest tightening when a shy smile blossomed on her face—"and Team James!"

Teddy raised his hands victoriously even though he'd been behind the bar during all the trivia rounds.

"Go on." Wilbur pushed on Owen's shoulder. "You go get the prize."

Owen stood and made his way through the crowd, falling in step behind Alice. She startled as she looked over her shoulder, a red flush creeping up her neck. He snapped his eyes to the back of her head and swallowed.

They stepped up onto the small stage in the corner of the room.

"Given it's Alice's first win, I think we should let her have the meat tray tonight. What do you say, folks?" Everyone cheered. Alice's blush deepened. "You don't mind if she has your meat, do you, Owen?"

He didn't, which was fortuitous considering she didn't seem to want anything from him.

"THE LIGHT'S so pretty in this one." Eloise angled her laptop towards Alice, pointing to a picture of her candle range. The background was dusky; the sherbet-coloured sky was streaked with soft pinks and purples. All five candles were lit, the rose gold on their labels shining thanks to the light Alice had held just out of the shot.

"I love them all." Alice sat on her hands so she didn't wave them around excitedly. "Thanks again for doing this. I don't know how you work full-time while studying and moonlighting as a photographer and web designer."

"I like to be busy." Eloise dragged and dropped images

into the beta version of Alice's website. "I think you're ready to send this baby out into the real world. One last check?"

Eloise pushed her laptop towards Alice, stretching back until she was leaning against the sheepskin that covered her chair.

"Oh, no," Eloise said.

"What?" Alice asked.

Eloise held up her phone. "My dentist appointment tomorrow has changed; now it clashes with my knitting circle at the Somers Gully Nursing Home."

"I can do it," Alice volunteered.

"Really?"

"Sure." Alice shrugged. She needed a break from pouring candles, and she loved to knit. While Eloise rang the nursing home and explained she wouldn't be there tomorrow, Alice scrolled through the site, checking all the links worked and nothing looked out of place. It was perfect. She'd been teasing The Emancipation of Alice logo for the last few days and would reveal it tonight when most people were likely to be on their phones. Tomorrow, she'd share the launch date. Which was only a few days away. She gulped and tucked her hair behind her ears. She'd written her media plan weeks ago, and now it was almost time to let everyone in on what she'd been up to; she wasn't sure she wanted to. The thought of sharing herself again, even if she could control how much this time, filled her stomach with butterflies. Who was she kidding? They'd been there ever since she sent Owen away.

She rubbed her face, needing to do something— anything—with her hands. The knitting circle would be good for her too. "I can't believe it," she said. "It's come together so well."

Eloise tilted her head to the side. "Is everything okay? I

thought you'd be a bit more excited. You've worked really hard on all this, Alice. You should be proud of yourself."

Alice was. She'd worked harder on this than ... well, anything ever. But ever since the other night, she'd been distracted, unable to focus. She'd avoided Owen, convinced he would agree that it had all been a mistake. He might even ask her to move out, and then she'd be in real trouble. At least she could hide in the shearing shed for a few days. God knows she'd been there from dawn until well after dark for days now. Her phone buzzed, and she looked at the screen.

Chris. Again. Now Phoenix was waiting to hear if he'd get bail, her old manager had been calling, trying to coax her back into the fold. He texted again immediately, another five-figure offer for an interview.

She tried to smile, but her face was all wobbly. "Got a lot on my mind."

"Anything you want to talk about?" Eloise asked.

Alice looked at the vintage rug under their feet. It was a mixture of pastel triangles—blues, pinks, and purples—with frayed edges the colour of dried wheat. She'd bet it was from Lulu's.

"Oh, no. I don't—" she started, the urge to tuck her hair behind her ears again so strong she had to settle for biting her lip. "It's fine. Thanks for asking, though."

Eloise smiled, her delicate features softening as she squeezed Alice's arm. "Sure? I'm here if you ever change your mind."

Alice swallowed and licked her lips. Could she? She hadn't had a friend to confide in ... in years. Well, except for Dougie and Rico. And as much as she loved them, the thought of ringing them now, interrupting their fancy pants jobs and telling them she'd slept with her 'hot' lawyer ... after Phoenix came to her for help but got arrested, filled her with anxiety. Yet another dramatic turn of events she could have avoided if she'd only used some commonsense years ago.

She took a deep breath, the lavender flowing from the diffuser in the corner tickling her nose. "I slept with Owen," she blurted.

Eloise blinked twice and then burst out laughing.

Maybe Alice had been wrong. Friendship was overrated.

"I'm so, so sorry. I'm not laughing at you, I swear."

Alice stared at her fingernails, the coral polish she'd applied last night was already chipped.

Eloise reached for her hand. "I'm sorry. I shouldn't have laughed. I was just wondering what took you so long based on the way Owen always looks at you. I'm sure he's very happy this happened."

Alice fiddled with the pile of proofs Eloise had printed for her.

"Did he say something afterwards that made you think he wasn't?"

"Teddy came home unexpectedly, so Owen snuck out. We haven't spoken since." She tapped the pictures against Eloise's desk, making sure the edges were straight. "I've been avoiding his calls." She hadn't even responded to his message telling her that the fourteen-year-old who over-dosed was going to be fine.

Eloise clucked her tongue, and Alice dragged her gaze away from the photos. "Trust me," she said. "Owen James doesn't ever do anything he doesn't want to. None of the James brothers do. Believe me. I know all about that, but this isn't about me. You should talk to Owen."

"But what would I say? 'Hi, the sex was great. Can I have some more, please? Oh, but by the way, I don't want anything serious because I'm still married to the guy in jail. Call me!' Going to be super hard for him to resist me."

Eloise leant back in her chair. "You won't know if you don't ask him."

The problem was Alice didn't know which answer would be better for her new life. Owen was already so far under her skin it was scary.

20

Owen scrolled through his emails as he waited for Lulu to return with the items she'd chosen for his new house. *Exactly how many cushions does a person need?* She emerged with two bags, the muted cream fabric of the top cushion coordinating nicely with the mustard blanket next to it.

"You sound a lot like your father," she said.

His fingers stilled. "What?"

"There's no such thing as too many cushions."

Owen hadn't realised he'd said it out loud. Chalk yet another thing up to the haze of distraction he'd been stuck in all week.

"Did you find someone for the race?"

"Not yet."

"What about—"

"Don't say Alice," he cut her off, grabbing for the bag. Lulu held on tightly. Her eyes narrowed, lips pursed.

"What about me?" Alice poked her head out of the store-room. "Oh, hey." She clutched two candles to her chest and offered him a polite smile. She was wearing her glasses, ripped jeans and a bright yellow jumper.

Owen looked back at his mum who smirked. Nice of Lulu to mention Alice was here.

"Hi," he said. Owen had been trying to reach her for days, and now she was right in front of him, he didn't have the foggiest idea of what to say.

"Owen needs a partner for a charity race in August. You should do it. Be excellent exposure for The Emancipation of Alice and aligns nicely with your new charity objectives. It's win-win."

Alice set the candles down on the counter. "Race?"

"It's an overnight adventure obstacle course thing with some running."

Her face drained of colour when Lulu said 'overnight'. Yep. She'd definitely thought the sex was bad. Was he so out of practice he'd imagined how much fun she'd had? He'd only rushed out of there like his pants were on fire because she'd been so worried about Teddy finding them in a compromising position. And he'd tried to call her. Make sure she was okay. *She* was the one who'd been ignoring him.

Owen slid his phone into his pocket, both hands reaching for the bags on the counter, keen to escape but Lulu refused to let them go. "I'm sure I'll find someone."

There.

He'd given her an easy out. He could ask one of the paralegals from his old firm who was obsessed with having zero body fat. This would be right up his alley.

"We're hoping to raise enough money to do some work out at Kathleen's Place," Lulu said. "Be great publicity for us and for you as well."

Alice fiddled with the candles, her thumb smoothing over the embossed foil logo on the front. The telltale flush spread across her neck.

"Just think about it. Now, can I pinch one of those? I promised Joan I'd save her one." Lulu pointed at the candles in front of Alice.

"Sure." She slid one across the glass cabinet top to Lulu before she turned back towards Owen, sucking her bottom lip into her mouth. "Maybe we could talk later?"

Was that hope on her face? But ... *what?* She'd made it clear this week she didn't want to speak to him. Hell, he wasn't even sure he was still her lawyer. Some of the calls she'd ignored had been about papers that needed signing. "About the race," she added. "And everything else."

"Okay." He nodded.

"All done back there?" Lulu nodded towards the storeroom, and Alice held up her phone.

"Yep. Got a few shots of everything all boxed up so I can share them on my socials. I'll come back to set up the display the night before. I'll leave you guys to it." She picked up an oversized tan leather tote he hadn't noticed on the countertop and looped it over her shoulder.

Crap. He'd forgotten about her launch next weekend. Owen was such a dick. She'd probably been running around trying to get everything ready, and he'd been bitching to himself about how she hadn't called him back.

Alice pulled a candle out of her bag and thrust it towards him awkwardly, avoiding his eyes. "This is for you. To thank you for all your help. I thought you might like it better than the other ones."

Their fingers brushed, and he swallowed before flipping the box over. A small smile tugged at his lips when he read the gold foil that said *Sporty McSports Sports Ball.* It reminded him of something musky, like the trails before a huge rainstorm, and something citrusy, maybe lemon.

"It's one of the new scents I've been working on. If you like it, maybe I'll make some more."

Hope flared in his chest, the first flicker of a candle being lit. "Thanks," he said. Thanks? *Idiot.*

"See you Friday," Alice said to Lulu before hustling towards the door.

Owen stared at the candle. Had she been thinking about him as much as he'd been thinking of her? He grabbed the bags, brushing a quick goodbye kiss across Lulu's cheek. "Alice, wait. Do you have a few minutes now?"

Lulu snorted. So much for subtlety.

Alice paused, hand on the door handle, shoulders rising as she took a deep breath. Her face was free of make-up, the freckles scattered across her nose reminding him of the constellations he'd been obsessed with when he was a boy. When she looked him up and down, her cheeks flushing the delicate shade of pink he now knew covered her whole body, he readjusted his grip on the bags. If his mum wasn't watching, and/or texting the Old Girls' group chat about how she'd been right all along, Owen might've asked if he could kiss Alice, apologise for being a selfish ass and check if she needed any help.

"Sure," she said.

He wouldn't make the same mistake twice. The spark in his chest became a full flame.

THE FIVE-MINUTE WALK BACK to the apartment was like swimming through honey. A few cars passed them, their headlights lighting up the footpath before disappearing around the bend towards Somers Gully. The air was humming, charged with something that wasn't there when she was with anyone else. Something equally exciting and terrifying.

"I spoke to Phoenix's lawyer today," Owen said.

The energy in the air dipped, weighed down by her past. She kept her eyes firmly on the ground. So, this was what Owen wanted to talk about. "What did he say?"

"Phoenix wants a meeting with you once he's out on bail."

Rocks crunched under their feet as they walked down the driveway to the car park behind the office. "Did he say why?"

"Nope."

She stopped. It had to be the photos. There was no other explanation. "What happens if I refuse?"

Owen paused, the bright white lights from the security lights making his features seem more angular. It also made the shadows under his eyes more pronounced, and her heart thumped against her ribs. She wasn't the only one who'd lost sleep since the night they were together.

He stepped towards her, close enough that she could smell the masculine scent that had inspired her new candle. "Nothing happens," he said. "You don't have to go, but if you did, I'd go with you."

It was his earnest tone that did her in. Alice pushed her chin forward, one last defence. Asked the question that had to be answered before anything else could happen. "Because you're my lawyer? I thought you'd be quitting on me after ..."

Owen's eyes darkened at the accusation. He stepped closer, set his bags down, not noticing when one tipped over. A cushion flopped onto the gravel driveway, narrowly missing a puddle from the earlier rain. "Is that what you want? For me to find you someone else?"

She shrugged nonchalantly, but it was pointless. Owen's gaze never left hers. "I don't know," she mumbled, her words as feeble sounding as she felt. Playing chicken with Owen had bad idea written all over it. Her gaze dropped to his mouth. She watched as his lips parted, his tongue dragging across his bottom lip.

"I think you do," he said.

She was shocked to see wariness in his eyes, a small frown pulling at the corners of his mouth when she didn't reply. "What do you want, Alice?"

You, she thought, but he wouldn't make this easy for her. Had she, *gulp*, hurt him by ignoring him? Alice wasn't used to telling people what she wanted. Even less so, having them listen to her. "What do you want?" she parroted back.

He stepped towards her, a big hand cupping her jaw. Damn her reflexes for immediately nuzzling into his touch. She'd been lying to herself about how greedy she was for more of it.

"I want whatever you want," he said.

A soundless laugh escaped her, his other hand landing on her hip. "What does that even mean?" she whispered.

He stepped closer, pushing her back against the brick wall behind her. "You set the rules here."

"Rules?"

"If you say I'm your lawyer, I'm your lawyer. If I'm something else, I'm something else. Doesn't have to be one or the other. I'm working on being flexible, remember? Changing my ways."

The intensity of his gaze stole her breath. "What about your policy against being involved with clients?"

His thumb caressed her cheek. "Maybe it needs to be updated, just for you. No one else."

"You'll go along with whatever I say? Play it fast and loose? You're a planner. I bet you separate your whites from your colours."

She could tell he was fighting a smile.

"You don't?" he asked.

Alice snorted. "I chuck it all in and hope for the best."

Maybe she should do that now: *hope for the best.*

Amusement traipsed across Owen's face, all his stoic pretence gone. She slipped her fingers through his belt loop, pulling their pelvises together. The amusement disappeared, replaced with heat. He tilted his head towards her, and she could see the stubble that lined his jaw.

Before they did this—whatever this was—she had to be sure. Alice spoke slowly, weighing each word before it left her mouth. "And if I don't want to label this?"

His fingers flexed on her hip, sliding up her back, drawing their chests together. She went willingly. "Then we don't."

His mouth was almost on hers when she pulled away, her hair catching on the rough bricks behind her. "And you're still my lawyer?"

"I'm whatever you need me to be."

She grabbed his tie—thank God he still dressed way too formally—and crushed her mouth to his. The kiss started out frenzied before Owen took charge, slowing things down, savouring her. Her bag slipped off her shoulder, catching in the crook of her elbow. Without breaking away, Owen untangled it, dropping it to the ground.

"Wait," she cried out. Her lady parts were crying too. "There isn't a good way to say this, so I'm just going to say it."

Owen let her go and stuffed his hands in his pockets.

"Can we keep this between us? With the divorce and everything. You being my lawyer." She had to clench her fists to stop dragging her hands through her hair.

"Then you'd better come up with a good reason for us to spend a lot of time together because I've got plans for you, honey," he said, his voice a low growl. If Owen was embarrassed about the term of endearment slipping out, he didn't show it. He pressed a firm kiss against her lips, and Alice melted against him.

"I'd like to do things right this time. I'm sorry our first time was on your kitchen counter."

Maybe it was remembering how their bodies had moved together. Or maybe it was the fire in his eyes, the warmth of his breath against her cheeks, but it all added up to heat pooling low in her belly.

"Guess I'd better sign up for the run thing," she whispered against his lips. "And for the record, I had no complaints that night. Just a mild freak-out after but I'm good now. It takes me time to make decisions." Especially the ones that involved trusting her instincts.

Owen brushed her fringe away from her eyes. The tender move made her clench her thighs together, giving her the courage to take a chance.

"Do you want to come upstairs?"

He pressed a gentle kiss behind her ear and dropped another on her neck. "I can't tonight, but how about dinner tomorrow?"

"What about Teddy?" She gasped when he bit her gently.

"I'll cook. At my house," he said.

"It's a ..." She almost said 'date', the unspoken word hanging awkwardly in the air between them. His Owen smile was as glorious as she remembered. Small and secret and only for her.

"I'll text you the address. We can talk about the race."

He walked her to the bottom of the stairs and kissed her softly, his lips lingering against hers.

"Tomorrow," she said.

"Tomorrow."

21

D amn it. Alice glanced at the clock before getting out of her car. She was fifteen minutes late.

"Hey." Owen walked towards her. The sun was setting, its last few golden rays framing his head in a halo. Her gaze drifted to the small cottage behind him. It was so *not* where she'd pictured him living.

"Hey yourself," she replied, passing him a bottle of rosé.

"You look great." Owen reached for her hand, laced their fingers together and gently tugged her closer until the soft cotton of his charcoal jumper brushed against her forearms.

"Are you going to kiss me?" She buried her head in his chest, hiding her face. "Oh my God," she breathed. "Shut up, Alice."

"That was the plan."

"Can we start over?" she mumbled. "Pretend I'm not an idiot."

"Nothing about you is idiotic," Owen said firmly, his eyes earnest.

"You might be the only person who thinks that." She laughed, trying to lighten the mood, but his grip around her waist tightened as his other hand snaked up to cradle her jaw.

"Then everyone else is wrong."

Unable to stop herself, Alice brushed her lips across his. When he leant towards her, she pushed up onto her toes, not pulling any punches this time, launching into a searing kiss. He went with her, taking control and she forgot everything she'd ever said before. He pulled away, panting and they stared at each other. Then he swiped his tongue along the seam of her mouth, sucking on her bottom lip until she opened for him again.

Somehow—she didn't know, her brain clearly wasn't getting enough oxygen—Alice ended up with her legs around his waist, the heat between her thighs pressing against the tightness in his pants.

"Owen," she moaned.

"Hmmmm?"

"Do you think we could go inside? Contrary to popular belief, I'm not actually an exhibitionist."

A thrill swept through her body as he blinked twice and looked around. They were standing in the middle of the doorway. The chances of anyone seeing them, who didn't hop on their hind legs and appear on the Australian coat of arms, was negligible, but she could never be too careful.

Gingerly, Owen unwrapped her legs and helped her down.

She gestured towards his home. "This is not at all what I was expecting. Teddy said everyone was surprised when you bought this place."

Owen cleared his throat and adjusted his pants; his cheeks tinged the sweetest pink. "There's another house—a proper one, well, it will be soon—over the ridge line." He pointed towards the copse of gum trees blocking most of the house from view. "It's an old barn. The main house on the property burnt down years ago, and the barn was partially renovated before I bought it. Hopefully, it will be finished soon, and then I'll move in there." He pushed the screen door open and gestured for her to head inside. "Can I get you a drink?"

She followed him to the kitchenette. "Sure." She shrugged. "What's this place then?"

"It was added by one of the previous owners as an art studio for her wife."

Alice spun around, her gaze bouncing around the open plan space. Her eyes zeroed in on the neatly made bed with its plain grey quilt cover.

"Do you want the wine you brought? Or I found a few others you might like. Mineral water?"

Alice dropped onto a bar stool, one leg bending so she was sitting half cross-legged, the other dangling towards the floor. "Wine, please. Any's fine." She snuck a piece of grated cheese off the platter, her finger tapping her chin as she chewed.

"Dinner won't be long. I've triple checked everything is gluten free, too."

Warmth filled her chest. Being a coeliac wasn't the end of the world, but it meant a lot when someone cared enough to cater for her properly.

"Thanks. I haven't eaten since breakfast. Got distracted doing a promotional shoot, and then I wanted to make a few more candles. And I'm finalising stuff for a charity auction I'm doing for the kid's hospital. Your mum and Joan have been a huge help. Eloise, too." It felt good to be achieving so much.

Owen leant across the bench, brushing their lips together like they'd been doing this for years. Not days. He passed her a glass of rosé. Alice buried her smile in her wine.

"Mum said she's earmarked a bunch of jackets from your sale."

Alice snuck a few more pieces of cheese, and he pushed the chopping board towards her. "Everyone's been so nice."

"That's Wattle Junction. It's why I wanted to come home." He smiled. "How are preparations for the launch going?"

She chewed carefully, her eyes drifting closed as she swallowed a sip of wine. "Oh, this is my favourite," she said. Knowing Owen, that was no accident. She'd bet he had quietly asked Wyatt for recommendations. Warmth spread throughout Alice's body. Soon she'd be so warm she'd probably have to take all her clothes off. "I'm as ready as I'll ever be."

Owen bent to pull taco shells out of the small oven and *oof*, his ass looked good in those pants.

When he turned around, her eyes flew to his face before dropping back to the bench. Busted. He smiled widely at her blush.

"Um, tell me about this race thing. I looked it up last night. Have you done it before?"

Owen set the oven tray on top of an oven mitt covered in cartoon koalas. Who was this guy? Seriously? He pulled plates from the overhead shelf and grabbed the sour cream and homemade guacamole from the fridge. "Raff and I raced it years ago. We came second."

"Second!" Her eyes widened. "You should lower your expectations then, like, by a lot."

His chuckle made her heart speed up. "Can I tell you a secret?" he murmured.

She nodded.

"The real money is in all the sponsorships you secure before it. The prize money's the cherry on top. I think we could raise a fair bit, but really, I'd be happy to have some fun."

Alice bit her lip. "Because you're such a fun guy, Boy Scout?"

"I have my moments." He tossed her a wink, and she worried a river of drool might escape as she remembered the *fun* they'd shared on her kitchen countertop.

Alice crossed her fingers. Hopefully, there'd be plenty of fun after dinner.

LATER, once they'd finished eating and Owen had vowed to himself to never again serve Alice a meal that involved her licking her fingers regularly, he led her to the couch and grabbed his laptop. She scooted closer, her thigh pressed against his, ankles crossing as she rested them on his coffee table. She was wearing Christmas socks. In June.

"You follow this track for twenty-five kilometres." Owen pointed at his laptop. "These are the campsites. Whoever arrives first gets to choose which one they want. These three"—he moved his hand—"are the best because they're the most protected from the wind and closest to the drop station. The river's not far too."

Alice looked a little pale.

"Tents and overnight food are taken to the drop bag station here." He moved the cursor. "And you collect them from there."

"It's quite serious, isn't it?" She rubbed her face, leaning back against the couch, a bit of space appearing between them. Space he didn't want or need.

The urge to comfort her overwhelmed him, and he draped his arm across her shoulders. He relaxed when she leant into him. "It's not as full-on as it sounds, I promise. At each checkpoint, you collect a page from a book to prove you've been there. You get your page number at the start of the race. The hardest obstacle is the climb, and it's not that high."

Alice's shoulders tensed. "Climb?" she squeaked.

"Right before the finish. See here?"

Alice chewed on her bottom lip.

"What's going on?" he asked.

"Don't laugh at me, okay? The running and hiking are fine. Well, maybe 'fine' isn't the right word, but with some extra training—"

"I can help you with that," he interjected.

She smiled softly, her hand landing on his leg. "—but I haven't ever been camping and ..."

"We can do a practice run here. I'll get Raff's tent next time I see him."

Her smile didn't meet her eyes. "Maybe."

Something else was bothering her. He could tell. "What else?"

Her thumb brushed across his jeans, and he waited.

"I'm not great with heights."

He opened his mouth to speak, but Alice cut him off, shaking her head quickly. "Please don't say we can practise that. I'm not 'not great' with them. I'm terrified, and I'm pretty happy being terrified of them. There are a lot of things I need to work on about myself, but this isn't one of them. If heights and I are never friends, it's okay with me." She pushed her fringe away from her face and clasped her hands together.

"Alice, honey," he said. Apparently, that name wasn't

going anywhere. It slipped off his tongue like he'd been calling her that forever. He wasn't complaining. "Only one team member does the climb."

"Really?"

"And guess what?" He tipped her chin towards his face until their gazes met. "I love rock climbing."

She exhaled loudly, and he swallowed a chuckle. When she lifted her shoulder, his gaze dropped to her bare skin, the green bra strap that had been teasing him all night. "I mean, if you insist, it'd be okay with me."

He tipped his head back and laughed. Relearning how to have fun with a woman, this woman, made him happier than he'd ever imagined. "Cheers," he said. "Very kind of you."

"I'm a nice girl," she said and *fuck,* the breathiness in her voice did things to him. He'd been waiting for another opportunity to kiss her properly again, not wanting to push or make her think he was only interested in one thing. But when Alice grinned at him, her hand sliding up his thigh and brushing over his rapidly hardening cock, he couldn't wait any longer.

The look she gave him was pure lust. Her eyelids were heavy, her lips parted enough that he could see her tongue. He pushed forward, remembering how sweet she tasted and twisted his body so he could pull her into his lap. She slotted into place so easily it was like they'd been in this position a million times before.

Her chest pressed against his as her fingers swept up his arms. As she twisted them in the short hair at the back of his neck, Owen closed his eyes, rolling his head from side to side. The bite of her nails against his scalp made him shudder. He sensed her moving closer, her breath warming his face before she brushed her lips against his.

Owen told himself he'd go slow.

Make it good for her.

Be the kind of guy she deserved.

A gentleman.

Alice kissed him again, a firm press against his mouth, a little tug from her fingers in his hair. Moved her mouth to his ear to whisper, "Get naked, Boy Scout. I can't wait."

Owen's gentlemanly intentions took a solid hit.

He slid his hands underneath the back of her fuzzy jumper. He rubbed his fingers across her bare skin, enjoying the way her lips parted a little more and she squirmed on his lap, rocking against him.

"This couch looks pretty comfy."

"I know somewhere better." He hooked his hands under her butt and carried her to his bed.

He tossed her onto the bed gently, and she scooted backwards. Wrapping his fingers around her ankle, Owen pulled her down the bed until she was underneath him. Careful not to put too much weight on her, he dropped to his elbows, his thighs pinning her in place. She reached for him immediately, her palm cupping him through his pants.

Owen slid a hand up her side, under her shirt, over the lace covering her breast, and she shivered, arching towards him.

When Alice tried to take her top off, Owen's nose dropped to her collarbone, breathing in her unique smell. He hadn't been able to place it before, but now he recognised it. A field full of wildflowers. Her skin was warm like she'd been basking in the sun all day. Alice gave up on her top, her hands clawing at the bottom of his instead.

"No," he said.

"No?" That one word was full of so many questions.

"I want to take my time tonight, honey. Do everything I

should've done the other night." Fuck it. He should just update her name in his phone, especially if she continued to press her chest against his, making that soft mewling noise.

His hips pushed against hers, her gasp spurring him on. A tingle ran down his spine, spreading through his limbs. He wanted more of her noises, more of the way her body shuddered underneath him.

They moved together, their hands learning each other's bodies, tongues stroking each other languidly. He couldn't remember the last time he'd spent so much time getting to know a woman this way. Usually, he was focused on having a good time and making sure his partner did as well. But every little gasp or hitch of Alice's breath made his balls pull tighter, his chest lighter.

When her fingers tugged at his shirt, he pushed it up and pulled it over his head. Her gaze blazed a trail over his exposed chest, and suddenly, it was like he'd been standing in the sun all day too.

She finger-walked her hand down his chest to his jeans. Sucking her lip into her mouth, she pulled the button free, shoving his pants down to his hips. His cock swelled, and he groaned when she palmed him through his boxer briefs.

Almost all the thoughts emptied from his mind, but one remained. *She's wearing way too many clothes.*

When her hand skated under the waistband of his underwear, Owen pulled away from her. Her disappointed sigh was music to his ears. He moved his hands underneath her jumper, the material collecting and gliding across her soft skin. It bunched under her breasts, and he kissed her, marvelling at the goosebumps that pebbled across her ribcage. Her scent was stronger here, and he chased it until he found himself between her tits. There was a bow in the centre. Not the usual small decoration on women's bras but a larger green velvet one. The idea of Alice thinking of herself as a gift made him harden painfully. Owen added peeling her bra off her ever so slowly to the list of things he wanted to do to her, but first, he wanted to taste her. He'd been dreaming about it since the last time they were together like this. Her tits heaved as he lowered his mouth to the left one. Sucking her through the material, he rubbed a knuckle over her other breast.

"You smell so good."

Her grip on his shoulders tightened as he blew on her nipples.

"May I?" He tugged lightly on the ends of the bow.

"Please."

It wasn't quite as spectacular as he'd imagined. Behind the bow was a metal clasp. He fumbled with it, and as the cups fell away, he buried his face in her luscious chest.

"Alice ..." he breathed.

She laughed softly, tugging his head until he looked at her. "You act like you haven't met the girls before."

"Last time was such a rush. This time I want to see you. Make it special."

She used her feet to try and push his jeans to the floor, but they ended up in a tangle of limbs and denim. He pulled away from her, her groan and outstretched hands pulling a grin from him as he stood and kicked off his pants. Any trace of disappointment on her face disappeared as she rose to her knees.

He sucked in a deep breath and reached for her, but she shook her head, a mischievous glint in her eyes. Owen's hands fell to his side. If she wanted to take control, he was more than happy for her to.

He clenched his jaw when she pushed her jeans over her hips, down her strong legs. Her sheer panties matched her bra, a tiny little green velvet bow in line with her navel. He gripped himself when she hooked her fingers in the sides of her panties, dragging the flimsy material down so fucking slowly. After what felt like an eternity, she was gloriously naked. This was how someone lost in a desert must have felt when they finally found water. Owen had never seen anyone so perfect.

His hand moved up and down his shaft, the cotton of his underwear rubbing against him.

Alice picked up her panties, her whole body flushing as she sling-shotted them at him. "Your turn," she said.

Owen caught them with his free hand and resisted the urge to smell them. Just. *Christ.* What was she doing to him?

Alice laughed, the light sound hitting him square in the chest. And he realised. She was unlocking him. Freeing him from all the stupid rules he'd made for himself. Showing him how it could be.

He had to have her. He'd waited long enough.

Apparently, so had she. She crooked her finger towards him and settled back against his pillows. Her hair spread out on his pillow like the flames of a dying fire. Her mouth dropped open into an 'o' as he stepped out of his boxer briefs.

"Ready?" he asked.

She licked her lips. Nodded slowly, dragging her eyes back to his face.

Owen prowled towards her, cataloguing the way she squeezed her thighs together before letting them fall open. He nestled his dick against her wetness. She looked up at him, blue eyes full of trust, short puffs of her breath skating all over his skin.

He took her mouth gently, pressed their chests together, tried to tell her how special she was without words. Trailing wet, open-mouthed kisses along her neck, he squeezed her breasts. Her skin was so soft. It was criminal.

She tilted her hips. The head of his cock slipped low. She was right there. Offering herself to him.

"Condom," she whispered. Her hands roamed across his shoulders.

"In the bedside table," he said more gruffly than he meant to but *shit,* he was mere seconds away from plunging into her, claiming her before he embarrassed himself.

Alice twisted underneath him, stretching out as she rummaged through the drawer of his oak bedside table.

Desperate to taste her again and make her writhe against his face, Owen slipped down her body, arranging her legs so they were on his shoulders.

"Oh God," she moaned when his tongue flattened against her. He circled her clit and she started to move against him, nonsensical babble falling from her lips. He pushed one finger inside her, then another, coaxing more of the sounds he wanted from her.

"Owen ..." The desperation in her voice made him lift his gaze. She was smothering her face with one of his pillows.

"Cry out, honey," he said, pumping his fingers faster. "Make as much noise as you want."

"I can't ... I ..."

He dropped his head. Found that hard little nub, sucked on it until she broke above him. Her legs clamped around his head, blocking out the rest of the world.

When she stopped trembling, he gently put her legs back on the bed and crawled up her body.

"That was ..." She sounded a little orgasm drunk. Her eyes were glassy.

"Better than good?" he teased.

She covered her face with her hands. "Yes. So much yes."

He picked up the condom she'd dropped next to the pillow and sheathed himself.

"Wait," she said. "What about you?"

"Plenty of time for that later."

When she pushed him away slightly, he panicked. *Fuck.* Too much? But then he realised she wanted to get on top.

He held the base of his cock as Alice lowered herself onto him. She was so wet and warm. God, he'd love to be in her bare. He'd never trusted anyone enough to do that before.

Her eyes widened as she took all of him. Owen started with a shallow thrust, but it immediately wasn't enough. He gripped her ass, watched her tits bounce. He must've looked like an idiot because he couldn't stop smiling. It had never been like this before. No one would ever compare to Alice.

He knew it the second Alice decided she'd make him come. She didn't just start to move; she began to grind. Letting go of his pecs, Alice cupped her tits, threw her head back and rode him.

Let the official record reflect it was hot as fuck.

Owen's balls clenched, white-hot need accumulating. Shifting his hand, he rubbed her clit. Her gasp spurred him on, and he fought against the tide of pleasure threatening to drown him.

"Oh my God, Owen ... I'm going to ..."

"Alice," he gasped.

His orgasm hit him squarely in the spine, and she clenched around him.

She didn't stop moving, her hips rocking as she took everything he had. His heart felt like it would crack open his chest, bust out.

Oh boy, was he in trouble.

22

"This is your idea of fun?" Alice followed Owen up a steep climb. They were almost finished with their training run—their second since she'd agreed to do the race—and she was flagging. The first had been an easy five kilometres around the fire trail at the bottom of the Wattle Valley Ranges. But this one? He'd had her scrambling over rocks, the route far more technical than she'd anticipated. Alice blinked, wiping the sweat off her brow. Her pocket water bottle was empty, or she would've reached for it.

"Want to lead?" Owen ran backwards. Up the trail. *What an athletic asshole.* But then he winked and smiled at her, and she forgot her legs were made from cement.

"I thought you wanted to be distracted this morning?" he said, a teasing whisper in his voice she'd never have thought possible when they first met.

"I meant with sex! Or more pancakes."

Owen had made those for her last night for dinner. Another thing she never would've dreamt he'd do. Sure, they'd been mostly banana and he'd covered his in fruit, nuts and seeds, but he'd bought ice cream for her and three different types of syrup. All gluten free. All delicious.

"Maybe you should spend the night at my place, then."

"I can't leave Murphy overnight," she huffed. Where the hell was the crest of this hill? "And Teddy would wonder where I was."

"Bring Murphy." Owen shrugged. "I don't mind."

"But what if he saw us ... you know." She raised her eyebrows. What kind of dog parent would she be then? He still wasn't toilet trained properly either.

Owen laughed loudly, the sound bouncing off the trees all around them. "He can sleep in the bathroom."

Leaving Owen last night, all rumpled in his bed with sex hair and chocolate syrup on the bedside table had been harder than she wanted to admit. "Maybe," was all she said.

The trail widened, and he waited until she pulled up next to him. She was surprised to see there was nothing flirty about his expression. "Nervous?" he asked.

She avoided his gaze, pretending to check the ground for loose rocks, roots or other tripping hazards.

"It's normal to be nervous," he said softly.

Alice tried to laugh, to play it off, but she knew he saw right through her when his mouth flattened. "Honey," and *ooof,* there went her heart, "you're going to be great. You've been amping the launch up online, you've got the whole shebang planned at Mum's and those newspaper folks are coming."

He was right. Her social media had been going off ever since she shared the logo for The Emancipation of Alice and teased her candles. Her last post, a cartoon picture of a pair of budgie smugglers covered in cocktails with the matching candle, had been shared thousands of times. It was the first time she'd been excited about going viral in ages.

Owen slowed to a walk, and she followed his lead, breathing deeply. She pulled at a loose thread on her coral-coloured top. The cool breeze hadn't bothered her when they were running, but now a chill crept over her skin. "But what if …"

"… it doesn't go well?"

She nodded, not wanting to give her fears more room inside her mind by voicing them.

"I'm going to tell you what every business owner I know said when I opened my firm. Okay? It's clichéd and annoying and stupidly, frustratingly true."

He waited until her gaze met his. His eyes were full of golden flecks today, and his running shirt clung to his chest, which rose and fell steadily. No hint of exertion or worry.

"These things take time."

"I don't want to fail …"

He looked around the trail, checking they were alone before he pulled her into his arms. "You're not going to fail. Didn't your last post have a gazillion likes or something?"

She mumbled against his chest. "Just because people like something doesn't mean they're going to buy it."

An alarm went off on his phone, his arms returning to her waist once he'd silenced it. "It's going to be great. You've worked hard, done your research. People are chomping at the bit to support you. Put on something sparkly and gorgeous and Alice-y and be yourself. You'll smash it."

She leant into his embrace a little more, focusing on the steady beat of his heart against her cheek.

"Something Alice-y, huh?" she whispered.

His voice lowered, like whatever he was going to say was

only for her, even though no one was around. "I like all your shiny, bright clothes."

She cocked an eyebrow at him. "You thought they were stupid in the beginning. I could tell."

The now familiar curl of his lips sent a thrill through her. "I didn't understand them, that's all."

"And now you do?"

Owen brushed his lips across her forehead, and her heart went *boom, boom, boom.* "Your clothes are a part of you, honey. They reflect your lightness and exuberance, how you want to make people smile. At least they always make me smile."

She'd always thought of her clothes as a defence or her armour. A distraction. No one would ask the girl wearing a burnt orange dress and tights covered in sequined pineapples how she planned to solve world hunger. She wasn't expected to be clever. It didn't hurt they were fun to wear and always cheered her up. Knowing Owen liked her clothes made her love them even more.

They ambled towards his Jeep, the only car in the car park, his arm firmly around her shoulders. "I thought I might shower at your place this morning if you were still looking for a little distraction," he whispered against her hair. All her senses fired up, energy flowing through her tired limbs as she leant away from him. "But Teddy will be there."

"And Murphy. I guess you'll have to be quiet," he teased before his expression grew serious. "I believe in you."

Those were dangerous words. How long had she been waiting to hear them? She cuddled back into his chest, savouring the strength of his body under her cheek. His heartbeat was strong and true, just like his words.

"I believe in me too," she whispered.

THE SOFT JAZZ Owen was used to at Lulu's Boutique had been replaced with the buzz of chatter and eighties tunes. He spotted Alice in the corner, her face alight with happiness, hands dancing in front of the display as she showed people her candles and smiled for selfies.

"Owen," Lulu called, and he tore his gaze away from Alice. His mother beckoned him towards the register where she kissed him on the cheek quickly and took the tray of coffees out of his hands. "Can you get another box of candles from the back room? We're almost out. Again. I think we might sell out!"

"Sounds like a good problem to have." He scooted behind the counter.

"Alice is a hit! I knew she would be!" Lulu cheered, and he didn't even try to stop his grin.

Owen had known it, too.

"Grab some more bags while you're back there too, please, darling."

He disappeared through the beaded curtain hanging across the storeroom doorway, scanning the room for the boxes of Alice's candles. Once Owen had one, he ventured back out into the store, walking to the corner where her display was.

He was about to say hello to Alice and ask where she wanted the candles when Eloise grabbed his arm. "Thank God. We're getting slammed. Can you get another two boxes of the charity ones and I'll put these out? One lady wants twenty!"

The woman Alice had been chatting with moved away,

and his mouth went dry when he saw the rest of her outfit. She'd paired a cropped tan leather jacket with a black minidress that was just long enough to be decent but short enough for him to admire her lithe legs. Legs that were clad in glittery black leggings and sparkly gold heels with chunky rhinestones on the strap that tied around her ankle. *There she is.* He made a mental note to ask her to leave those shoes on the next time they were together.

"Owen?" Eloise snapped her fingers in his face.

"Right, yes. More boxes. Got it."

Alice finally noticed him when he returned, her face a mixture of pride and surprise.

"Looks like it's going well." He tightened his grip on the boxes so he didn't do something reckless like kiss her in front of all these people. She pressed her lips together, her tongue darting before she dragged it across the bottom one, a tantalising flush hitting her skin. Did she want to kiss him too?

"Would you excuse me for a second?" she asked the lady with short hair she'd been talking to. She ducked past Eloise, promising to return in a second, and led him into the back room.

As soon as they were alone, Alice did an adorable little shimmy, bouncing around on the balls of her feet. "My website crashed!" she whispered as she looked over his shoulder. "And *The Age* sent a reporter earlier. I told them all about the race and how important Kathleen's Place was. And I've almost sold all my charity candles! All gone! That's ... I can't, maths is ugh, but yay!"

Her deep blue eyes framed with thick dark lashes called him home like a lighthouse guiding a ship to safety. Owen had to touch her.

"I don't want to say I told you so ..." His hands rested on

her hips. She hooked her fingers behind his belt, pulling him so close he felt her soft exhale against his neck.

"I'm so happy I wouldn't even care if you did." She laughed. "My phone's been going off. This could work, Owen!"

"Honey." He dropped his head until their foreheads were pressed against each other. "It is working." He wasn't only talking about the candles anymore either. If anyone had told him he'd care this much, so quickly for someone, he'd have never believed them. It was hard to fathom they'd only kissed for the first time less than two weeks ago. Once she was divorced, they could do this. Be like this always. He just had to wait for her to catch up and realise that staying in Wattle Junction could work. Staying with him could work.

Her lip gloss smelt like strawberries and shimmered under the fluorescent lights. One quick kiss and he'd let her go back to her launch. Her celebration.

"I'm so proud of you," he said. And did he think she was beaming before because, *hell*, sunshine and happiness and everything good in the world was pouring out of her right now. If they'd been somewhere more private and it didn't involve stealing her away from her moment, he'd have really shown her how happy he was for her.

"Me too." She giggled and wrapped her arms around his neck. "I didn't ever think ..." She trailed off, and he rubbed his thumb across her mouth, sticky lip gloss be damned.

"Think what?" He brushed his lips across hers.

Her breath hitched, her fingers twisting in his hair. "Nothing. I didn't think people would like the candles this much."

He wanted to press her, to ask if that's what she really

meant, but he had to trust that she'd tell him when she was ready.

Alice pulled on his tie until he covered her mouth with his. The kiss was soft, gentle ... familiar. No promise of anything else. It was the most dangerous one they'd ever shared. He was about to pull her in closer when someone gasped.

23

Owen and Alice sprang apart.

"Sorry! I saw you come in here, Owen, and I just wanted to have a quick chat," Camille said.

"It's fine. We were just talking." Alice's cheeks were bright red, her shoulders rigid; Owen's stomach dropped to his feet. He was about to say something—what though?—when the beaded curtain that separated the storeroom from the main store was pushed aside.

"Darling, where have you been?" Lulu bustled into the back room. "We need candles and ba—" His mother froze when she saw the three of them.

"Camille was just leaving, Mum. I'll be right there."

The glare Lulu gave Camille made Owen grimace. His mother was scary when she wanted to be. "Only staff are allowed in the storeroom. Out you go, please." She even made a shooing motion.

"I just need a minute of Owen's time."

Lulu snorted and shook her head, and jeez, she was the best. "That won't be happening. Not under my roof. I'll walk you to the door."

"What are we going to do? What if she tells people what she saw?" Alice hissed as soon as Lulu and Camille were out of earshot.

"Nothing. Camille might not live here anymore, but everyone knows the Arturos love to stir up trouble. If anyone says anything, we can just roll our eyes." Dear God, please let Camille keep her big mouth shut.

"What do you think she wants to talk about? Do you think she wants you back?" Alice sucked her bottom lip into her mouth, worry still etched across her beautiful face.

"Hey," Owen said, closing the distance between them, noticing how easily Alice slipped back into his arms. His thumb traced her lips. "I don't know what Camille wants to talk about, but it doesn't matter because she doesn't matter to me."

He leant forward, needing to kiss Alice and prove to her that everything he'd just said was true, when a soft cough from the doorway interrupted them again.

Jesus.

"Excuse me." Lulu didn't even try to keep the glee out of her tone. "I just need to get those bags."

"Why don't you head back out there?" Owen's hand settled in the small of Alice's back as he pushed her towards the door.

She nodded, smoothed her hair and scuttled out of the storeroom.

Owen picked up a box, adjusted his grip and waited.

"Do you have something to tell me?" Lulu asked.

"Nope."

Her smile disappeared, replaced with a frown. "I thought I taught you that lying was wrong."

Owen sighed loudly. "I need you to forget what you saw."

"But why?" Lulu protested, the lines of her forehead deepening. "This is wonderful news. Everyone's going to be so happy for you both. I knew there was something going on!"

She was probably right. People would think this was nice. Now that Alice had shown everyone that she was committed to using her platform for good and was starting to take part in local events, her popularity had increased significantly. Once Owen had switched to local suppliers for the final few things for his new house and made it clear he was back for good, Owen's had gone through the roof as well.

But then he remembered Alice's stricken expression when she'd realised they weren't alone. His stomach clenched. She wasn't ready for a whole swag of reasons ... she might never be ready.

And he wouldn't risk anything derailing whatever it was they were doing.

"Mum." He licked his lips. They were still sticky. Strawberry lingered under his nose. "You can't say anything, okay? You have to promise me. With her divorce and everything ..." His voice cracked, and the box slipped. How could he lose this when they'd barely gotten started?

"Oh, darling." His mum's frown returned, spurred on by the seriousness of his plea.

"Not to anyone. Especially not the Old Girls."

She patted his arm. "I won't. But you know secrets have a way of getting out. I'm always here if you want to talk, right?"

He nodded. "I should go."

"Do you want me to take them?" Lulu pointed at the stock he was carrying.

"No, it's okay. I can do it." He wanted—no, *needed*—to make sure Alice was okay.

His eyes found her as soon as he stepped back into the store. She was in her corner, laughing at something a lady with frizzy hair said, but there was a brittleness to her smile that hadn't been there earlier. Her movements were jerky, almost manic.

"Here he is!" Eloise descended on him with scissors in one hand. "We need another Kathleen's Place candle for the reporter." She snipped through the masking tape, pulling out a candle box decorated in wattle branches.

"Owen's going to partner with Alice in the Wattle Valley Ranges Charity Adventure," Lulu said, and Owen shot her a look. So much for playing it cool.

"I wouldn't have picked you as the kind for an adventure race," a tall guy with a recording app open on his phone said to Alice, hastily tacking on a "no offence."

"That's a fair assumption." Alice laughed, more like her normal self. Owen tried not to believe it was because his presence soothed her. That was a dangerous thought. "I couldn't refuse the opportunity to support a cause as brilliant as Kathleen's Place. They've been providing a place for the community to gather since the sixties. I caught the tail end of an art therapy session the other day and what struck me most was the sense of belonging everyone there had. It's something that"—she took a deep breath, her hand settling on the display shelf next to her —"everyone needs. Even if it's a stepping stone to some-where else."

Owen's stomach clenched, but he pushed the worry away.

"I can't think of a better organisation to be the charity recipient for my first 'Alice Loves' candle and our race fundraising. We've been so lucky to have some great spon-sors come on board, too. The local hotel and footy club have been great, but we're always looking for more. Every dollar counts."

Owen had never seen her like this. Her eyes sparkled, and she was so calm, so confident. Hearing Alice speak so eloquently and emotionally about a place he'd loved all his life made Owen want to tell everyone the truth about his feelings for her. Or at least tell her.

"You guys should get a picture." Eloise pointed at Owen and Alice. "For the article."

Owen thought he saw Alice's eyes widen a fraction before her big, toothy grin slipped back into place.

"An excellent idea," Lulu said.

"Sure, sure," Alice said, her words rushing out on top of each other. He watched as she took a deep breath, her face flushing. "This guy's going to have to listen to all my whinging during the race, after all. He deserves some recognition. In fact, Owen's only recently opened his law firm here in Wattle Junction, but he's been supporting Kathleen's Place for years now, offering free legal advice and sitting on the Board of Directors. I can't think of a better partner ..." Their gazes met before she looked back at the reporter. The cheeky gleam in her eyes gave him ... *feelings*. So many feelings. "He's promised to do all the heavy lifting and sing pop songs when I need a pep up."

Everyone laughed, and Alice tilted her head towards the space next to her. Owen stepped around the table, all the different candle scents making his head swim. At least, that's what he told himself. It wasn't because she'd called him her partner. Nope. Not that.

"Right, you stand here." Eloise shifted Alice towards the light, ignoring the photographer who'd come along with the reporter. "Owen, you here." She shifted out of the way, handing him an *Alice Loves Kathleen's Place* candle, checking the label was towards the front.

He stood stiffly next to Alice, her wildflower perfume mixing with the heady scent of the candles. *Don't look like you sucked chocolate syrup off her tits last night, don't look like you sucked chocolate syrup off her tits last night* marched through his mind.

"Big smiles," Eloise said, her grin a little too big ... suspiciously big, actually, as she snapped a few pictures on her phone.

Owen blinked when the camera flashed, looking down at Alice. She was still smiling at Eloise, a few loose strands of hair escaping from behind her ear. His fingers itched to smooth them, tuck them away. To touch her in a way that made it clear to everyone she was his, and he was hers.

But he knew that wasn't what she wanted, not yet. The debacle in the storeroom had made that perfectly clear.

"And now some of Alice on her own," the reporter said.

Owen leant forward and put his candle back on the table. He settled on a polite nod as he said goodbye, wishing everyone luck for the rest of the afternoon.

Silently, he wished himself luck as well. He was going to need it.

IT HAD BEEN the perfect day, except for when Camille and Lulu had caught her and Owen together. "About before"— Alice cleared her throat as she and Lulu were wrapping up for the day—"with Owen."

Lulu patted her hand. "No need to explain."

"He's so great, but it's ... complicated." Alice sat on one of the fluffy stools behind the counter, reaching for her glass.

Lulu clicked on the screen, finalising the day's sales before answering. "Alice, it's okay. I promised Owen I wouldn't say anything."

"Thank you."

The printer spat out a long receipt, and Lulu pulled a small canvas bag from the drawer under the till. She shook it out, plastic cash bags and rubber bands tumbling onto the counter. "Why don't you take off? I'll tidy up in the morning. I've got an early delivery."

"Are you sure?"

Lulu winked. "Go celebrate and have some fun. Maybe put Owen out of his misery. He worries a lot more than he lets on."

"About us? Not that there is an 'us' technically." Alice swallowed her last sip of drink, the taste souring as she tried to glibly dismiss what they shared. She didn't want to cheapen it, even if she wasn't sure exactly what it was. Sure, they were playing by her rules, but her heart kept moving the goalposts.

"I think you'll find Owen disagrees," Lulu said as she tipped out all the two-dollar coins and started counting them. She grouped them into piles of five—little gold towers all in a row.

Alice ran her finger around the base of her champagne flute. "You do?"

Lulu laughed, nodding towards the open bottle of fizz. "Take the rest of this with you too. I'll be asleep before my dinner if I have any more."

"Thanks again for everything," Alice said.

She grabbed her bag from the storeroom, smiling at the empty corner where her stock had been, tucked the flowers her family had sent—organised by Rico she'd bet—into the crook of her arm and picked up the champagne bottle. She had a huge few days ahead of her now, making more candles and mailing all the orders she'd sold but right now, she knew exactly who she wanted to celebrate with.

Scratch that. She'd stop at home first to pick up Murphy and take him to Owen's with her.

Waking up in his arms for the first time would be the best reward for all her hard work.

24

The next six weeks were a blur of sleeping with Owen, making candles until Alice's fingers hurt and she almost lost her sense of smell, mailing orders, restocking Lulu's and her website, training for the race, finding sponsors and trying to keep on top of all her social media promotions and campaigns. Not to mention ignoring all the whispers online about her sexy training partner, who Alice constantly stressed was 'just her friend'. That was what she was trying to do now, replying to a comment with a string of laughing emojis, her legs sprawled across Owen's lap. Murphy was asleep at their feet. Stretched out like he was, the pup was now significantly longer than the coffee table.

It was exactly the kind of lazy evening she'd always imagined with her boyfriend.

Wait.

Owen wasn't supposed to be her boyfriend. When had she started to think of him that way?

She must've made a sound because he looked up from his notes for a custody trial that started tomorrow. He'd been careful not to say anything, but the tension in his shoulders told her everything she needed to know. Owen was stressed. She'd overheard the tail end of a phone call the other day, and she had a feeling his client had unrealistic goals. That was something she knew a bit about too. Up to her eyeballs in wax most days—or at least it felt like it—Alice had been dragging her heels with her divorce. She was crossing her fingers that Phoenix's other legal problems, which were multiplying at an alarming rate despite the recovery of the child who overdosed on his drugs, would cause him to lose interest in fighting with her. As far as she was concerned, no news about their divorce was good news.

"What?" he asked, all boyfriendy, in a tone she wouldn't mind hearing every day for the rest of her life.

"Nothing!" Her response was too loud, too quick. She adjusted her glasses, rubbing her eyes; Owen's brow furrowed. Why'd he have to be so perceptive all the time?

"I forgot to order something," Alice lied. She pulled up the bookmarked screen on her laptop, tapped a few keys and ordered some boxes for the final items she still had to post from her clothing auction. With any luck, she'd be dropping the cheque for fourteen thousand dollars plus change over to the hospital by the end of next week.

Damn it, she'd better get some more candle jars as well. She was almost out of those too. She opened another tab, logged in and scrolled quickly through the list of supplies available. The next charity candle would be for the volunteer regional firefighters, and she was still finalising the scent, but candied orange and cedar was her current favourite.

Owen didn't say anything, picking up the printout of his opening argument. His thumb rubbed across the top of her shin as he wrote a note in the margin. She lost herself in watching him, the way his jumper clung to his chest as it rose and fell, how he'd tap his pen against his bottom lip when he was mulling something over. She laughed softly when he looked up, catching her, and sent her a wink.

Alice typed loudly on her keyboard, keeping up the pretence of working, quickly ordering more candle jars and hitting save on all the social media posts she had scheduled for the following week. She'd spent more time doing admin since her company launched since ... well, ever. When she stood and stretched, folding her body in half and touching her toes, her tired muscles lengthened and relaxed. The fifteen-kilometre run yesterday after a strength session where she lifted more than she'd ever managed before was catching up with her.

The sound of shuffling papers and the quiet skid when they landed on the coffee table made her heart rate speed up. She shifted forward even more, her top slipping and pooling around her chest. The red lace of her bra would be peeking out. Through her legs, she watched Owen stand, rising on his toes as he stretched his arms above his head, a sliver of toned stomach with a dusting of hair making her lightheaded. He squeezed her butt, his strong arms encircling her waist as he bent forward to pull her up until her back was pressed against his chest.

"Are you ready for your surprise now?" he whispered in her ear.

She wiggled a little against him to see if it was in his pants. The cheesy line would be out of character for him, but she wouldn't mind. She couldn't get enough of Owen. "Is that what the kids are calling it these days?"

Instead of leading her to his bed, Owen pushed the big sliding door open and pulled her outside, one hand lingering on her hip. Murphy followed, and Owen clipped him onto his long lead before he could escape. Once they'd each slipped on an old pair of runners, Murphy trotted ahead, barking at shadows. Alice shivered, the wind piercing through her jumper and leggings. They ambled over the spiky grass around his place until she stopped.

She thought he'd forgotten.

Behind his funny little studio, was a tent strung with fairy lights and a lantern propped against the entry flap. Owen wrapped his arms around her, his hands rubbing up and down her arms when she shivered again.

"Raff finally dropped it off, and I thought we could practice sleeping in it."

"What about—"

"There's room for Murphy as well. Come see," he said, nudging her closer. She allowed him to lead her into the small space, her knees sinking into the big air mattress that took up two-thirds of the tent. Two sleeping bags rested on top of it with the pillows from his bed. There was another lantern and a small oil heater in the corner near the front zip, both plugged into a big orange power box. Warmth spread throughout Alice when she saw the dog bed in the corner. The fluffy blue blanket he'd been using to cover Murphy's crate, so he didn't get cold on the nights they spent at Owen's place, was also there, folded neatly. Murphy obviously approved, flopping down on his bed and rolling onto his back.

"What do you say?" Owen sat on the bed, the air in the mattress shifting underneath her. He rested his chin on her shoulder. "Ready for your first night of pseudo-camping?"

She twisted around, taking a moment to marvel at how this was her life now. When Owen looked at her like that, Alice was ready for anything. And when he kissed her, soft and sweet, their breath mingling, she never wanted to leave.

A teeny, tiny voice in the back of her mind reminded her this couldn't last. It would eventually fall apart, like everything else in her life always had.

Alice needed to lighten the moment. Push aside her worries. She scooted up the bed, bouncing around. Owen threw her a flirty smile, and she waved a finger at him. "Oh no. No funny business in front of the dog. I'm not that kind of girl."

Owen laughed as he stretched out next to her, biceps flexing as he rested his arms behind his head. She drank in his relaxed form, her eyes drifting over his slouchy navy jumper and dark grey tracksuit pants. There was something extra sexy about him in his grey tracksuit pants.

"I remember. It doesn't have to always be about sex, you know." He winked at her, and she flushed, pretending to study the stitching on the top of the tent.

When was the last time she'd slept next to the man she was seeing—because *damn it,* she was seeing Owen—and not *slept* with them? In fact, before Phoenix, she hadn't had a proper boyfriend since high school. All her other conquests had been hook-ups, plain and simple. What was the point in wanting more when she'd never been enough before? The only time she'd thought maybe she was wrong had been with Phoenix. And everyone knew how that had ended up.

When Owen stood and reached for her, Alice hesitated. Maybe it would be best if she ended things now. Business was consistently busy, and she could afford to rent an office closer to the city and shift her operations there. Pull out of the race. Find a new lawyer.

Protect Owen from the inevitable fallout that'd come from being involved with her.

But as he smiled down at her with a wry smile on his face, the lights from the fairy lights and lanterns casting a magical glow throughout the tent, she couldn't deny the truth any longer. She wasn't going anywhere. She'd let herself enjoy this for a little longer.

"Alice?"

She placed her palms in his and let him pull her up. Leaning into him, her face resting on his chest, she closed her eyes, savouring this perfect moment of time in their bubble.

"Everything okay?" Owen rubbed her back, his hand slipping underneath her jumper.

She nodded, not trusting herself to speak.

For the first time in forever, everything was okay. She had a job she loved, super fun sex with the hottest, sweetest guy she'd ever known, real friends, her family weren't worried about her all the time, and she controlled her own life. The words Owen had said to her at her business launch came to mind again.

This is working.

Her new life was working.

And she loved it.

25

Everything was not okay.

Exhibit A: the massive delivery truck in the car park outside her apartment. Exhibit B: the dour-faced man with a large moustache and bushy eyebrows sighing loudly. The truck's rear doors were open, and ten pallets of boxes wrapped in thick plastic were waiting to be unloaded.

"I didn't order this." Fingers of panic curled in Alice's stomach.

The man, a blob of high-vis yellow and orange, didn't look up as he manoeuvred the pallet jack into place. "This is the address on the order."

Each pump of the handle made her heart thump harder.

"Don't unload anything yet." Alice pushed her wet hair behind her ears. She'd been in the shower when the driver had arrived.

The man sighed again and pulled out a pack of gum, popping two pieces into his mouth.

Alice scrolled furiously through her emails on her

phone, all the words blurring together until she finally found her order confirmation.

Oh no.

She hadn't ordered a thousand new jars. She'd ordered ten thousand. "Oh my God," she whispered.

"Watch out." The truck's motorised tailgate whined and started lowering. "Because of the gravel, I'll have to leave the pallets here." He dumped it in the middle of the car park.

"You have to take them back. I didn't mean to order so many!"

His eyebrows raised, two hairy caterpillars on his forehead. "Sorry, love. No can do."

The tailgate grunted, its motor clanging as it started ascending.

"But ... but ... what am I supposed to do with them?" Alice rubbed her forehead. Right. She'd call her supplier and explain. If she had to pay a small fee to have the jars returned, then that was unfortunate, but it wasn't the end of the world.

Her front door banged open, and Teddy clattered down the steps, his uni bag slung over his shoulder. "Whoa," he said, eyes wide as he surveyed the scene in front of him. His car was blocked in by the truck. Another pallet thudded onto the gravel.

"Um, Alice, first of all, it's nice to see you," he teased. "It's like I live by myself these days."

She shifted her weight from one leg to the other, the gravel cutting into the soles of her bare feet. "I've been doing lots of hours."

"Sure, you have." What? Did Teddy know? She knew she shouldn't have let Owen convince her the shower would muffle her moans in the mornings after their runs.

"Listen, I hate to be this guy, but I've got to go. Like, now. I've got a prac today."

Of course he did. The stupid truck's stupid tailgate groaned again. Alice squeezed her eyes closed. "Okay. Let me think for a second."

Owen chose that moment to poke his head out of the office's rear door. "What's with the truck? It's blocking the driveway."

"There's an issue with my delivery." Alice tried to keep it together, but her voice wobbled. She blinked furiously. How could she have been so stupid?

"Chin up, Al." Teddy looped an arm around her shoulders. "These things happen. Any other day, I'd happily skip uni, but I can't miss this morning." He was lying about skipping university, but Alice appreciated Teddy's attempt to brighten her spirits.

"Here." Owen pulled his keys out of his pocket and lobbed them to Teddy. "Take the Jeep. I'm parked out front. I'll swap them this afternoon."

Teddy squeezed Alice's shoulder. "See. You can always count on Owen to save the day."

Great. She didn't want him to even see her messes. Having him help her clean it up was too much.

The final pallet hit the gravel.

"Sign here," the delivery man said, thrusting a clipboard at her. She scrawled a barely legible version of her signature.

"I'm so sorry, Teddy. I hope you're not late," she said as he passed his keys to Owen.

"Don't stress." He waved before disappearing inside the office.

Once Teddy was out of sight, Owen crossed the car park

to stand next to her. "You okay?" he asked softly, his hand settling into the small of her back.

Alice nodded twice before her face crumpled. Her voice broke. "I ordered too many candle jars and put down the wrong address."

So, help her God if he called her *honey* right now, she'd go to pieces.

"That's all candle jars?"

"I'm such an idiot," Alice muttered. She doubted he'd even heard her over the rumble of the truck's engine as it started.

Owen's hand slipped to her hip, and she leant into him automatically, but the clean scent of his aftershave was immediately swallowed up by the fumes from the truck's exhaust.

"Call Mum and ask if you can borrow her van for the shop. We'll load as many of these into it as we can and take them to the shearers' shed this afternoon. I should be back around three o'clock. And I've got a few hours before footy training. What doesn't fit can go into my storeroom until we can ferry them across."

Alice swiped at her eyes. He made it sound so simple. "But what am I going to do with them all? It'll take me forever to sell these." She didn't have enough supplies to make a third of these candles.

Owen spun around, wrapping her up in his arms. Alice wanted to collapse against him, but her body was stiff. All her old wounds were reopening. She'd been waiting for something to go wrong. And a mistake like this had the power to undo all her good work.

"It'll be okay," he said. "We can sort it out."

She *knew* he didn't mean it that way—the way that implied

she couldn't fix it by herself, the way so many people had said it to her over the years—but Alice couldn't stop the words from escaping. "*We* don't have to do anything, Owen. I'll fix it."

She heard the office door bang open, and Owen's body tensed. Alice pushed away from him, putting some distance between them. Still, it hurt when he frowned at her, so she turned around and stared at the bugs stuck in the grill of Teddy's ute.

"Owen?" Frankie called, curiosity heavy in her voice. "Jessica's here and so is Camille. What's all this?"

Alice held her breath. Great. Not only was Frankie getting a front-row seat to this train crash but now Owen's ex was back. *Again*.

"I'll be there in a minute, Frankie."

"I put a fresh coffee on your desk, and there are some of those all-bran muffins you like in the kitchen if you're hungry. Should I call someone about this?" Frankie asked.

Alice buried her face in her hands. When she was little, and she'd play hide and seek with Dougie, she'd believed if she couldn't see him, he couldn't see her.

"No need, Frankie." Owen's tone was firm, definitive.

"It's no problem. You know I'd do anything to help my favourite boss. I could ring my brother ..." Her flirty tone rankled Alice. But really, what claim did she have to Owen? She wasn't even able to tell him about her ever-increasing feelings for him, let alone everyone else.

Frankie's voice was louder; she must've stepped around the pallets. "Oh, sorry! I didn't realise you were out here with Alice." All the flirtiness was gone, replaced with something Alice recognised immediately: jealousy.

"Thank you, Frankie," Owen snapped, and Alice cringed. She didn't want to feel sorry for Frankie, but she couldn't blame her for being surprised. As far as Frankie knew, Owen was an available, successful, hot guy. What single lady in their right mind wouldn't flirt with him? Alice clenched her jaw, furious with herself. She focused on her breathing, but her body wouldn't cooperate.

"We need to be more careful," Alice muttered once Frankie had closed the door behind her.

Owen's sigh made her purse her lips.

"Of standing near each other in an empty car park behind my office? Besides, Frankie doesn't care ..." he said.

Alice's head snapped up, and she spun around so quickly that she almost lost her footing. "She's probably already texting people, Owen. She hates my guts, and she's your number one fan. What do you think the coffee and special muffins mean? All the offers to get your lunch for you. And why is Camille here?"

He rolled his eyes and shook his head. "I have no idea what Camille wants. Frankie's just being friendly. That's what people do here."

Alice snorted. How could someone so smart be so oblivious? "They sure do. I was so overwhelmed with friendliness when I arrived, especially from you." She tried to swallow the bitter taste in her mouth, immediately regretting the low blow.

Owen's jaw clenched. Maybe when he finished with Jessica's case, he could cut some granite with the hard line of his jaw. "That was different."

"Was it, though? You thought I was a spoiled rich kid who had never worked a day in her life. Guess I could only pretend to have my shit together for so long. Now you get to see the real Alice."

How embarrassing. Mason jars and women she knew Owen wasn't interested in at all were sending her spiralling. So much for personal growth.

He strode towards her. "I never thought that. Not even the first time when I stopped to help you with your car ... after that, I was being professional," he breathed out roughly, his hands tugging at his tie before settling on his hips.

"Whatever; I've worked too hard to lose all of this over a silly mistake."

They looked at each other, locked in a staring contest. Owen broke first, his expression softening. "Why are you trying to start a fight right now?"

Alice dragged her foot through the gravel, shoulders sagging as all the anger left her body. "I'm not doing anything." She hated how small her voice was.

"That's not true and you know it," he said. God, couldn't he let her get away with it? Give her a free pass this one time? She knew she was being a cow.

"I know you're having a bad morning and these last few months ... years ... have been really hard, but lashing out at people who are only trying to help isn't a good idea."

"Because I always need help? Which is why it's so weird someone like you would be interested in me?"

Christ. What was wrong with her? She was reverting to a version of herself who she hadn't been for a long time. This was exactly the kind of argument she used to have with Phoenix. About her weight or when he flirted with his fans.

"Where did that come from? That's not what I mean. I think you're amazing. If anyone's keeping secrets here, it's not me. Okay? I told you at the start of whatever *this* is that I don't play games. I care about you a lot. But I don't like this." He gestured between the two of them. "You deserve better, and so do I."

"I should make some phone calls." Alice stared at the gravel.

"I'll leave the back door unlocked. If you want help later, let me know."

Owen was way too good for her. It had never been more apparent.

She swept her foot across the gravel again, in the opposite direction, smoothing the mess she'd made. If only the same could be said for the jumbled thoughts in her mind. "It's okay. I'll sort it out."

He nodded once, disappearing into the building without a goodbye.

Alice spun on her heel, deflating when she saw the pallets.

Right. One disaster at a time.

"What do you want?" Owen said once Camille was in his office and the door was shut firmly behind them.

"I can't even stop by to say hi?"

Owen dragged a hand down his face and undid his tie. Stupid thing was suffocating him. "I have a client waiting."

Camille shifted forward so she was sitting on his desk. She flicked her hair over her shoulder and crossed her arms. "I need your help."

Owen paused and looked at her. Really looked at her. Her clothes were wrinkled, and there were bags underneath her eyes. Despite her standard bravado, Camille was missing some of her usual polish.

She pulled her phone out of her bag. "I want you to convince my mother she needs to divorce my dad. Come back to Queensland with me."

Owen didn't hesitate. "I can't do that."

"Can't or won't? She needs help, Owen. Someone who

can explain the process and how it will work. Someone who cares like you do."

Owen picked up his tie and retied it, hoping Camille would pick up on the subtle hint. "It wouldn't be appropriate for me to get involved."

"But you owe me! I didn't tell anyone about you and Alice when I could have. Hooking up with her lawyer wouldn't be a good look for her."

How could a day go so far off the rails before it was even nine o'clock? Owen took a deep breath and forced himself to release it slowly. He made sure his words were even and calm, the opposite of the feelings swirling inside his body. There was an immediate need to protect Alice. Followed by the desire to protect the honour of the business he was working so hard to build and the complications it would have for Raff if Owen suddenly started working for the Arturos.

"I don't owe you anything."

With a heavy sigh, Camille tossed her mobile back into her bag. "Can't you just do it because it's the right thing to do, then?"

It was like someone flicked a light bulb on in front of Owen's eyes.

It had to be the right thing for *him*.

And this just ... *wasn't*.

Nothing was more important to him than his family, and he'd do everything he could to always protect them. He realised with a start that when he thought of his family, Alice was right there too. She was already more important than anyone else had ever been. Regardless of what had happened just before, he still wanted her more than anything. Wanted his new life to keep growing and getting better and better.

He wasn't going to blink just because Camille tossed a thinly veiled threat his way. "I can suggest some lawyers who may be able to help you, but that's it."

"What if I—"

Owen cut in. He wasn't even prepared to let Camille finish her sentence. "I won't change my mind. No is my final answer. You can see yourself out because we're done here. We're done. Do you understand me? I'll take my next meeting in the conference room."

And he strode out of the room without a backwards glance.

THIS WASN'T the first time Owen had made a grown man cry. It probably wouldn't be the last, either. Owen waited for Rob to get a hold of himself. The rain tapping against the windows of the courtroom mirrored Owen's mood.

"I'm sorry. I understand you have to ask these questions but I've changed. Sam has two parents who love him."

Owen resisted the urge to straighten his tie, tap his fingers on the wooden table in front of him. His argument with Alice had tipped him off-kilter and still lingered in the back of his mind. Made him question if there was any possibility that this could end well for him. His feelings were already too big, too much.

Jessica's laser-focused determination to fight for Sam made perfect sense to Owen. Sure, she was probably going to be disappointed by the outcome of this custody case. But she was there next to him, shoulders straight, eyes forward. She was unapologetically going after what she wanted. The shitshow with Camille this morning was similar. Even if it had been one of the easiest 'no's of Owen's life, he could still understand why his ex had asked him to help, appealing to what Teddy always called his 'saviour complex'.

Rob blew his nose loudly.

Owen shifted in his seat. This was the part he was struggling with. The unexpected greyness of the situation. He'd never expected to find himself in this position, sympathising with a gambling addict. Back when Jessica had first explained what had happened, it was easy to cast Rob as the villain. Even when he'd analysed the situation from different angles or played devil's advocate, there was no avoiding the fact that it was the actions of the guy sitting in the witness stand, gently weeping into a crumpled tissue, that had brought them all to this moment.

But still, Rob had showed up. Made changes that seemed genuine. He was trying to right all his mistakes.

Shades of grey were creeping into all the facets of Owen's life. He couldn't help but think of Alice—there was no point pretending she wasn't always on his mind—and how quickly she'd unravelled this morning. Her embarrassment colouring all her decisions. Helping her realise there was nothing she couldn't conquer was the one problem he couldn't seem to solve.

Jessica's chair creaked. Owen swallowed. Personal feelings aside, he had a job to do. "You originally wanted equal custody. Why did you change your mind?"

"I had an unrealistic view about how this was all going to work out," Rob said.

"What does that mean?"

"I was thinking about what I wanted. Not what would be best for Sam. He doesn't know me. We need to rebuild our relationship, and that takes time. I can be patient. But I can't do it if I'm not even allowed to see him."

Owen frowned at his notes. Every word out of Rob's

mouth chipped away at their argument. What was he supposed to do? Drag out all of Rob's past indiscretions and failures? Take him apart on the stand? Hit him with statistics about the chance of addicts relapsing? Try to undermine the man's confidence which could have a devastating impact on his sobriety? That's what Malus, Mendax and Associates would've expected of him.

It was also exactly why he'd left to start his own law firm.

Owen blinked, refocused. He wasn't going to move backwards. "No further questions, thank you."

The judge nodded and told Rob he could return to his seat before calling a recess.

"You ready?" Owen murmured to Jessica once they were outside, huddled in a corner of the hallway.

She fiddled with the collar of her blazer. "I'm going to lose, aren't I?"

"It's unlikely the judge will give you sole custody." Which was what he'd been saying ever since she'd decided to go for full custody.

"And whatever she says is binding?"

"You could always appeal. But that will involve doing all this again and proving the judge's decision wasn't fair. It's not impossible, but honestly, it's not an easy process."

"Do you think I'm a terrible person?" she whispered. "I could've saved us all a lot of time if I'd just agreed to this when you first suggested it. They didn't even mention my criminal record when they questioned me."

That had surprised Owen, too. He swallowed, giving himself a second to choose his words. Regardless of his own feelings, Owen had a duty to Jessica. "I think you've been in an impossible position. Rob turned your and Sam's world upside down. But it seems like he's gotten himself back on track and there are lots of systems in place to keep an eye on him.

"Based on the evidence they've presented and the way the court will always try to preserve a child's relationship with both parents, as long as it is safe to do so, I don't think you'll get full custody. And, in my professional opinion, it would be pointless to appeal joint custody immediately. You'd need to wait for Rob to fail to meet his terms of the agreement."

Jessica nodded before biting her lip and releasing a shaky exhale. "He's right, you know. Sam deserves two parents. I'm putting my fears in front of his needs. And now I might have to share Sam more than I originally wanted to."

"We can still offer a different custody split if there's one you think you'd prefer now."

Rob and his lawyer walked towards them. Jessica picked up her phone, Sam's cheeky face filling the screen.

"Four days a fortnight, no overnights. Not initially. And I want a transition period that includes supervision so Sam can get to know Rob again."

"You're sure?"

"Make the deal, Owen. It's time to start rebuilding our lives properly. I'm sorry I didn't listen to you when you first suggested the different options."

He blinked. Took a long breath. That's why this morning's fight with Alice had caught him so off-guard. He thought they were building their lives together. Chipping away at all the obstacles in front of them so they could have a future together when she was finally free of Phoenix, but Owen had forgotten something essential.

What if that wasn't what was right for Alice?

And he was left on his own.

Again.

26

Alice was halfway through trying to figure out how much more wax she needed to order when the door to the shearers' shed opened. She rushed forward, careful not to trip over Murphy. She'd been practising her apology all day, spurred on by the deep embarrassment that had settled over her skin as she thought about how she'd treated Owen.

Eloise poked her head through the doorway, and Alice sighed. "Hey," she said. "What are you doing here?"

Eloise grinned, stepping into the mess. The heavy boxes of candle jars hadn't made it more than a metre inside before Alice had decided that was where they could stay for the time being.

"Good. You're still here. We were hoping to catch you before you left for the day."

Alice looked around, past the old wool sorting table covered in candles that had set but not yet been boxed up and the metal shelves she'd bought to store her wax and other supplies. Where else would she be? Owen would be busy with footy training for another hour or so, at least. And

—she swallowed—he might not want to see her tonight. Not after the way she'd behaved earlier.

"What's going on?" she asked as Eloise pushed the door wide open. Lulu, Joan and a few other of the Old Girls walked in. They were carrying boxes of takeaway pizza, bottles of wine and grocery bags. Murphy leapt to his feet, following his nose until he was wrapped around Eloise's jean-clad legs.

"We heard you had a rough day and thought we'd come and keep you company," Joan said.

Alice blinked back the unexpected tears. "That's so nice of you all."

"Is there somewhere I can put these?" Lulu held up a cupcake box. "They're from a box mix because I wanted to make sure they were totally gluten free, but Wilbur tried one and said he couldn't tell the difference."

"I'll make space." Alice reached for the Tupperware container.

"Now, how can we help?" Eloise asked.

"You ladies don't have to do anything."

"Nonsense. Drink this and then put us to work." Lulu thrust a plastic cup of white wine into Alice's hand.

"I've always wanted to learn how to make candles," Joan said, looking up from where she was assembling a cheese platter. Alice's mouth watered at the array of hard and soft cheeses, salami and prosciutto.

"Everything I bought said gluten free on the packaging. Nothing from the deli, so there shouldn't be any cross conta-mination," Joan added, answering the question Alice was about to ask. Constantly having to be vigilant about her diet could be exhausting but little extra acts of care like this? It helped her not feel so different from everyone else.

"Seriously, what can we do?" Lulu asked.

"Well, I guess these need to be boxed up so I can sort them into their orders tomorrow." Alice pointed at the wool sorting table. That would make space for the next round of candles she needed to make.

"On it." Lulu dragged a stool over to the table and started assembling the pretty candle boxes covered in wattle flowers.

"And we could get a head start on pouring tomorrow's candles. If you're sure you wouldn't rather sit and relax. Have some of the food you all brought?"

"Please." Joan tossed her a wink. "We're women. We can multi-task, especially when wine and carbs are involved. Let's make some candles! And Lulu can tell you all about the time she ordered five thousand shopping bags instead of five hundred."

"I still maintain that extra zero was a glitch in their system."

"Was this when you were in denial about needing new glasses?" Joan teased and Alice giggled. The easy friendship and warmth the women had brought into her cold, little shearers' shed chased away some of the disappointment in herself that she'd been unable to let go of.

"Possibly." Lulu winked at Alice.

"See," Eloise whispered, nudging Alice. "These things happen. It's not a big deal."

Now all she had to do was make things right with Owen. Explain to him why she'd twisted herself into knots in front of him and hope he would understand.

"This is a surprise," Wyatt said when Owen pushed

through the front doors of the Wattle Junction Hotel. "You never come to drinks after training."

"Felt like a beer tonight." Owen slid onto a bar stool next to Nate. Teddy was sitting on his other side checking his footy tips. Owen nodded at his teammates who were playing pool.

"What'll it be?" Wyatt flicked the rag he'd been wiping the bar down with over his shoulder.

"Whatever's going."

Nate passed Wyatt a couple of notes. "Give us three of the new red ales. Owen will like it."

Wyatt placed an icy pint glass under the beer tap, and Teddy looked up when the drink was placed in front of him. "He does seem to have a thing for reds at the moment, doesn't he?"

Owen ignored the joke, swallowing a long mouthful of beer. When he looked back up, both his brothers were watching him closely. In his peripheral vision, Owen noticed Wyatt quietly drift down to the other end of the bar, giving the brothers privacy.

"Alright, O. That was a subtle opener. We can be more direct. Want to talk about your lady problems?" Teddy leant forward, resting his elbows on the mahogany bar.

"I don't have a lady. I had a long day at court. That's all," Owen grumbled, trying to deflect.

"But hypothetically, if you did have lady problems"— Nate smirked and did air quotes—"would that explain why you tackled Jack so hard tonight he's still limping?"

Owen tapped the side of his glass, his gaze sliding over to where Jack was walking around the pool table. He *was* favouring his right side. "I'll pay that it wasn't my best tackle."

"We're not surprised," Teddy said. "About you and Alice."

Owen pushed his drink away, his thirst evaporating. He lowered his voice. "Jesus, Ted. She's my client and keep it down, would you?"

Teddy scoffed. He helped himself to a bag of peanuts, tearing it open and tipping a small handful into his cupped palm. "Maybe Alice should keep it down when she showers after her morning run. You know when she's in there all alone?"

Owen dropped his head into his hands.

"Seems like her divorce is taking a long time," Nate said.

"We're headed to court next month." Although Phoenix was still asking Alice for money and she was ignoring him. Even Owen was annoyed by the big sigh he couldn't stop escaping.

"Why don't you go and see her, mate? Sort out whatever problem you're having." Nate gestured for Teddy to wing him a packet of nuts.

"She's working."

Teddy raised his eyebrows. "So, go and help her. Jesus. You lot act like I'm the family idiot but *hello*."

Owen sipped his beer. "No one thinks you're an idiot. We think your hair is idiotic."

"Yeah, well, so is your face, asshole."

Owen shook his head, a small smile pulling at his lips. He could always count on his brothers to pull him out of a bad mood.

"The way I see it, you can sit here with us and pretend everything's fine, or you can go find Alice. A blind man could see what's going on between you. Even Raff's figured it out, which is impressive because he's living and breathing work right now," Nate said.

Owen stared at the drink mats lined on top of the bar. They'd been so careful. Only spending time at his place or hers when Teddy was out or supposedly asleep. And yeah, there had been that time in his office—he shifted on his seat thinking about it—but Frankie had been wearing headphones, transcribing a deposition. The bite marks Alice had left on his shoulders when she came had been worth it.

"There's nothing going—"

"Whatever. Fine. There's nothing going on. I guess I'm not used to seeing this Owen. Not since Camille, anyway." Teddy threw his hands up in the air and stomped around the bar to sit next to Nate.

His family needed to stop acting like he was carrying around a barely bandaged together heart because his ex-girlfriend had dumped him. This idea he'd been so damaged, he'd been unable to form connections with women ever since was shit. He'd had plenty of consensual, no-strings-attached fun over the years. The no-strings aspect was purely convenience focused. That was all. End of story.

"Camille's got nothing to do with this. Besides, you were about six months old when all that went down."

Teddy threw a peanut at him. "I was seventeen, dumbass, and you were heartbroken."

"I was fine." Owen turned to Nate. "Tell him I was fine."

"You were pretty cut up about it."

"See!" Teddy stole Owen's beer and finished it.

Continuing this conversation would be like banging his head against a brick wall. Still, something Teddy had said rankled Owen. "What did you mean when you said you weren't used to seeing 'this Owen'?"

"Since when do you not go after what you want?"

Owen's phone rang, and Alice's picture flashed on the

screen. In it, she was snuggling Murphy, curled up in the corner of his couch. They were both asleep.

Teddy grabbed the phone and held it up. "You'd better get this. The woman you're not seeing has been breaking into your place and napping on your couch."

Owen stared up at his brother blankly. "But she set the rules."

It was like they'd all swapped spots and Teddy and Nate were his older, wiser brothers. The looks they gave Owen were a hair's breadth away from pity.

"Since when are you afraid to renegotiate?" Nate said, passing him his phone.

Owen nodded, his throat thick. "Hey," he answered the call, pushing off his stool and waving farewell before he stepped outside.

"Where are you? I'm at your place, but you're not here."

He stared at the night sky, the crisp, cool air filling his lungs. "I stopped for a drink after training."

"Will you be back soon? I have good news," she sing-songed, her enthusiasm cutting at him like a knife. "And I want to hear about how your big case went."

Owen exhaled. It was pointless pretending he didn't want to see her, and he'd promised that he wouldn't play games. "Give me fifteen minutes."

Alice's voice deepened, reminding him of how she sounded when she woke up. "Hurry, please. I owe you an apology."

OWEN'S MOUTH went dry when he saw Alice. Her hair was mussed, like she'd been running her hands through it and her cheeks were pink. Even in the low glow filtering out from his little studio, he could see how bright her eyes were. When Murphy ran towards him, tail wagging furiously, Owen was glad. He needed a minute.

"Hey buddy," Owen said as Alice stood and smoothed out her jacket.

As if she knew what he needed to hear, Alice stepped closer, a nervous expression on her face. "I'm sorry about this morning," she said.

"I was only trying to help."

She tugged his hands out of his pockets and linked their fingers together. Alice lifted her face to his, her skin clean, scrubbed free of make-up. This was his favourite Alice, the one not many people got to see.

"I'm not good at accepting help." Her voice was quiet, but she didn't look away from him. "Never have been. And you're the last person I want to see my mistakes."

"Why?" His gaze dropped to her neck, knowing the delicate skin there would flush if she was embarrassed. It was another little Alice secret he'd been collecting, adding to his treasure trove of information about her. The telltale pink tinge warmed him, reaffirming he wasn't wrong. He knew her.

She dropped her chin and sighed, her grip on his hands tightening like she was gathering her courage. "Because I don't want you to think I'm stupid."

There it was again. That word. *Stupid.* He shook his head, unable to believe it had taken him so long to figure this out. When she'd first referred to herself as stupid, he'd brushed it away, not able to fathom why she'd think that ... which, ironically, was *stupid* of him. But this was a bigger issue than he'd realised. Alice had been made to feel this way her whole life.

He opened his arms wider until she got the hint, stepping into his embrace and wrapping hers around his waist. "I will never think that," he punctuated each word with a kiss to her forehead, her cheeks and then finally her lips. "But I would like for you to talk to me." He cleared his throat. "In the past, I've not always been good at doing that myself. Maybe we could try together?"

Alice nodded, brushing her lips across his before resting her head against his chest. "I can do that." He guided her to the Adirondack chair next to his front door and pulled her onto his lap.

He traced her lips with a finger when she shivered. "Cold?" he asked.

Wordlessly, she shook her head, pressing their foreheads together. "Something really good happened today. Something I never imagined. Maybe I could tell you about it?"

"I'd like that," he murmured.

"Lulu, Joan and Eloise rallied the troops for an impromptu candle making class tonight."

His shoulders relaxed.

"We made so many that I've run out of wax. And packed all the orders from this week. All these people turned up to help me unasked. I mean, there was a killer grazing plate and pizza and a fair bit of wine, but ..."

"I don't think they were lured in by carbohydrates and charcuterie, honey. They wanted to help you, not because they could," he corrected her, "but because they like you and want you to do well. We look after each other out here. Look at what everyone's been doing lately for you."

Oh, well done, asshole, Owen said to himself. Reminding Alice about her freak-out over her mistake wasn't a smart idea.

Alice's quiet laugh and teasing eye roll surprised him.

"We, huh? Do you mean the town or you and me? Are we a 'we'?"

"Uh, both? Maybe?" Owen rubbed his neck.

Alice surprised him again, pulling his face towards hers. "Good."

Good? What the hell did that mean?

"Okay?" Later, once he'd figured out what was going on, Owen would revisit how he managed to pack so much doubt into one four-letter word.

She smacked him lightly, rolling her eyes again. "Stop panicking. It's okay for us to be a 'we'."

"It is?" His voice cracked like he was thirteen years old again.

"I think we might be dating, Owen. Is that okay with you?"

He took a steadying breath of her flowery shampoo. "Sounds good to me."

Alice pinched his side, her eyes sparkling. Seeing her so happy and relaxed was dangerous. His mind was liable to run away from all common sense, letting all the wishes he hadn't verbalised to anyone, least of all himself, run rampant.

"It's so different here," Alice said quietly as she looked out at the inky blackness in front of them. "I'm not used to it. The niceness, I mean."

"Do you think you could get used to it?" he asked. It didn't take a genius to figure out the barely concealed message hidden in his words.

"I'd like to."

So would he.

"Hey Owen ..." she said, her fingers scratching at the longer-than-usual hair curling at the nape of his neck.

"Mmhmm." He twisted his head, encouraging her to scratch harder while he waited for her to finish her thought.

Alice breathed out slowly, her fingers stilling. She was going to say something important. He'd bet all the stars in the night sky.

"What do you want?" she asked.

Owen remembered his brothers' words and made a silent wish that this wouldn't be too much.

"You."

27

Alice pushed open the door of Owen's place, warmth spreading through her chest when he looked up and smirked. Just like she'd known he would. Murphy sprinted past her, leaving muddy footprints all over the polished concrete floor.

"Didn't want to do two trips, huh?" Owen's long strides ate up the distance between them, and he took the hessian bags full of groceries out of her hands and lifted the multi-coloured tote she always brought with her when she stayed over off her shoulder.

"Wanted one of these more," she said, wrapping her now empty arms around his shoulders. She pressed her lips against his, immediately sliding her tongue into his mouth. He let her dominate, groaning against her mouth. Her grip loosened, and they broke apart when a bag of rice flopped to the floor. She giggled before kissing him again. When she pulled away, his eyes filled with heat and a pang of longing burnt low in her belly.

God, she was so happy.

"You know," he said, the hint of playfulness in his voice that would never not thrill her, "I have rice here."

"You have brown rice." She wrinkled her nose at him. "It's not the same thing."

Owen followed her to the kitchen and started unpacking the ingredients for a chicken stir fry. As she poured them each a glass of wine, she told him about her day. A few women staying at Kathleen's Place had come by to help pack orders, and then she'd gone out to the nursing home teaching knitting again. Alice's voice rose steadily, her cheeks flushing as she described how the day had flown by before she stopped. This was the hard part. Hard because it had been so unexpected. She paused. Took a deep breath. Reminded herself that unexpected wasn't always bad.

Owen stopped slicing mushrooms. "What?"

Alice skirted around the bench, her hand lingering on his hip. It'd be easier if she was touching him.

"Then my parents came by," she said. A little wine slopped over the side of her glass when she put her drink down.

"They came out here? Did you know they were coming? Were they impressed?"

She watched as he lifted his wine and took a drink. The tip of his tongue appeared, chasing a drop across his full bottom lip. *Don't get distracted.*

She started to shrug but stopped, shoulders up near her ears. "Sorry," she whispered.

"What for?"

"I was going to say I didn't know if they were impressed, but that would've been a lie. Can I?" She gestured for him to open his arms.

"Always."

Her heart rate slowed the second she was in his embrace. Regardless of what happened, her parents' visit had been a good thing. They'd had a nice time together for the first time in as long as she could remember. Until right at the end.

"My parents have a friend keen to invest in a small business."

It might be a good thing. And she could say no.

"And they're interested in The Emancipation of Alice?" Why did it sound like he had to force the words out? Did Owen think it was a ridiculous idea?

She burrowed her face into his chest, focused on the steady beat of his heart, the familiar feel of his jumper under her cheek. "Seems so."

"That's ...." *great*, was what she was hoping he would say. "Wow," was what he went with instead. "What did you say?"

She shrugged, not lifting her face. "Nothing, really. I was too shocked."

"Whoever this friend is should really give you a proper business proposal, spell out the percentage they'd want to purchase, what their financial contributions would be, whether they'd be a silent partner or expect to make decisions as well." Alice swallowed the small taste of disappointment that filled her mouth. It made sense that the lawyer inside of Owen took over because the *boyfriend* part was still so new and secret.

"I think I just wanted them to come out and see what I've done and be proud of me."

He pressed a kiss against the crown of her head, and she melted against him.

"Sounds like they were, though, doesn't it?"

"You think so?"

"Absolutely. If they thought you were wasting your time,

they wouldn't be encouraging a friend to go into business with you. It's a compliment, really. A very well-deserved one."

This time she did look up. Warmth and familiarity were etched across his face, reinforced by the way he was stroking her back, how she fitted so perfectly against him while he said what she needed to hear.

"Would you help me figure out what to reply to this investor dude's email with? Should I meet with him, maybe?"

He cupped her jaw, coaxing her forward. Not that she needed any convincing. "I'll always help with whatever you need."

Alice swallowed. It was time to come clean about the pictures. Phoenix's threat. Keeping it from Owen for this long had been foolish, but with the court case coming up next month, she owed the truth to both her boyfriend and lawyer. "There's something else I need to tell you."

"I have some news for you, too."

He snagged their glasses off the bench. "Come sit with me."

OWEN TRIED TO SMILE, but his mind was reeling. An investor could be a game changer for Alice's business. And it could take her away from him. Couple that with the news he had for her, and he was grateful they hadn't eaten yet. Some of the tension in his shoulders eased when she cuddled up next to him, her hand sliding over his thigh. He twisted so they could see each other.

"I heard from Dean Malus today." There went her bottom lip, just like he'd known it would.

"And?" she asked.

"Phoenix will agree to the divorce terms we set forward, but he still wants forty grand. He's got some debts he needs to pay, and this is a direct quote: 'he's not going to protect you forever'. He wants your answer by next Friday."

Alice's mouth twisted to the side as she mused over what he'd said. When she finally spoke, her voice was calm and measured, but the flush on her neck gave her away. Owen's gut told him there was something she was keeping from him.

"What would you do?"

"As a lawyer, I'd look at the probability of the judge siding with us while weighing up the court costs and everything you stand to lose. We haven't spoken about this in detail yet, but he might be planning to go after The Emancipation of Alice. Claim you're profiting from your reputation, which he is partly responsible for. Think about it. He's desperate for cash, and his brand's in the toilet."

"But he hasn't had anything to do with this. This is all mine."

Owen brushed his thumb across her palm, linking their fingers together. He took a deep breath and asked the question that couldn't be avoided any longer. "Is there anything else he could try to use against you?"

He tried not to read too much into the way her gaze dropped to the floor, how she avoided his eyes.

"It's embarrassing," she mumbled.

"Honey," he said softly, doing his best to quell the warring emotions in his chest to protect her while wanting to gently force the truth from her, "there's nothing you can tell me that will change anything between us. You need to know that, okay? I'm here, and I'm not going anywhere. Whatever you need to tell me, it's going to be okay."

She tucked her face into his neck. Her breath made goosebumps prick along his skin. The only sound was Murphy's panting breaths.

"There might be some ... compromising photos," she whispered, and Owen's heart stopped. Those weren't the words he'd been expecting. Visions of Alice in his bed filled his mind, her gorgeous body and how willingly she offered herself to him. He wasn't an idiot. Everyone had a past. Owen had a past. But this ... he was ashamed to admit how his baser instincts roared to life, almost drowning out any common sense.

Christ.

He focused on softening the edges of his words. "Might be?"

She took a deep breath, her voice thick with tears. "From when we were first together. It was a mistake."

"It'll be okay." He held her tightly. "When you're ready, can you tell me exactly what happened?" He wanted to spit the words out, douse the anger at Phoenix that was scorching through his veins but he focused on his breathing, reminded himself that problem-solving was his thing. They'd get an injunction. There was nothing he wouldn't do to protect the woman he loved.

Owen blinked up at the ceiling.

Love.

He'd known it for a while now, but he'd managed to avoid labelling his feelings. But there was no denying it anymore. He loved Alice.

And based on the moisture running down his neck and how Alice's shoulders were trembling, she didn't need her lawyer right now, she needed her guy. And Owen was her guy. He stomped down the urge to ask more questions. What sort of pictures? Was her face visible? What other body parts? Was she on her own? Was there a video as well? Were there any copies?

"I'm not naked or anything, but my bra is kind of sheer, so I might as well have been ..."

A wave of sadness smothered Owen's anger. To have her trust broken so completely by someone who was supposed to love her.

"It'll be okay. There are legal things we can do to stop him from releasing them. A reminder to him that revenge porn is a crime. I won't let him hurt you."

But shit, how could Owen promise that? After they got through the race, they'd have to figure out all these messes. She'd have to make a decision about her divorce.

"But won't people know? Would there be a record of it?" There it was. Her ever-present worry about what people would think.

"Why don't we go for a walk? Get some fresh air?" God knew he needed some. "We can figure out all the details once the race is finished. You've got until next Friday to respond."

Alice wiped her eyes, and he kissed her forehead. "That sounds like a plan."

In fact, he knew exactly how to distract her while also reinforcing that this didn't change how he felt about her. "Do you want to come and see my new house? It's almost finished. I'm just waiting on the certificate of occupancy to be granted."

If Alice was going to be a part of his future—and he really hoped she was—then he'd better start sharing his plans with her. And maybe one day it'd be her house too?

Owen slipped his hands underneath the back of her fuzzy jumper, the warmth of her skin calming him down. Reminding him she wasn't going anywhere yet but if this potential investor turned into something serious ... or Phoenix released her photos ... a flare of panic raced up his spine. "I promise we'll figure it out. There's nothing we can't figure out together."

Alice tipped her head back, some of the light back in her eyes. "Okay, Boy Scout. I trust you."

28

*C*ome do a charity race, they said.

It'll be fun, they said.

You'll raise money for people who need it, they said.

All of Alice's muscles and bones and limbs and *hell*, every part of her body was mutinying against her. Thank God for Owen's ass in his running shorts. Without it, she'd have flagged this whole thing hours ago.

Alice shrugged out of her running vest, coughing when she necked herself with the tube from her Camelbak.

"It's not much, but it's home for the night," Owen said as she looked around their campsite. By some small miracle, they'd made it to the first crop of tent sites, the ones near the river and—she shuddered—the long drop toilets.

The sun was slipping towards the horizon, the shadows of night creeping in and chasing away the last fingers of stubborn daylight. Rafferty's tent, an esky and some fire-wood were stacked next to a ring of stones. After being on her feet for over twelve hours scrambling over rocks, canoe-ing, working through a rock maze, running along fire trails, and hiking more hills than she realised were in the range, it looked like heaven.

Owen stowed their collection of page thirteens from the random books at each checkpoint in the front pocket of his vest. He tilted his head towards hers and pulled her closer. "You ready for an adventure?"

She tried to raise her arms out wide but *tired, so very tired.* "Haven't we been doing that all day?"

He chuckled, dropping a featherlight kiss on her lips. The warmth of his hand blazed through the sweaty patch on her back where her pack had been all day. His hands met on her shoulders. He applied just enough pressure to make her forget she was a sweaty, gross mess while he looked like he could still run a marathon.

"We have, yes." His warm breath danced across her skin. *What were they talking about again?*

"You're very good at this," she murmured.

He laughed, the sound giving her a burst of energy she wouldn't have thought possible an hour ago.

Alice wrapped her arms around his waist, resting her cheek against the spot on his chest she was starting to think belonged to her.

"Raff and I camped here the year we raced as well. There's a creek nearby. Fancy a dip?"

She pulled away, jabbing Owen in the side when he laughed at her. "But it's so cold!"

He raised his eyebrows in challenge. "I'll warm you up after," he promised. "Be good for all your sore muscles ..."

"It's getting dark. Shouldn't we start a fire? Rehydrate food for dinner?" Her stomach rumbled. All she'd eaten since lunch had been a few jellybeans, some energy gels, and boiled, salted potatoes. The potatoes had been surprisingly good.

"This will take ten minutes, tops. It'll be fun."

"I think you just want to see me all wet."

Owen smiled wolfishly, his hands venturing to her front, stopping shy of cupping her breasts. Maybe she wasn't that tired after all.

"I absolutely do. What do you say?"

ONCE THE TENT was up and a fire had been set for their return, Owen took Alice's hand and helped her down an embankment covered in ferns.

"Are you sure you know where you're going?" Alice looked over her shoulder in the direction of where they'd left the trail behind five minutes ago.

Owen stifled a smile. Her nervousness was more adorable than he'd expected. "It's all here on my watch, honey. I loaded all the maps on to it." The pet name slipped off his tongue extra easily and he thrilled at how her cheeks flushed a deeper red, still tinged from the day's exertion. "That's where the campsites are." He pointed. "We're down here."

Running water bubbled in the distance, and birds sang to each other as they settled down for the night. Something rustled in the long grass on the other side of the creek, and Alice clutched his arm. There was no hiding his smile this time.

"Is that a snake?" she hissed.

"Probably a roo," he said calmly. "I won't let anything happen to you."

She huffed but didn't let go of his arm. When he looked down at her, the waning sunlight highlighted all the golden strands in her hair. Dirt was smeared on her cheek and forehead. She'd never looked better.

They stopped next to a moss-covered boulder, and Owen toed off his shoes and peeled his socks off. Alice followed suit, stepping warily onto the small rocks, leaves and twigs that covered the riverbank.

"You ready?" Owen asked. He leant away from her, needing to see her face. He'd pull the pin on this idea if he caught even a whiff of discomfort from her.

"I didn't bring swimmers, obviously." Her gaze searched through the thick wall of tall trees.

He hooked his fingers in the side of his running shorts, planning to swim in his boxer briefs.

She bit her lip. "No one's around?"

He spread his arms open wide, spinning in a circle. Aside from a few cockatoos in an old gum tree with a blackened trunk, he couldn't see anyone or anything. "It's just us here, honey."

She looped her arms around him, her hands sliding past the waistband of his shorts and underwear.

"Really?" He looked down at her, searching for any sign she was doing this to make him happy, but there was nothing.

"Well, you did promise me an adventure." Her smile was pure mischief. It might've been the best one she'd ever given him. He let her push his clothes to the ground and stepped onto the slippery riverbank. She swayed away from him, pulling her shirt and sports bra over her head. The crisscrossed straps had left marks on her skin, and Owen dropped a kiss on each of her shoulders as she peeled herself out of her panties and running shorts.

"God, you're beautiful," he murmured, breathing in the salty tang hovering on her skin.

"Ready, Boy Scout?"

He guided her further down the bank to a big rock near the edge, pointing out where the deepest point of the creek was.

Alice shivered as a cold breeze rolled across the water. He tried not to notice how her nipples hardened into points, but his cock stirred.

"You jump first," she said.

Owen shook his head, linking their fingers as he stepped onto the rock. "We jump together."

He waited until she nodded. "Three, two, one ..."

And *oh, God,* the water was so much colder than he thought it would be. His muscles seized, a shudder rolling through his body. Alice's laughter was the first thing he heard when he broke the surface. She flung her arms around his shoulders, wrapped her legs around his waist and the weight of the moment and their shared happiness almost pushed him back under.

"I knew you could do it!" He smoothed her hair away from her face before fusing their mouths together. The kiss was slow and gentle, their tongues stroking each other softly, no promise of things escalating now. But when they got back to the campsite ...

When they broke apart, Alice laughed again. The sound was bigger and freer than before. If Owen wrapped himself in that sound, he'd never be cold again.

"You owe me at least five orgasms," she teased.

He rubbed his nose along the column of her throat, his lips skating across her skin as Alice arched her back, encouraging him to bite her gently.

"Guess we'd better get back to camp so I can make dinner and pay my debts, huh?"

"Hurry," she said, breaking away from him and swimming towards the shore.

It was his turn to laugh when Alice saw the 'towel' he'd packed. She scoffed, calling it 'nothing more than a face cloth', but any complaints died on her lips quickly when his hands caressed her skin as he whispered promises for the night.

Owen knew he had her when she blushed, drops of river water falling from her lashes and tracking down her rosy cheeks. Away from all the distractions of everyday life and the little bubble they'd created over the last few months, they were so raw, so honest out here.

To hell with it.

He'd tell her.

Trust it wouldn't be too much.

Owen loved her, and it was time she knew.

29

I t was official. Alice was sure there wasn't anything Owen wasn't good at. Like everything he did, he moved methodically, blowing on the flickering baby flames, balancing bits of slightly larger wood on top, poking the coals with a long stick. The fire grew steadily, making light and shadows dance across his face. Somehow, they softened his features and defined them sharply at the same time. It was like they were showing all the sides of Owen at once. The serious, honourable man who fought for what was right and the soft, sweet guy with a wild side that simmered under the surface. Sparks flew into the air as he put a big log onto the fire, the embers shifting and cracking. A soft wind rustled the leaves in the shadows.

Alice watched as Owen held out his hands out, checking the fire was hot enough, and then he started warming the pot. He opened and closed the esky, adding containers of things he'd pre-cooked or pre-planned to the pot as he stirred it occasionally. Alice had been expecting sandwiches —never a good gluten-free option—because they were easy.

Trust Owen to go out of his way to make something nice for her.

She watched as he twisted around, dusting his hands against his tracksuit, smiling when he saw her.

"There's something I didn't tell you," he said, crawling into the tent. Alice's stomach twisted, and it had nothing to do with hunger.

She wet her lips and sat up properly, shifting over to make room for Owen. "What?"

"Dinner's going to take a while."

She laughed softly, rubbing her face like the movement would erase all her fears. *Something's got to give*, that evil little voice in her mind whispered. *Nothing's ever this easy.* "That's okay."

"Didn't want to make you eat gluten-free muesli bars, stale sandwiches and jerky when we could have a proper camp meal."

Warmth spread through her body so quickly she could jump back into the freezing creek and not notice the water temperature. She scooted closer, her foot catching in her sleeping bag, but Owen freed her, settling her in his lap, their bodies aligning in her favourite way.

"Thank you," she whispered against his lips, enjoying the scratch of his stubble against her sensitive skin. Her fingers skimmed along his cheeks, tracing the hard angles of his jawline before moving to his neck. He smelt like smoke and the outdoors, a whisper of salt lingering on his skin despite their impromptu swim.

Without breaking contact, he lifted them both, rising onto his knees. They both laughed when their heads hit the roof of the tent. Alice's giggles died on her lips when he ground his hips into hers, his fingers digging into her butt. He sat back on his heels, his mouth capturing hers as he lowered her to the mattress. The kiss started out soft and slow, leisurely strokes of his tongue matching the slow, *so slow*, way he moved against her. Despite all the layers of clothes between them, he managed to work her into such a frenzy she could barely think straight. He increased the speed, his hands guiding her over his dick.

Damn. Dry humping had never felt like this in high school. Just when she thought it couldn't get any better, he slipped a hand under her jumper. His fingers left a trail of fire behind them. Owen pinched her nipple, and Alice moaned loudly as a spike of pleasure zapped around her body, pooling between her legs.

"Owen—" Her nerve endings were about to self-combust. The breathiness in her voice must've spurred him on, his hips moving relentlessly against hers, his hardness hitting just the right spot.

"I think ... I'm gonna ..." Her muscles coiled, tightening almost painfully as Owen's hot breath washed over her face. He palmed her breast, pulling at the nipple with the exact right amount of pressure. He always knew exactly how far he could push her, never stepping over the line that would make her uncomfortable.

"Come on, honey," he murmured, burying his face in the crook of her neck. His voice was pure sex and all hers. It was the 'honey' that sent her spiralling.

Pleasure flooded her body, her back arching and hips jerking against his. Owen looked up, dropping the sweetest, softest kiss on her lips as he brushed her fringe away from her eyes. Alice's breath heaved in and out.

"That's one."

"Wha—"

He pulled down her pants with one hand and pushed a finger inside, twisting it so it hit the spot inside she couldn't reach on her own without her plastic friend. Her toes curled automatically, the sounds of the outside world disappearing, replaced with her thundering heart.

How could it be this good every single time?

"Five, yeah? That's what I owe you?"

Mischief dripped from his words, a throwback to her teasing at the river. She rode his hand, tried to tell him he didn't owe her anything, but all she could do was gasp his name.

In no time, the familiar tightness spread throughout her body. She yanked at his pants, but he twisted out of reach.

"Not yet." His kiss swallowed her growl of protest, and he added another finger. "This is all about you."

She bit her lip, trying to keep herself from crying out.

His eyes zeroed in on where her bottom lip was caught between her teeth, freeing it with his thumb. "It's only us. Don't hold back."

So, she didn't, moaning loudly as she toppled over the edge, his fingers stroking her slowly, *reverently*, as she rode out her orgasm.

Owen rolled onto his back, tucking her under his shoulder and tilting her face towards his. "Two," he whispered.

Alice's arms wobbled when she pushed up on them. "Three's going to be a team sport," she said with all the sternness of a tiny kitten.

"Is that so?" The dimples in his cheeks popped, and if she was wearing pants, they would've melted off.

"Team sports with you are my favourite," she said.

"That's convenient because everything with you is my favourite."

Jesus. If he kept saying sweet shit like that, she was going to have to tell him how she really felt about him.

She settled for something safer, a husky voice she barely recognised as her own. "Take your pants off."

Owen's smile widened; his face bathed in the golden glow from the lantern in the corner of the tent. "Your wish is my command." He lifted his hips, shimmying underneath her as he kicked his pants off, and she ground against him. He tipped his head back, jaw clenching as where he was hardest, thickest, nestled against where she was softest, wettest.

"More please," he groaned. His voice was so deep, one octave above a growl.

"Like this?" she whispered, sliding along his dick, stopping shy of where she knew he wanted to go. He groaned and reached for a condom.

"Do we need that?"

Owen froze underneath her. "Do we not?"

"You know I'm on the pill. And I'm clear. I haven't been with anyone but you for years. I don't want anything between us."

The way his Adam's apple bobbed made her roll her hips.

"I've never done this without one." His hands gripped her hips. "You're sure? It'll be messy."

She slipped down his length, the head breaching her entrance and enjoyed the way Owen sucked in a deep breath, his eyes darkening.

"We can handle messy. Don't you think?"

His eyes turned the colour of golden whiskey as she hovered above him, not moving, waiting for a sign from him. Her arms shook, and she bit the inside of her cheek. Owen lay perfectly still, his chest rising and falling. Then, without warning, he pushed up and she sank down. A startling thought ripped through her.

If I could do this every day for the rest of my life, I would.

"Oh my God. This is amazing. You're amazing," he said.

Alice paused, reality hitting her hard. The barriers around her heart had taken a hit each time Owen was sweet to her, but for the first time, she realised they were all gone. He hadn't even stolen her heart. She'd given it to him willingly.

"Honey ..." Owen reached up, cupping her cheek tenderly. All his hard lines and rough edges were gone, replaced with sweetness and concern. "It's okay if you've changed your mind. If this is too much, I'll get a condom. We can stop."

This was it. She could say it now. Look down into his eyes, filled with golden flecks and worry, and tell him she loved him, but something stopped her.

The fire outside popped, and she shook her head, breathing deeply. If he rejected her, and anything short of a declaration of love would be a rejection, the next twenty-four hours would be unbearable.

"Thought I heard something," she lied, looking over her shoulder to where the tent flap was zipped shut.

"There's nothing out there to worry about." He pulled her against his chest, rolling them over so he was on top. His eyes searched hers; no need for him to verbalise the question in them. Alice nodded, and Owen started to move, sliding almost all the way out before he pushed deep, hitting all the hot spots that turned her into a quivering, gooey mess. She matched his rhythm, opening herself even more to him. His skin was dewy, muscles tensing under her fingers as they swept across his back, his breathing erratic.

He didn't stop when she fell apart again, calling out his name. He sped up, pushing deeper, chasing his release. When his rhythm faltered, Alice knew he was close. A low moan erupted from his mouth as he stilled. He dropped to his elbows, mashing their chests together, hearts beating wildly against each other.

"That was amazing." He licked the sweat from her collarbone, and Alice's stomach growled.

"Let's clean up and eat." He laughed. "You're going to need your energy tomorrow."

As Owen ladled beef and vegetable stew into chipped camp bowls, Alice knew what she had to do. About everything. Phoenix. The investor for her company. How she wanted her future to look.

"Hey," she said, waiting for him to look up. "Let's file the injunction as soon as we get back. Tell Phoenix I'm not offering a financial settlement."

She just had to trust that it would all work out the way she hoped it would.

30

Owen could pinpoint the exact moment Alice saw the rock-climbing course in the distance. Red flags hung at varying heights, flapping listlessly in the breeze. She faltered, loose rocks skittering off the side of the trail they'd been following for the last hour, but she didn't stop. The voices of the team behind them—a pair of paramedics—weren't far away. Nine new page thirteens were tucked neatly in his running vest. His hands ached from using a rock to dig the last one out of the ground.

"Boy Scout," Alice whispered, dropping back so they could run next to each other. "That's pretty damn high."

"You'll be on the ground the whole time, remember?"

"But what if you fall?"

"That's not going to happen." His chest tightened at her concern for him, followed by regret because he'd chickened out last night, keeping those three little words to himself.

The sun dipped behind the thick treetops of the next section of trail, the temperature dropping. Tree branches and limbs twisted around each other, dappled sunlight pushing through the gaps in the canopy.

"Passing," a man called, a smile in his voice Owen didn't need to turn around to see. *Shit.*

"Oh, hell no," Alice muttered when the two guys pushed past them, their steps even, arms pumping. "They're not beating us."

She tossed a determined look his way and raced after them, fatigue evident in her sloppy stride. But that didn't stop Owen from grinning and shaking his head as he chased after her.

Of course, the woman who hated to lose was perfect for him.

Sticks, leaves and rocks crunched under his feet. He blinked when the trees thinned out, sunlight burning his eyes. He'd never admit it, especially not to Alice, but the cliff face looked a lot taller than he remembered. The paramedics were snapping harnesses and pulling gloves on. Cheers from the volunteer course marshals—headed by Nate's best friend, Charlie—distracted him.

His runner clipped a long, scraggly exposed tree root, hooking behind the gnarled and twisted wood and Owen lurched forward, arms flailing as the ground rushed up to meet him. Pain shot through his body, his knee popping when he hit the trail. He knew that sound.

"Fuck," he grunted, rolling to his side. His right wrist throbbed, but it was nothing compared to the fire inside his knee.

"Oh my God!" Alice skidded to a stop next to him, her hands hovering above him like she didn't know where she should touch him. "What can I do? How can I help?"

Heavy footsteps rumbled towards them, and Owen realised the paramedics had come to help. Alice withdrew her hands when they crouched down next to him, burying them in her hair. He hated she still felt like she had to hide who she was to him around other people.

"It's my knee," he ground out, his breath hissing between his teeth.

In his heart, Owen knew he'd torn the ligaments he'd spent so long trying to strengthen after his surgery two years ago. He mashed his lips together, trying to swallow the wave of pain.

They were so close to the finish line, almost guaranteed a place.

"Can you hop over there if we lift you?" one of the men asked. "Be a bitch to try and get a gurney down here."

Owen nodded, gritted his teeth, and they each grasped him under the armpit. Sweat ran down his face, sunscreen burning his eyes. He blinked furiously, trying to clear his vision.

"Wait a second," Alice cried, her hands digging into her pack. She pulled out a buff. "Here." She wiped his forehead and his face. "Better?" she asked quietly.

Owen nodded; his mouth felt like it was full of sand. They were going to lose. Shit. He'd gone to sleep last night with Alice in his arms convinced they were going to win the race, finalise her divorce and tell everyone the truth about their relationship. He had it all planned.

Owen blacked out when the paramedics hoisted him up, the ground shifting beneath him like quicksand.

"It's going to be okay." Alice was walking backwards, her eyes never leaving his face. "You'll feel better soon, I promise."

He watched her through half-lidded eyes as she fumbled for her phone.

"I'll call your mum. Tell her to meet us at the hospital."

"But the race ..." he said, breathing deeply when they

reached a chair near the climbing stations. "We're so close. I can still do the climb."

The urge to throw up had passed, which had to be a good sign, right? And it wasn't *that* far to the first or second flag. Climbing *was* mostly upper body strength.

The steely expression on Alice's face told him she wouldn't let him off that easily. "You can do the climb?"

"It's the last clue. The finish line is right there." He jerked his head towards the row of miniature orange flags flapping next to a trail marker. It was fifty metres away. Hell, he could hop there.

Probably.

Maybe.

"You're going to climb that"—she pointed up—"and run over there?" Her hand moved to the right.

When she said it like that … He jutted his chin forward. "It won't be pretty but maybe."

Alice knelt next to him. "It's only a race, Owen. We still get all our sponsorship money, even if we don't finish."

He scrunched his eyes closed, another wave of pain stealing his breath. God, even he knew he was full of shit. "I really hate to lose," he grumbled. "And Kathleen's Place could use the prize money for so much stuff."

A wry smile blossomed on Alice's lips, and he wanted to return it, but everything hurt too much.

"Fine." Her voice caught as she toed off her runners. Her socks were covered in bits of leaves and dirt. She shoved her feet into his climbing shoes, snatched the harness off the ground and stepped into it. Charlie helped her wind the rope through the carabiners.

"What are you doing?" Owen asked.

"I'm doing the climb, Boy Scout. Get ready to hop your ass off."

"Oh, honey, no." He didn't care if anyone heard him call her that, but her flinch told him they weren't on the same page. "I didn't mean ..."

"It's fine," she said. "Take these"—she thrust two painkillers into his hand—"and pray they kick in before I get back. Kathleen's Place is special to me too."

Her hands were shaking so badly she couldn't tighten the straps on the harness properly.

"Let me," he said, checking the harness carefully. "You don't have to do this."

Alice looked up at the cliff face and swallowed deeply, and he wanted to kiss her so badly that it almost hurt more than his knee did.

"I'll be fine. Worst case scenario, it's the second flag."

Charlie stepped into the spare harness, ready to help as their belayer. Owen was fuzzy on whether the rules allowed that, but he wasn't going to question it.

Alice clipped her helmet into place, hands trembling as Charlie slackened the line. The smaller paramedic was already climbing up the cliff face, his red helmet bobbing with each movement.

"Any other advice?" she asked him, sucking on her bottom lip.

Guilt coursed through his veins, mixing with pride. He was so proud she was even prepared to try and do this. Bright red spots covered her arms and chest. "One hand in front of the other and your legs will follow. I know you can do this."

She nodded once, her eyes closing. If the media weren't here, he would've kissed her. Poured everything he had into it. But there was something else he could do for her. For himself too, really.

"Come here a second," he whispered, and her eyes

popped open. Time slowed, and the pounding in his ears drowned everything else out. Alice leant forward, and Owen swallowed the ball of nerves lodged in his throat. "I love ..."

Alice's mouth dropped open, and, in the background, Owen heard the voices of another team arriving.

"... how brave you are. You've got this."

THE FIRST PUSH OFF the ground was the hardest. Not helped by the fact that, for a split second, Alice had thought Owen was going to say he loved her.

Each movement was unnatural; every part of her body convinced she shouldn't be doing this. But Owen's voice was calm and steady, directing her to different hand and foot holds.

"There's a good one on your left." His voice was quieter already, but she didn't trust herself to look down. The sun was hot against her back, dirt and fragments of rocks clinging to her hands. The air smelt different up here. Fresher, devoid of any other scents. Or maybe the fear thrumming through her body was smothering all her other senses? Her arms shook, and she rested her face against a flat section of rock.

"His rope is tangled. You can pass him. Two more big pushes, Alice," Owen yelled. That explained the colourful language to her right.

"We're not having a baby here," she called back, the titter of laughter from everyone on the ground distracting her for a millisecond. She looked up, craning her neck as far back as she could. The red flag was still out of reach. She pushed forward, the sharp edge of the rocks biting into her knees. Her hand stretched as far as it could, the tip of the flag brushing against her fingertips. If she could just stretch ... She gritted her teeth, pressed up on her toes.

"Careful!" Owen yelled, and she slipped, the rope pulling taut, holding her steady.

"What the hell, Owen! You scared me!"

"Sorry. Try going up one more spot. You'll be able to reach then."

Without thinking, Alice looked down. Black spots popped in front of her eyes. All the breath left her body.

High.

So very high.

Owen was a blob on the ground.

"Hey, Boy Scout ..." She was too far into her fear to be embarrassed about the tremors in her voice. Strands of hair stuck to her face, little pinpricks against her skin.

"You're okay, Alice. Focus on the things you can control, remember? What can you smell? I can smell eucalyptus," Owen yelled. "And I can taste excitement. We're so close."

She thunked her helmet against the rock face, a few tears sliding down her face.

"Alice." Owen's voice cut through the fog. "What can you see?"

All she could see was herself plummeting to her death, Owen never knowing how she really felt about him.

"I can see a beautiful woman facing her fears. Doing her best for everyone else even though it scares her."

He always knew the right thing to say.

"I know you're nervous, Alice, but you haven't let this beat you yet. You've got this, honey."

Honey.

It was scary how much one word could make her believe she could do this. That they could do this. To think there wasn't anything they couldn't tackle together. Her fingers loosened slightly, and she looked up, figured out her next move.

A shadow fell across her body, the sun disappearing behind the paramedic. No way was he going to beat her. Not now.

"What can you touch?" Owen's words spurred her into action. Alice propelled herself forward, shoulders aching, head pounding. Her shirt caught on a sharp edge, but it didn't matter. Nothing else mattered.

"I can touch the flag." Her fingers closed over the fabric, and she yanked it free.

Owen whooped, and she sagged down into her harness.

"Let's get you down here so we can win this thing," Owen called.

All the residual elation disappeared, her limbs turning to cement.

Down might be her least favourite word ever.

"See if you can push off the wall as Charlie lowers you."

Alice tried, but her legs wouldn't cooperate. Each time her feet connected with the cliff face, it was like her lower half was made from jelly.

Somehow, she managed it, the sounds around her growing sharper, louder. Owen's hand was on her before she even touched the ground, two roughly hewn branches clasped in his other hand. So that's what he'd been doing. Always the multi-tasker. The air between them crackled.

"You're amazing," Owen said as he undid the carabiner, disconnecting the rope from her harness, his walking sticks clutched to his chest. His eyes dropped to Alice's lips, and her heart started to race for a very different reason. There would be *so much* kissing later.

So. Much. Kissing.

A bellow of victory from above spurred them both into

action. Alice looked around, finally able to take in her surroundings properly. Three other teams had arrived and were in various stages of the climb. They had to move.

"Let's go." Owen hobbled towards the finish line.

Alice couldn't see anything but the row of flags in the distance and the group of people waiting. Owen was breathing heavily, punctuating each step with a groan. Her harness dug into her hips uncomfortably. But they didn't stop.

Maybe they could actually win this thing? As soon as the thought entered her mind, reality caught up with her.

Thunderous, elephant-like steps made the air around her shake. They were two metres away from the finish line when the paramedics sprinted past them, bursting through the winner's ribbon.

31

They crossed the finish line three seconds later, and Alice tipped forward, hands braced on her thighs. She dimly registered someone calling her name, but she ignored them, steering Owen towards the first-aid tent. Once he was seated, his bad leg stretched out in front of him, she took her first deep breath since his fall.

Second place.

Better than she'd dared to hope for. Her hand settled on Owen's shoulder, his large palm automatically covering hers.

"How are you?" she murmured.

"Coming second hurts more than my knee," he joked, but his voice was pinched, pain smothering his usual vibrato.

"Is there something you can give him? For the pain?" she asked the woman taking Owen's pulse, but she didn't hear her answer.

"Alice! Oi, Alice! Over here!"

She spun slowly, noticing several cameras were trained

on her. No one seemed to care about the winners, which was ... *unsettling*. And unfair.

A male reporter she recognised from an online music chat show caught her eye; his mobile pointed squarely at her. He'd always had a massive hard-on for Phoenix, mimicking his shaggy blond hairstyle and hipster beard. "How long have you been lying to everyone, Alice?"

She pulled her hand off Owen's shoulder.

Owen leant to the side, looking around her. "What's going on?"

"Nothing. He's a dick," she replied. "Ignore him."

"Come on, Alice," the guy called. "You must've known you couldn't keep it a secret forever."

"What's his problem?" Owen reached for his walking sticks. She moved them away, stowing them on the other side of the tent. She ignored the annoyed sound Owen made, her attention drawn back to the reporter when he called out again.

"When did you first realise you had a problem with drugs?"

His question echoed like a cannon blast. Time stopped. The lady filling out the novelty cheque dropped her Sharpie, a long black line marring the cardboard.

"What did he say?" Owen asked. The little colour left in his face disappeared.

"Stay here," she ordered Owen and stalked over to where the reporter was standing. "What are you talking about?"

"The video. Where you're high as a kite. It was leaked yesterday. Phoenix said you got him hooked on drugs." He shoved his phone even closer to her face.

Is that ... holy shit, he was streaming this live.

Alice breathed out slowly, tried to reassemble her game

face. The number of viewers was climbing steadily. She couldn't afford to make a mistake right now.

"Here." Someone passed Alice a phone. She stared down at the video paused on the screen.

Her old hair was scrunched up in a rat's nest, her eyes droopy, mouth slack. Video Alice giggled drunkenly and tried to wipe her face but missed, spurring another round of giggles. "*Sötnos?*" she slurred at the camera.

Oh God.

"This is some good shit," she said. The camera panned out. The table next to her was covered in pill bottles, take-away wrappers and Uber Eats bags. In her hand, she clutched something green, but it was impossible to see what it was. A wine glass with bright red lipstick smeared on it stood like a sentinel in the middle of the mess.

But ... *What? When? How?* The sexy photos would've been less damaging. To think she'd actually believed she could break free from her past. Old Alice slumped to the side of the screen, eyes glassy. "Everyone should be doing this. I'm floating."

"Alice, ho—" Owen called out again. She watched as he snapped his mouth shut, stopping himself from calling her honey.

Her beautiful, sweet Owen who always tried to do the right thing. Her heart broke when she thought about how she'd misjudged him at the start. He might show the world his serious exterior, but he was the most encouraging and supportive man she'd ever met. She'd been fooling herself, thinking she could be his. She didn't belong here. She never would.

And she loved him too much to drag him down with her. To have them dig through his past, whisper about him behind his back—and worse, to his face—when he'd done nothing wrong.

She wouldn't do that to him. Not when the mistake was hers.

The weight on her chest was suffocatingly heavy. Alice had worked so hard to rebuild her life, to convince people she wasn't the reckless woman she used to be ... to show them who she really was. And now, everything was about to be taken away again. Over something she didn't even remember doing, but clearly, she had. The truth was right there, beamed over the internet for the whole world to see. Again.

THE FLEETING PANIC on Alice's face was enough to propel Owen out of his chair, crutches wobbling as he stuffed them under his arms. He should've watched the ground, but he couldn't tear his eyes away from Alice. With each step he took, she transformed.

Gone was the exhausted woman who'd pushed herself to her physical limit for the last two days.

Gone was the woman who laughed and joked like one of the locals.

Gone was the sparkle in her eyes, replaced by the hard glint of defeat.

His injured leg shook when he stopped in front of her, the heavy bag of ice strapped to his knee with thick medical tape pulling painfully as it sagged.

"Don't," she said as he opened his mouth. There was no emotion in her tone, just the weary resignation he remembered from when they'd first met.

Gone was the woman he loved.

And he'd never even told her.

Owen's grip on his crutches tightened, his vision blurring. "Is it …"

It must've been the pictures she'd warned him about. Fury threatened to consume him at the thought of her privacy being violated so hideously, but he forced himself to rein in his reaction. Phoenix had broken the law by releasing private images of Alice without her consent.

Owen would sue.

He would fight.

He'd fix this. He had to.

But Alice shook her head.

He held her gaze for a few beats before looking at the phone clutched in her hand. "Please." Maybe it was the gentleness in his voice that broke her. He hoped it also reminded her she wasn't alone. They were in this together, for fuck's sake.

She passed him the mobile silently and closed her eyes like she couldn't bear to see whatever it was again. "People are watching us," Alice whispered.

The tenuous hold he had on his emotions snapped, and Owen switched into protector mode. It should've felt like slipping on a second skin, a return to his real self, but his skin burnt, his head pounded. An image of Alice was frozen on the screen. Her hair was a mess, and she looked pretty wasted. Critically, he watched the clip, his pulse spiking when she made a joke about the drugs being good.

At the sound of her voice next to him, not on the screen, Owen tore his eyes away from the video.

An apologetic expression was on Alice's face, a total juxtaposition to the woman on the screen.

Sirens went off in his mind.

"Listen," she said.

She was going to run. Leave him.

"I don't know who you are …" Owen turned towards the reporter, his words louder, more powerful than hers.

"Owen, stop, please."

He ducked his head, lowered his voice. "I've got this," he told her.

Alice straightened her shoulders, a spark of fire returning to the bright blue pools he loved so much. He'd tell her the plan once they had some privacy. "Don't tell me what to do," she said.

She was in shock, clearly.

He barely even tilted his head towards her when he spoke. "Let me handle this, honey."

He knew he'd fucked up before he'd even finished saying 'honey'. Calling her that so publicly, in a way that sounded like he was trying to keep her in line, like everyone else in her life had always tried to.

One of his crutches fell to the ground as he reached for her. "I didn't mean …" he started, but it was too late. Alice's face had shuttered, and she lurched away from him. And maybe he imagined it, but a faint whiff of her wildflower scent lingered in the air where she'd been standing.

"Don't," she snarled before shifting her attention back to the media pack. "This is a silly video of a stupid girl. I mean, we were all young once, right? We've all made mistakes. This girl"—she jabbed at the phone screen—"was trying to be who she thought she should be." She brushed her fringe out of her eyes and looked straight at the camera phone still pointed at them. "I'm so sorry to everyone I've disappointed, but I can assure you all this is behind me. It doesn't reflect who I am now and I'm committed to doing the work I need to earn back your trust."

"To earn back their trust?" Owen couldn't stop the words from tumbling out of his mouth.

When she didn't look at him, he knew it was over. But no. Just no. It wasn't over until he'd left everything on the table.

"This isn't real," he said hollowly. "We have to fight, Alice." He shifted his attention to the asshole holding his phone in their faces, weird hearts and comments streaming onto the screen. "My client is clearly overwhelmed and needs time to process the allegations levelled at her. If you'll excuse us."

"Just stop," Alice murmured. "You're making it worse."

"I'm making it worse?" Owen spluttered, lowering his voice. "You're making it worse! Would you please listen and stop reacting from a place of panic? As your "—she'd kill him if he said boyfriend right now—"lawyer ..."

Calmly, Alice smoothed the dirt off her running shorts.

"I need you to listen to me," she said to Owen. "I'll handle this, okay? Your services are no longer required."

The ground dropped out from underneath him. "I thought ..." he started before he stopped, shaking his head. He looked over at the crowd and then back at her.

She sniffed, wiped her eyes, cheeks reddening. "This was a mistake. This whole thing." She was pretending to talk about the video, but Owen knew the truth. She didn't want him anymore.

He swallowed rapidly, his Adam's apple bobbing. "You don't mean that."

"I do," she whispered.

He ground his crutch into the dirt, hearing the crunch of twigs and leaves snapping underneath it.

An ambulance pulled into the car park.

"Take my car," he said, not looking at Alice. She might

not want him anymore, but he couldn't leave her here with nowhere to hide from the cameras. "The keys are in my drop bag. Give them to Teddy when you get home."

"Owen ..."

"Don't." He threw her previous plea back in her face as he turned away. Charlie passed him the crutch he'd dropped, and he hobbled away.

It was almost funny, really.

His brothers were always telling him he couldn't save everyone. Why did Alice have to be the one who proved them right?

32

Owen was already awake when the short, sharp knock sounded on the bedroom door. He blinked, staring at the timber walls of Nate's bedroom. His family had met him at the hospital yesterday, their faces lined with pity and worry, unspoken questions filling the room, mixing with the heavy smell of antiseptic.

"O? It's after eleven. Do you need help getting up?" Nate asked.

Owen threw back the covers and sat up, shuffling over to swing his legs over the side of the bed. "I'm okay," he said, wincing at how rough he sounded. He cleared his throat as he braced his palms on the mattress on either side of his thighs. Once he'd had his MRI, he'd go into the office and grab everything he needed to work from home for the next week or so.

Nate pushed the door open, a cup of steaming coffee in one hand. "Here." His hair was wet, his feet bare. He crossed the room and set it down on the dark oak bedside table.

Owen sipped the warm drink and tried to act like he

hadn't been awake all night. The room was dark, thanks to the blockout curtains. His clothes from the race were crumpled in the corner near the en-suite door. He vaguely remembered arguing with Nate about sleeping on the couch when they'd gotten home from the hospital around one in the morning. But his brother had insisted on taking the couch. Said he'd be up half the night readjusting to Australian time anyway.

Nate picked up a fleecy black blanket that had fallen off the bed and draped it around Owen's shoulders. It smelt like the lavender laundry detergent their mother used. Owen always bought the same one, too. Maybe things other than DNA were hereditary as well. Like showing up and caring for family when they needed it. He scrubbed a hand across his chin, feeling the beginnings of his beard. "Sorry about last night. I shouldn't have said that stuff about you and Eloise." He'd lashed out when Nate had tried to talk to him about Alice.

Nate shrugged. "You were hurt ... in more ways than one. You get a free pass."

"Still, it wasn't fair. How you live your life is your business."

Nate's chest rose, and he looked out the window. "It's okay. I know it doesn't make sense, but I can't give her what she wants. Doesn't seem fair to waste her time or jeopardise our friendship."

The blanket around Owen's shoulders itched. How wrong he'd been to think he could provide Alice with what she needed. He shook his head, focusing on his brother. "How do you know you can't give her what she wants?"

A sad smile bloomed briefly on Nate's face before it disappeared. "I just do."

Owen stared at the floor, one hand clasping the blanket around his shoulders, the other holding his coffee cup. "I watched the video someone took of us after the race last night," he confessed.

"Of you and Alice?"

He nodded. He'd watched it twice, the volume on silent because he didn't need to hear her tell him to get lost again.

"What are you going to do?" The air around him shifted, and Nate sat down next to him, his long torso stretching forward as his elbows rested on his knees.

"I have no idea," Owen said.

And that was the truth.

"YOUR DOG PEED ON OUR DISHWASHER," Rico said.

Alice flopped back on the pull-out sofa she'd spent so much of the last three days on. Rico had started calling it 'Alice Island'.

"Sorry." She cringed. Poor Murphy was bored. He'd gotten far too used to their nights at Owen's where they'd go for a long walk before bed. Dougie and Rico's small court-yard couldn't compete, and their cat, Mr Whiskers, was totally disinterested in the boisterous puppy. Alice sat up and rolled her shoulders. Dougie swore it was the best sofa bed on the market, but her neck and back didn't agree. She shoved her feet into her brother's Uggs and pulled an old jumper over her head. "I'll take him out back."

"Why don't we all go for a walk?" Dougie asked, poking his head around the wall that divided the kitchen from the study where Alice was bunkered down. He and Rico had been working from home so she didn't have to be alone. They'd even packed up all their sample invitations and magazines, limiting their wedding talk to when they thought she was asleep.

"I can't."

Rico rolled his eyes. "Still sticking with the plan to never go outside again, are we?"

Easy to say when it wasn't his life in ruins around him. Alice had only checked her emails once since she arrived, and she'd lost a swag of her new clients. There had been two emails from companies that sponsored her and Owen for the race, but she'd been too chicken to open them. Same for the messages Eloise had been sending each day.

Alice took a deep breath, but it didn't have the desired effect. Stale, tangy air burnt her nose, her throat closing as she sucked it into her lungs. What was that smell?

"It's you," Rico said. "A shower would also be an excellent idea. Why don't you do that, and we'll start dinner, and then we can take Murphy out before we eat."

Alice voiced her fear. "But what if someone sees?" Which was ridiculous because, seriously, what could anyone see now that would make things worse?

"No one's going to see. It's dark. One block and then we'll eat something with actual vegetables in it. I promise it'll help."

"That's unlikely."

Rico propped himself against the wall, his arms folding. "Because you're embarrassed about the first video or second video ... are we still counting the video of Phoenix as the first one? I'm confused. Or, God, the video with Owen?"

"Don't, please," Alice whispered. She couldn't talk about what had happened with Owen. Not yet. Maybe not ever. She pulled a crumpled-up tissue out of the pocket of her borrowed tracksuit pants. She was too far into her shame spiral to care if it was weird she was wearing her brother's fiancé's tracksuit pants. "I never deserved him."

"And what exactly is it you think he deserves?" Rico asked. She'd expected Rico to fall into his cheerleading routine and tell her that, of course, she had deserved him. Obviously, he thought Owen was too good for her too.

"I don't want to talk about it."

Rico's mouth twisted to the side, his gaze drifting to the ceiling before looking at Dougie, who raised his eyebrows. "Can we ask you another thing?"

Alice nodded because words were too hard right now.

"Why does he deserve more than you do?"

She hadn't said that. She'd said she didn't deserve him, which wasn't the same thing. Was it? But as she fiddled with the cream-coloured tassels on the edge of the throw blanket she'd been using as a tablecloth when she ate all her meals on Alice Island, she knew Rico and Dougie were right. If he was too good for her, the flipside was that she wasn't good enough for him. She pushed her thoughts aside and narrowed her eyes at Rico because this was too hard. The fragile shell she'd rebuilt around herself over the last three days was about to crack, and then she'd never be able to put her messy self back together again.

"This is partly your fault, you know."

Rico pushed off the wall and wrapped his arms around Alice. He didn't even complain about how much she stank. "Please don't remind me. I still feel terrible about that."

It hadn't taken long for Alice to figure out the video Phoenix released—number two for those playing 'The Many Disaster Videos of Alice Aspinall's Life' at home— where she looked high, was from when she'd fallen over after her appendix surgery and torn all her stitches. The paramedics had given her a green whistle while they prepped her for transfer back to hospital. Phoenix had been away performing, and Rico had sent it to him, thinking they were still happy and in love.

"You do realise you could explain what happened? You can see the whistle if you look for it." Dougie crossed the room and sat on her other side.

Alice had been on a total social media blackout since the race. She knew if she looked, she'd get sucked into doom scrolling which would only make things worse.

"It doesn't matter."

Dougie bumped his shoulder against Alice's. "It does matter. C'mon, Alley Cat. Shower. Walk. A meal that isn't ninety percent Cheezels. Then we'll figure all of this out."

Right there in front of her was something Alice could control. "Can you please not call me that? I hate it. I always have."

Dougie leant away and frowned. "I thought you loved it! You've never said anything before."

"Nobody ever asked me." Alice pushed up off her island. The throw blanket dragged along the wooden floorboards as she trudged to the bathroom, her brother's and Rico's footsteps following her.

"I'm sorry," Dougie said as Alice flipped the light on, cringing at her scungy reflection. "I guess we just assumed."

Drops of water splattered over her hands and forearms as Alice turned the shower on. "You don't need to apologise. I should've said something." She hoped the water drowned out the tremor in her voice.

There were a million things she should've done differently.

"How about we take Murphy out while you're showering? Try the walk tomorrow instead." Dougie closed the door quietly when she nodded.

Alice pressed her face against the shower door, the glass brushing her cheeks and breathed in the steam filling the small room. She'd started again so many times. She could do it again.

After she undressed, Alice sat down in the corner of the shower and cried because she was going to miss Owen every day for the rest of her life.

33

"Oh, Owen, you're here! Good. We've got lots to discuss." Mrs Mandrill smiled kindly at him. The rest of the Old Girls nodded or waved.

He'd been avoiding his mother's calls, but there'd been no getting out of today's committee meeting. Not when she'd turned up outside Nate's little log cabin and refused to leave without him.

"Yep. I'm here," he said without enthusiasm.

Seriously though, why was he there? They didn't need him to form a quorum, and he didn't hold any of the executive positions. But Lulu had insisted, probably because she wanted to get him out of the house. She was still campaigning for him to stay with her after his surgery next week.

He looked down at the table, clasped his hands in front of him and wished he'd brought some notes so he could pretend to read them. Or begged off and said he had to go to the office. Check out the damage after some idiot threw a brick through the front window overnight. But Frankie had insisted she could handle it.

"Right," Lulu said. "Shall we get started?"

Chairs scraped across the floor as everyone sat down. Hang on. Was the full committee here? But why?

Owen tuned out as Mrs Mandrill ran through the meeting formalities and the voting on the previous minutes. A burst of blue on the wooden windowsill captured his wandering gaze. A fairy wren hopped from one side to the other before flying away. Its feathers matched Alice's eyes, and he shifted in his seat, focused on the water glass in front of him. It'd been a week since the race, and he'd been—as Teddy so helpfully put it—'a sad fucker ever since'.

A swift elbow to his side pushed him out of his thoughts.

"Owen," Lulu said. "Do you know the final count from the race?"

He sure did. One hundred and ninety-two thousand dollars, a battered heart and one destroyed knee. Or maybe it was the other way around. A battered knee and a destroyed heart.

He cleared his throat, told the committee what they wanted to know and avoided everyone's eyes. Allowed their quiet congratulations to wash over him.

At least it hadn't all been for nothing. The shearers' shed was well on its way to being remodelled, and more people who needed help would get it.

"Now, what are we going to do about Alice?" Mrs Mandrill asked.

He didn't have to look up to know the rest of the committee were watching him. They were lovely, kind-hearted women, but they were predictable.

"I guess that's up to Owen," Lulu said.

His head snapped up, his throat all scratchy. Nothing about this had been up to him. Alice had made her plan and left him in the dust. He knew he'd fucked up accidentally outing their relationship to the media by calling her 'honey', but in his defence, he'd been pumped up to the eyeballs with painkillers, panicked he was going to lose the best thing that had ever happened to him. "The lease Alice signed is month to month. If you give her thirty days' notice, she has to vacate the property."

Then she'd really be gone. All traces of her time in Wattle Junction erased. Owen rubbed his chest.

Lulu's disappointed sigh echoed around the table.

"That's not what we mean." Mrs Mandrill leant forward, her hair now a faded pink, not the bright hue she'd had the last time he saw her. "How are you going to get her back?"

"Get her back ..." Owen raised his eyebrows.

"Yes."

"Uhhh ..." He gulped down a swallow of his water, looking over the rim of the glass at Lulu.

"Rumour is that video is rubbish," was all she said. "She'd had surgery, and her stitches tore. She wasn't high on drugs. Well, not illegal ones, at least."

He coughed. "How do you know that?"

Lulu threw her hands in the air, bracelets jangling with the exaggerated movement. "Because we're the Old Girls Gossip Brigade, Owen. Darling, catch up! We know everything, remember? Now, how are we going to make this right?"

Why hadn't Alice said that then? Or released a statement afterwards? Done something other than act like she'd done the wrong thing?

"Teddy said she hasn't been home since the race. Her brother and his fiancé dropped Owen's car off. They packed a bag for her and took all Murphy's things. I thought the two of you were so lovely together," Mrs Mandrill said wistfully, and Owen frowned at his mother. *So much for keeping their secret.*

"Don't you look at me like that, Owen David James." Lulu waggled her finger at him. "I didn't say a thing. You young people think you're so difficult to understand. We figured you'd tell everyone when you were ready. You know, with all the nonsense with her ex and everything. Everyone gives us a hard time about gossiping, but we can be discreet when we need to be. It was obvious to everyone that the two of you were falling in love."

He swallowed a bitter-tasting laugh. After all their sneaking around, everyone had known anyway.

"She said it was all a mistake." Vocalising the words hurt almost as much as hearing them had. He bit the inside of his cheeks and waited for the inevitable sighs of sympathy.

But they didn't come.

"So?" Mrs Mandrill lobbed across the table. "She was put on the spot! Ambushed. Of course, she panicked. Poor girl's probably got PTSD after the stunts her ex has been pulling."

"Imagine if you'd worked so hard to rebuild your life and it was all going to be taken away again," his mother said gently.

"Then why didn't she let me ..." He picked up his drink.

"Take over?" Mrs Mandrill shook her head.

"I was helping!"

"By taking over ..."

He put his glass down so quickly that water sloshed over the side. "Alice didn't want anyone to know we were ... that we'd been—"

"Falling in love?" Mrs Mandrill piped up.

"No!" Owen's face was on fire. No way was he going to admit that to anyone when he'd never even had the chance to tell Alice.

His old teacher stroked her chin. Said hopefully, "Having sex? Netflix and chilling?"

God, just kill me. Talking about his sex life with his mother, year three teacher and all the other Old Girls was not something he wanted to do.

"That's not ... that's not important. She didn't want people to know we'd been *involved* so I couldn't go over there and be her boyfriend. And as her lawyer—"

"—ha! But you *were* her boyfriend! You admit it." Mrs Mandrill grinned triumphantly.

"Joan," Owen barked, surprising himself. "Not the point right now."

"Of course it is." Lulu crossed her arms and sent him such a withering look of disappointment; it was like he was five years old all over again.

"If being her lawyer and doing my job was the wrong thing to do and I couldn't let on I was her boyfriend"—he sent a warning look at Joan because fuck it, now he'd snapped at her, he could allow himself to use her first name —"what was I supposed to do?"

They gaped back at him like he was an idiot. Finally, his mother spoke. "If you can't figure it out, then we're not going to tell you."

Owen growled, and they actually laughed at him. Right to his face.

"Excuse me," he said tersely, pushing back from the table and grabbing his crutches, pretending he needed to go to the bathroom. Really, he just wanted to get the hell out of there.

He was halfway down the hall when he spotted Jessica sitting in the lounge room by herself, staring glumly out the window. "Hey, you okay?" he asked.

"I should be asking you that. Sounds like you've had a bad week."

Owen eased himself slowly into one of the grey armchairs opposite the couch. "It hasn't been great."

"I'm sorry about your knee. And everything that happened with Alice. You two seemed so well suited. At least, I figured she was the reason you started smiling so much."

Good God. Was there anyone in Wattle Junction who hadn't known they were together?

Owen changed the subject. "Where's Sam?"

"It's Rob's afternoon."

Ah. "How's that all going?"

Jessica fussed with the cushion next to her. "Okay, I guess. Sam's having fun and seems to be adapting well. Which is all I care about. I've actually got a job interview tomorrow. At the pub. Waitressing. It's not ideal, but Wyatt said he'd work around Sam's schedule."

"That's great news. I'll ask Teddy to put a good word in for you, if you'd like."

Jessica's lips twitched. "You can't help yourself, can you? You're always trying to help people."

Fat lot of good it had done for him with Alice, though. A pang of sadness hit Owen square in his chest, and he shifted on his seat, tapping his phone. Alice hadn't called. Not that he expected her to.

"Do you have any regrets?" Owen asked Jessica, the words escaping before his brain caught up with his mouth. "About not pushing for full custody?"

He'd done everything he could to help Alice, and it

hadn't been enough. He hadn't been enough. His regrets kept him up at night.

Jessica shook her head. "Not really. I told myself that I was doing my best to protect Sam, but really, I was trying to protect myself. Rob's not a bad guy. And he always loved Sam so much. His addiction was just too strong back then. It took everything from him. From us. And when he came back, I panicked. Thought he was trying to take another thing from me. I couldn't see past my own fears. But I really appreciated that you were upfront and honest about what the law would allow while letting me make my own decision. I needed that extra time to come to terms with it. Find my peace."

It was like someone had thrown a brick at him, instead of his office, and knocked all the air from his body. How had he missed this?

I should've given Alice time to make her own decision.

Just because he wanted to slay all her dragons for her didn't mean he should. He'd have to learn to be content with handing her the sword if she wanted it.

He'd forgotten this was what Alice put up with every day, even during the 'good' times. Each time she stepped out in public, people made assumptions about her and her life. No wonder she'd wanted to try and control the damage after the race, give herself a bit of time to figure out what to do. He still didn't agree with what she'd done, but that didn't excuse how he'd ... stormed in and steamrolled all over her. He was as bad as everyone else.

"I should get back to the meeting," he said to Jessica. "Good luck with your interview."

"I can't thank you enough for everything. None of this would've been possible without your help."

"Glad I could do it." And he was. If only he hadn't learnt his lesson way too late.

Slowly, Owen made his way back to the kitchen. Everyone stopped talking when he pushed the door open.

"It was her decision, not mine," he said simply, his heart closer to his feet than his chest. He'd really fucked this up.

The room erupted with surprised cheers, which, frankly, was quite insulting. They'd obviously thought it would take him longer to figure his shit out.

Lulu banged on the table and Joan—*Joan!*—pulled a bottle of prosecco out of her handbag. "We knew you'd get there eventually!" she said. "Now, we plan!"

Who *were* these women? Again, the answer he was looking for was right in front of him. They were the ladies who'd played such an important role in raising him and shaping him into the person he was.

"What are you going to do first?" Lulu asked.

"I don't know," he said truthfully, holding his hands up when everyone paused. "But I'm going to figure it out."

A champagne cork popped. "Right, well, while you figure that out, we'll let you in on our plan."

Owen knew what he wanted. Or, more accurately, who he wanted. And once he figured out how to get Alice back, he wasn't ever going to let her go.

He just had to hope she still wanted him, too.

Dougie pressed a mug of rosé into Alice's hand and checked his phone when it pinged. "Mum and Dad are almost here."

Wait, what?

"You can't avoid them forever, Al," he said. "They're really worried this time."

Thinking about how proud her parents had been only weeks ago had Alice blinking back fresh tears. She hadn't heard back from their friend who was interested in investing. Probably never would.

The apartment door opened and closed, and the low murmur of conversation snuck down the hallway. The kind you'd expect at a hospital after the death of a dearly loved friend or family member.

Her chest squeezed when she heard Rico say, "Remember, this isn't Alice's fault, okay? It was a misunderstanding."

"Oh, Alice." The softness in her mother's voice immediately knocked her off-kilter. Alice pulled the throw blanket around her shoulders even tighter, like it could stop her from falling apart in front of her family.

Dougie scooted to the side, making room on the couch for Marguerite.

"It's going to be okay. We'll fix this together," her mother said.

When Alice stole a glance at her father, he coughed and unbuttoned his charcoal suit jacket, shaking his head when Rico offered him a drink.

"If the kettle's still warm, I'll have a tea, please, Rico." Marguerite nodded at the mug Alice was holding in a death grip. Which was filled with wine because all the glasses were in the dishwasher because she was a shitty house guest. Marguerite picked it up and sniffed. Alice braced herself for the jab. *Here it comes.*

"Actually, wine would be better. Whatever Alice's having is fine."

Alice slid her eyes towards Dougie, who shrugged back at her.

"Alright. Now we've all had some time to get over the shock of what's happened, what's your plan?" Her father sat stiffly in the cream armchair to the right of the couch.

Huh. That was strange. They'd never asked her if she had a plan before. Normally, they'd taken over and she'd let them.

Alice blew her nose loudly, shoving the crumpled tissue into the bulging pocket of another pair of borrowed tracksuit pants. Neither of her parents commented. Dougie and Rico must've really read them the riot act. "I don't know." Fear of making another mistake had left her paralysed for days.

Her parents shared a loaded look, and Alice's heart sank when her father's lips clamped together.

"Because the video of you was distributed without your consent, there are some legal avenues we can pursue. Some things are ready to be deployed—" Marguerite raised her hands when Alice's mouth dropped open. This was so typical. They weren't really offering to help. It was just an act. "We're concerned, darling."

"But it's still your call," Dougie interjected.

"But how are things ready to be deployed? I asked you not to do anything!" Alice glared at her brother.

"And I haven't, but Owen reached out to see if you'd like him to pass on the paperwork he'd already prepared for your divorce. He won't give it to me unless you sign a letter saying I'm your new lawyer, though."

Owen's name was like a spear through her chest. Her head and her heart had been at war ever since she'd told him they couldn't be together. She was desperate to know how he was … if his knee was okay and if he was miserable too. She gulped down a mouthful of wine and swallowed without tasting it.

The room swam in front of her. "Why didn't anyone tell me they'd spoken to Owen?" she asked.

"Uhhh, remember how you've been leaving the room whenever we mention him?" Dougie muttered.

Alice pulled the blanket even tighter around her body. If they were going to talk about Owen, her heart needed all the protection it could get. She paused before she opened her mouth, waiting until she was sure she could speak. "Did he say anything else?"

"He told us to stop going behind your back and wait until you'd decided if you wanted to sue Phoenix for defamation, which, okay, I had sort of started loosely putting a case together for. When I asked him what he thought of that, he said you were capable of making your own decisions."

A galloping horse stole her heart, thundering away with it. A few tears leaked out, dripping down her cheeks. She wiped her face quickly, hoping her family would pretend they hadn't seen.

She cleared her throat. "Owen said all that?" Of course he had. While she'd been paralysed with embarrassment, heartbreak and anxiety, he'd been trying to fix things and realising he couldn't do it for her. He was so damn amazing.

Dougie squeezed her hand. "I know you haven't wanted to know what's happening online, but things have been pretty bad for him too." The horse in her chest was joined by the rest of its herd. Their hooves beat in time with the blood pounding in her ears. "He's been followed, and his office was vandalised a few days ago."

The pit in her stomach that was always there these days opened up. *God, if he was hurt …* "Is he okay? And Frankie?"

"Everyone's fine," Rico said. "Owen's working remotely."

Relief flooded through her quickly, pushing her back against the couch. "I just want it all to be over."

"Then finish it. No one else can do it for you," her father said. "Hiding will just destroy everything you've worked for. We don't always see eye to eye about your choices, but these last few months you've been so different, Alice. You seemed happy. Driven. If you don't fight this, you'll always be the girl who went on reality TV and married a guy who treated her terribly. Everyone will think you're a drug user who lies."

"Which we know isn't true," Marguerite said gently.

"But no one else does! You're so much more than who you think you are, Alice. Look at what you've done with this candle business. You know everyone's been buzzing about it if even I've heard about it! And your mother said you've approached her hospital about doing a special charity candle for them." Douglas dragged a hand over his face. "Don't give up because it's the easy option. Sometimes I think we made you feel like you were not enough or too different, but we were trying to protect you. You keep telling us you can fix things, Alice. I'd love for you to show us how."

The horses in her chest slowed to a trot, her cheeks aching from the salty tears she couldn't stop. Rico passed her a box of tissues. "But everyone will think ..."

"Who cares?" her mother asked, chuckling at the shocked look on Alice's face. "Don't look so surprised. I gave up caring what other people thought years ago. Do the right thing for you, Alice. Live your life by that motto and you'll be fine. I promise."

"Tell her about the messages now!" Dougie said.

Alice blinked, shaky hands wiping at her eyes. "What messages?"

"You've clearly made an impact on everyone in Wattle Junction. Aside from hearing from Owen, I've had calls from"—her father pulled a small notebook out of his breast pocket and flipped until he found the page he was searching for—"a Lulu Hampshire-James, Joan Mandrill, Eloise ..."

"... Hamilton," Alice finished for him, her chest squeezing. "What did they say?"

Everyone in Wattle Junction hated her now, surely? After what she'd done to Owen? He was one of them. All the friendships she'd built during her time there, despite her rocky start in the small town, would disappear now. If this were a divorce, and it hurt more than her actual divorce did, she'd lose custody of everyone and everything in Wattle Junction automatically. Her fingernails bit into the palms of her hand. Once she figured out a new location for her candles, there'd be no trace of her left in the place she'd thought of as her first real home as an adult.

"They wanted to make sure you'd seen the videos."

Jesus. Fucking videos. Alice never wanted to hear that word again. Her eyes met her father's.

"Here." Marguerite pulled her phone out of her small handbag and found a page she'd booked marked on YouTube.

The screen filled with images of Wattle Junction. The fountain in the park all lit up at night. Trivia at the pub, Teddy's blond hair shining behind the bar as he filled a pint. In the background, Wyatt was holding a cocktail shaker above his head.

Her shearers' shed. Boxes stacked on the shelves, the table covered in rows and rows of her candles all drying.

Text appeared, and she squinted to read it.

"Here"—her mother passed her glasses over—"we have the same prescription."

Did you know scrolled across the screen. Followed by *The*

Emancipation of Alice has donated over $10,000 to charity since its launch only three months ago?

The image changed to the racks of designer gear she'd auctioned.

Or that Alice organised and operated a wardrobe sale that raised over $14,000 for children in hospital?

The lounge room at the retirement home was next. The knitting circle were all there, big smiles on their faces, half-finished scarves and beanies hanging from their needles.

And she volunteers to teach knitting every week?

Tears dripped down her cheeks, her mother's glasses fogging up.

The next image caused a garbled sob-slash-snort. There she was, a small dot against the high cliff, one hand raised above her head, a red flag held triumphantly. In the bottom of the picture, so out of focus he was easy to miss, was Owen. She knew he was smiling up at her.

And she faced her fears to help raise over $192,000 for additional accommodation and services to expand Kathleen's Place, a community home for people who need a little help.

The image on the screen changed again to the lavender field at Kathleen's Place. The dam where everything had changed shimmered in the background.

The final image was a big group shot. The sun cast a golden glow over the people who had welcomed her into their lives and town. Several held signs that read 'Wattle Junction Loves Alice Aspinall'. And right in the middle, holding the heart, was Owen.

"See." Her father pointed at the screen. "These people know who you really are, and so do we. Now it's time to show everyone else."

Alice pressed her head into her hands. They were right.

Her family. Owen. Doing nothing was taking the easy way out.

This was her life, goddamn it. And she loved her life. She pushed up off the couch, stumbling to the side before she got her balance.

No one could fix this but her.

"I have to go and make some calls," she said.

"To Owen?" Rico said hopefully.

"There's someone else I have to speak to first." She raced out of the room and turned her phone on.

It was time to finish this, once and for all.

34

Owen eased himself out of Teddy's ute, ignoring the empty spot where Alice's car should've been. His brother passed him his crutches.

"Thanks for the ride," Owen said.

"Need anything else? I've got beers, but I'm guessing you don't want to come up ..."

Owen's gaze shifted to the apartment landing. The painkillers for his knee did nothing to help with the ache in his chest. Being there without Alice would be brutal. "Another time, maybe."

Tipping his chin towards the back door of his office, Owen said, "I won't be long."

Teddy didn't offer to go in with him. "Text me when you're ready, and I'll drop you at Nate's."

He waited until Teddy was up in the apartment, the light streaming out of the window a sharp contrast to the early evening darkness. Moving slowly and carefully on his crutches, Owen unlocked the office, leaving the light in the hallway off. Everything looked the same. Papers were stacked neatly on his desk, his spare jacket hanging behind the door.

He continued down the hall, smiling at the takeaway containers in Frankie's bin. Nothing had changed here, but everything was different for him. The light from the street shone through the new window, all traces of the vandalism removed. He turned around, returning to his office. Quickly he found the letter he was looking for and tucked it under his arm. He reached into his pocket for his phone and realised it must've fallen out in Teddy's car.

He noticed the white van parked in Alice's spot as soon as he stepped out into the car park. Cigarette smoke surrounded him.

"Brilliant," a raspy voice said. "Get him on camera."

An umbrella light flicked on, blinding Owen. A microphone was shoved in his face. A man Owen didn't recognise smiled lasciviously at him.

"How long were you having an affair with Alice?"

It was on the tip of his tongue to point out they'd both been single. Neither of them had done anything wrong. But the anguished look on Alice's face when she'd sent him away made him clamp his lips together. He eyed the stairs. He'd never make it up there on his own.

"Are you why she wouldn't get back together with Phoenix?"

Owen bit the inside of his cheeks, ducked his head.

"Do you sleep with all your clients? Is this why you were fired from Malus, Mendax and Associates?"

Sod it. He'd manage the stairs.

"Told you to get lost, didn't she?"

Twelve steps. That's all he needed.

"Probably already moved on to some other guy."

Owen's hands wrapped around the metal rail. He let his crutches fall to the ground. Inhaling deeply, Owen raised his bad leg onto the first step. Braced himself for the wave of pain.

"Rumour has it, she's never coming back."

Owen faltered, the toe of his sneaker slipping, but his forearms locked and he stayed upright.

"Not gonna say anything, huh?"

He gritted his teeth. Breathed through the next two steps. Ignored the footsteps behind him.

"Thought you'd try to defend her."

Teddy's shadow crossed the kitchen window, the fridge door blocking out the light as it opened. The dull ache in Owen's leg was eclipsed by the burning in his heart.

"Guess she didn't mean anything to you."

Owen spun around. His voice was firm and clear, ringing out through the night. He didn't give a shit who heard him. Hoped everyone would.

Hoped Alice would.

"Alice Aspinall is the best person I've ever met. And she's more than capable of defending herself. There's nothing she can't do."

He twisted around and gingerly climbed the last steps, ignoring the pain in his knee and heart.

"What's going on ..." Teddy said, mouth half full of rice and curry when Owen opened the door.

"There's a reporter downstairs who won't leave. I don't have my phone. Can you call Raff?"

"I can do one better." Teddy picked up his mobile and swiped through his contacts. "Hey Wyatt. Some idiot's harassing Owen at my place. Is the team dinner still going? Send them round, would you?"

Owen sank onto a kitchen chair, raising his knee onto

the opposite one. He accepted the bag of frozen peas Teddy passed.

"They'll be gone soon. The whole footy team's coming."

Calmness settled over Owen. "I appreciate it."

Teddy shrugged, passing him a bowl of rice and red curry. "It's no big deal. You're still one of us, even if you're out for the rest of the season."

THE ADDRESS PHOENIX had texted Alice was for a trendy townhouse a few minutes from the centre of the city.

"Sure you don't want me to come in?" Rico leant forward, his arms resting on the steering wheel. "I could snap Fuckface in half for everything he's done to you."

His protectiveness was a warm balm to Alice's frayed nerves. "I'll be okay." She smoothed a hand down her front, picking at a piece of lint clinging to the oversized dark green jumper she'd borrowed.

"Then I'll be waiting right here. Take your time."

Alice clipped Murphy's lead to his collar and opened the door, ducking her head automatically in case there were any hidden cameras.

A shadowy figure, half hidden by the elm tree in the corner of the tiny front yard, was waiting.

"I was surprised to hear from you," Phoenix said before releasing a cloud of smoke from the corner of his mouth. He looked terrible, his hair a mess and deep circles under his eyes. Two suitcases and a guitar case were next to him, his battered leather satchel on the table. He backed further into the corner when he saw Murphy.

Good.

"Are you going to ...?" She didn't finish her sentence, remembering how the word 'rehab' used to send him into fits of rage. Murphy laid down next to her feet, tail still, ears up.

"My parents are here," he said, and Alice understood the hidden meaning. They'd be watching him like a hawk. The curtain behind Phoenix twitched. "They've been helping me detox. Next stop is court-ordered rehab because I gave the cops some information they wanted." A dry laugh cut through the tension hanging in the air, and he flicked his cigarette ash into the small bowl next to him. "I'm officially not your problem anymore."

Alice stared at her unpainted fingernails. "We caused a lot of problems for each other. It wasn't right, what we were doing, lying to everyone like that. We never should've gotten married."

"No kidding," he snorted, running a hand through his hair.

"Staying together was the real mistake, though."

Phoenix scuffed his boots along the concrete path. "About the video ... I wasn't thinking clearly. I haven't been myself for a long time." He pushed his hair off his face, something like genuine regret in his eyes.

"It doesn't matter," Alice said softly. And it didn't. "I've sorted it all out." She'd gone live and told everyone the truth about the video after her surgery. How she and Phoenix had been unhappy for a long time. Trapped in a lie of their own creation, spurred by her fear that she'd never be good enough. It didn't matter if anyone believed her or not. She didn't care anymore. She just had one last thing to do.

Phoenix stubbed out his cigarette, flicking the butt into the garden. "What are you really doing here?"

Alice pulled a large envelope out of her pocket. Tossed it onto the table. "You're going to sign our divorce papers. Now.

There will be no financial settlement. I'm not taking no for an answer. Rico or your parents can be our witnesses. But this ends now."

Phoenix's lighter ticked, the flame blooming as he lifted another cigarette to his lips. "Is that so?"

"Yep. You know I didn't damage any of your stuff. And you've brought all this trouble on yourself. Last thing you need is for me to tell everyone what the last two years have really been like. Not if you ever want to work again."

She let her threat hang in the air. If he was going to continue to tell lies, it was time she stood up for herself. Made it clear her weapon of choice would be the truth. She watched as realisation rolled across Phoenix's face, followed by the smile she'd foolishly thought she'd once loved.

"You must really love this new boyfriend, huh?"

She'd never even gotten to enjoy telling people Owen was her boyfriend. Alice stared at her feet and bit the inside of her cheek. Hopefully, that would all change soon if things went according to her plan. "Just sign the papers."

"I'm going back to Sweden after I get out of rehab." His voice was low and stripped of all the snark and derision she'd gotten used to hearing from him. "It'd be easier if all of this was behind me."

"I'm glad you're getting the help you need."

Phoenix's icy blue eyes met hers. "Yeah, me too. Got a pen?"

35

Owen was staring at his dinner when the security light above his front door flicked on. All he'd wanted was to sleep in his own bed the night before his surgery.

"Are you expecting someone?" Lulu asked, her knife and fork poised over the plate of roast lamb and veggies balanced on her knees. Wilbur was squished on one side, Raff on the other. Nate and Teddy were sitting on the floor, their plates on the coffee table. Several moving boxes were stacked behind them.

"Nope."

A shadow stretched across the concrete. He recognised her immediately from her profile, the delicate slope of her nose, her full lips. Even in pitch black darkness, Owen would've noticed the redness in her cheeks, how her hand shook when she knocked.

"Want me to get it?" Nate asked.

"Nah, I got it." Owen pushed himself up and grabbed his crutches.

"Hi," Alice said when he opened the sliding glass door.

She looked over his shoulder, panic flaring in her eyes when she saw his family. Her wave was so awkward.

"Where's your car?" he asked.

She jammed her hands into the pockets of her fluffy lavender coat. "It broke down near the turn-off."

He looked down at the sequined sneakers on her feet. She'd walked almost three kilometres to get here. That had to be a good sign, right?

"I can come back another time if you're too busy."

Owen pulled his big puffer jacket off the hook next to the door, keenly aware of the silence behind him. "It's fine. Why don't we ..." His head jerked towards the patio area.

She nodded, stepping back to make room for him to pass through the doorway.

"How's your knee?" Alice asked as he sat on a painted white Adirondack chair. Her eyes darted around the area, looking everywhere but at him.

"It's fine."

From the corner of his eye, Owen saw her nod, her bottom lip tremble. He had to make this right. Tell her how sorry he was. "Alice, I wanted to—"

"Before you start. There's something I have to say. I'm so sorry about what happened. I shouldn't have done that." She paused, her voice cracking. "Treated you that way, said those things. I hate that I sent you away when you were hurt. It's the worst thing I've ever done."

He stole a glance at her when she sniffed, shaking her short hair off her cheeks.

"You deserved better. So did I," Alice said.

Owen nodded, swallowing the lump of gravel in his throat. He'd been about to tell her the same thing.

"I'm not very good at being accountable," she continued, her words tumbling out on top of each other. "It's not an excuse. I know it sounds like one, but I wanted you to understand. I never have been."

He turned towards her, unable to stop himself.

She sniffed loudly, her fringe brushing across her face as she bowed her head. "Staying with Phoenix and continuing to pretend everything was fine was the easy option because I didn't have to admit to my mistakes. But I don't want to pretend anymore."

She released a shaky laugh, a crumpled tissue appearing as she dabbed at her eyes.

The urge to touch her almost tore him in two.

"I know you reached out to Dougie. And I wanted to thank you for telling him to stop. To wait for me to decide. And I saw the clips. The group one and the one that was just you. You wouldn't believe how many people tagged me in them. Even after how I treated you, you were still looking out for me because that's who you are."

He tilted his chin down. He'd always want to help her, especially when he owed her so much. "I wanted to—"

"—but I've taken care of it. Phoenix signed the divorce papers this afternoon."

"Really?" His fingers curled around the fleecy inside of his hoodie's pouch.

"I made it clear I'm not going to take his crap anymore. That I was done protecting something that wasn't real. And I took Murphy with me because he's scared of dogs." She laughed lightly, the sound so soft anyone else might've missed it, but he'd spent the last few months noticing every-thing about her.

"Nothing's going to stop me now that I'm ready to fight for the best thing that ever happened to me."

Her hair skimmed her cheeks as she stepped towards

him. She pushed it away, tucking it behind her ear, the skin he'd kissed so many times.

"Honey," slipped past his lips before he could stop it. Alice's face pinched in pain, her shoulders drooping but she squared them and fuck, he loved her even more for the show of strength. This was hard. But she was here. Listening. If she could be brave and admit to her mistakes, he could, too. He'd spend the rest of his life apologising if she'd let him. He cleared his throat. "I wanted to explain about Camille."

It killed him how she froze at the mention of his ex, but he ploughed on. "It's a long story, and lots of it isn't relevant, but when she left me all those years ago, I thought it was because I didn't matter to her and looking back now, I can't believe I let that influence how I've been living my life, keeping everyone at arm's reach, burying myself in work, trying to solve people's problems for them. But then I met you, and you woke up something inside of me and I'll always be grateful to you for that. I shouldn't have done what I did after the race either. I should've supported you, not tried to take over. But I was just so scared I was going to lose you. If you ever need me," he choked out, "I'll always be here. Okay? You just say the word." He stared at the ground, her glittery sneakers sparkling under the outdoor lights.

"There's something else," she murmured, and his head snapped up. "I thought I didn't deserve you, and I'm not one hundred per cent sure that isn't true, but Rico asked me something the other day, and I haven't been able to get it out of my head."

"What'd he say?"

"He asked me what you deserved, and I was like, 'D'uh, obviously Owen deserves the world.'"

He smiled ruefully. It was all he'd ever wanted for her.

"You're so good and true and kind, Owen. And it really doesn't hurt that your ass looks great in your running shorts. Any pants you wear, really. And when you wear no pants? Wowsers."

His laugh caught him by surprise, puffing out of his mouth before he knew it was happening.

When their eyes met, hers were still too watery for his liking, but there was a hint of sparkle. A sign his Alice was still there. When she bit her lip, he knew there was more.

"What else did Rico say?"

Alice looked out across the dark field in front of them. There were a few wildflowers growing along the side fence where he'd set up the tent all those months ago. His mother had called them weeds and offered to pull them out, but he hadn't let her. He hadn't been ready to lose the little touches of Alice at his home. Her shampoo and conditioner were still in the shower, for fuck's sake. Owen had used his injury as an excuse to delay moving into his new house, too.

"He asked why you deserved more than I did."

Owen smiled. He really liked Rico. "That's a good question."

Two big fat tears rolled down her face, and he was on his feet, crossing the concrete to her within seconds. If his knee hurt, he didn't notice. There was nothing until she was in his arms, slotting into the place where she'd always belonged.

"I don't want to go back to the way things were." Alice rubbed her face against his chest. "I want things to be better. For us to both have what we deserve."

Owen's arms wrapped around her, and she melted into him. "You're sure? But what about what people will say?"

She looked up at him, her eyes clear, the freckles on her face calling to him like the constellations dotted across the night sky behind them. "I don't care what anyone says. I have a plan."

Another laugh erupted out of him and fuck it, a few tears as well. He sat down, pulling her onto his lap and pressed their foreheads together, felt their breath mix. "I love plans."

She smiled, properly this time, her cheeks stretching wide. God, his Alice was glorious.

"I've done a few things to clear up that drug video. Made sure everyone knows it's not what it seems like. I'm going to work with a few different drug charities as well."

Owen traced her cheek with his thumb. "That sounds good."

"And I'm going to woo you."

Another laugh. His chest felt lighter than ever before. "You are, huh? What if I want to woo you?"

"I'd like to take you on a date, Owen James. In public. I'd like people to know you're mine." The flush he loved so much bloomed again on her cheeks. "If you'd like to be mine. It's okay if you want some time to think about it."

He brushed his lips against hers, keeping the touch featherlight on purpose. "I've been yours since you thought I was a well-dressed murderer."

Alice's fingers twisted in the hair at the back of his neck, pulling him down towards her. "And I want you to know that I love you. So much."

Fireworks. Everywhere. Joy ripped through Owen so quickly he would've sworn under oath that the sky had exploded with colours. "I love you too, honey."

Their lips met, and it was like they'd never been apart. Where she led, he followed, his hands sliding underneath her jacket, seeking out her skin. She shivered against him, sucked his lip into her mouth and then she ... stopped. He groaned against her lips, but she didn't respond.

When he pulled away, her eyes were glazed, her cheeks his favourite pink.

"Your whole family is watching." Alice blushed.

Owen's grin might break his face. "I thought you didn't care." He nipped at her lips once more, and this time, she didn't resist him. She melted into his embrace. "Come have dinner with us."

"You're sure?"

"Never been surer of anything in my life. Besides, the Old Girls are probably fifteen minutes away if we're lucky. Finding a designated driver might slow them down a bit."

"We'll have to make sure they know I'm staying in Wattle Junction indefinitely. Next part of my plan is asking my landlord for a proper lease. None of this month-to-month rubbish."

He breathed her in, her wildflower smell soothing him. "I've heard your landlord is a big fan of admin."

Her coy smile made his heart swell. "You should know I'm a big fan of everything about you," she said.

"Oh, honey." Owen waited until their eyes met. "I'm your biggest fan and I always will be."

THE END.

EPILOGUE
(THREE YEARS LATER)

Owen hadn't set out that day to buy an engagement ring.

And he certainly hadn't planned on finding the perfect one at his mother's boutique. But when he saw the dark blue tourmaline surrounded by a halo of diamonds set in a delicate rose gold band, he *knew* it was the one. The round stone was the exact shade of Alice's eyes, and the shape made him think of wildflowers. It was as unique and gorgeous as she was. Actually, that was impossible. Nothing could ever equal the brilliance that was Alice Aspinall.

He checked no one was within earshot and ducked behind the counter. The only other customers were at the other end of the shop looking at Alice's candles. The Emancipation of Alice display spanned the whole back wall and included her skincare and homemaker products. Owen smiled, remembering how she'd pored over fabric swatches and samples before deciding which would be the best ones for her cushions and throws. Next month, she was adding a clothing range to her empire.

"I need you to stay calm," he said to Lulu.

"Oh my God! Alice's pregnant!" she crowed.

Owen fixed her with a hard stare despite the warmth that spread through his body at the thought of Alice carrying their child. "No, she isn't. And for the record, that's the opposite of calm."

"Well, what did you expect when you sauntered in here and said *that* to me?"

"That maybe you'd understand I wanted your help with something. And we needed to be discreet?"

Lulu rolled her eyes. "Really? You actually thought that would happen? Oh, my darling boy. No."

Owen chuckled. Now that he and Alice had been together for a few years, Lulu had been campaigning for grandchildren. Exhibit A: The table covered in baby gear sitting in the centre of the store. Exhibit B: The onesie hanging above it that said *If you think I'm cute, you should see my grandma.*

"Can you put that blue stone and rose gold ring aside for me? I'll come back at closing to pay for it."

Lulu's eyes widened, and she grasped his hands tightly. "Does this mean ..."

Honestly, he should've been expecting the whoop of joy that reverberated around the shop when he nodded. The women in the corner startled.

"My son won a big case, that's all. He's a lawyer. Nothing to see here, folks!" Lulu offered him a sheepish smile and lowered her voice to a whisper. "Sorry. But really, we can both agree that could've been much worse. Here, take it with you now." With shaking hands, she unlocked the drawer and slipped the ring into a small velvet pouch.

Owen bent down and kissed her cheek. "Thanks, Mum. I'll see you tomorrow night at dinner."

"You're sure we can't bring anything?"

"Nope, Alice's organised caterers."

Lulu raised her eyebrows.

"She feels guilty that we'll be away for Christmas." Two months in Europe beckoned, and he couldn't wait to have Alice all to himself every day.

"She shouldn't. You two deserve a proper holiday."

"And remember ..." He patted the pocket he'd put the ring in.

"Your secret is safe with me." Lulu tapped a finger against her red lips.

ALICE WAS SWIMMING when Owen got home, her body gliding through the water as she did freestyle. Pop music blared from the speakers on the deck, and all the citronella torches were lit, the flames dancing in time to the beat. Murphy was fast asleep on his outdoor bed, legs twitching as he chased after dream rabbits.

Owen stripped to his boxer briefs, hanging his trousers and business shirt over the back of a timber deck chair. He waited until she stopped in the shallow end and stood. The water lapped around her waist, her neon green one-piece glued to her curves. She said she liked the suit because it made her feel like a real swimmer. Owen liked it because it had a zip down the front that acted like one of those old-fashioned mood rings. If the zipper was up at her neck, Alice needed time to herself to focus, burn off some nervous energy. If she'd lowered the zip, she was in the mood for fun. And usually, it was the kind Owen could help with.

"Hey, Boy Scout." She grinned.

"Want some company?" he asked.

"Always."

Ever since they'd put the pool in, Alice had been obsessed with swimming each night. They still ran together a few mornings each week, but she said the calming, repetitive motion of the water helped her quiet her mind after a busy day. And right now, with everything they had going on, every day was a busy day.

Owen sank into the warm water and paused. "Is the pool heater on?"

Alice flicked her hair back. Drops of water chased down her neck, sliding between her breasts. The zipper was as low as it could go. "Only a little."

"It's twenty-four degrees today, honey."

She swam towards him seductively before wrapping her arms and legs around him. "You know I like things hot."

His smile was immediate. "I do know that."

He walk-swam them over to the far corner, behind the jumbo pots Alice had insisted on putting there. She said it was good feng shui. He knew it was because Murphy couldn't see them there from his bed. She kissed his neck, his chin, his lips. Ground against him. "Are you ready to be seduced?" she asked.

"Always."

Her giggle pushed his tiredness away. He pulled her closer, peppered kisses along her collarbone.

"Don't distract me," she groaned when he found the spot behind her ear he knew turned her bones to putty. "I worked hard on a surprise for you."

Owen lifted his head and met her gaze. "Okay, I'll behave. Show me what you've got, honey."

"It's inside, but I should warn you. I used Excel and alphabetisation to finish off the running sheet for tomorrow night. And I confirmed everything with the caterers."

Slowly, he climbed out of the pool with Alice in his

arms, wrapping them both in one of the fluffy towels she'd left on the outdoor table. "Are you trying to woo me with admin?"

Alice pressed against him, rocked against his hardness. "Seems to be working."

"Mmmhmm. Tell me more about these spreadsheets." He bit her neck gently, then used one hand to open the screen door.

"What about the floors? We're going to drip all over them."

"We can clean up the mess later." They'd gotten very good at cleaning up messes—both literal and figurative— together.

"Where are we going?" he asked her.

"To our bedroom. I thought you could help me pick something special to wear under my dress tomorrow night."

How'd Owen get so lucky?

EVERYONE ALICE LOVED WAS HERE. Cutlery clinked against plates and conversation mixed with the buzz of excitement around the long table. They hadn't bothered with place settings, preferring to let everyone choose where they wanted to sit to give the evening a relaxed, fun vibe.

Owen's warm palm settled against her thigh, his breath skating across her neck as he leant in close. "It's almost time. Ready, honey?"

With him by her side? Alice was ready for anything.

"Does anyone want a refill?" Owen asked, standing. Dougie and Rico held up their empty champagne glasses, engrossed in conversation with Eloise and Nate. Everyone else was huddled around Rafferty, watching something on his phone. Probably a video of his new puppy, Sweetpea. Contentment rolled off him in a wave.

Alice stood and slid her arm around Owen's waist. Pulled him down for a quick kiss. "You get the drinks, and I'll bring out the cheese boards."

"Need any help?" Marguerite offered.

Alice waved her away. "It's already done. Keep chatting with Lulu. I'll be right back."

She headed for the kitchen where she'd stashed her make-up and a mirror in the walk-in pantry, but Owen grabbed her hand and pulled her down the hall and out through the laundry door. "What are you doing?" she whispered. "I need to fix my face."

"This will only take a second, and you look perfect. You always do. No one else could wear sequins and feathers to a barbeque and not make everyone wonder what they're missing." He led her towards the field behind their house. Wildflowers swayed in the gentle breeze.

"I wanted to give you something." Owen pulled a little velvet pouch from his back pocket and reached for her hand. "Please don't be mad."

That wasn't what she'd expected him to say.

"I'm going to make some promises in front of our guests in a few minutes, but I wanted us to have a moment together first. Something just for us."

Alice said a prayer for her waterproof mascara and swallowed a happy sob.

"There are so many things that I love about you. And I'm going to spend the rest of my life making sure you know how special you are every day. Not only to me and Murphy but to everyone. Celebrating all the goodness and sweetness that shines out of you like the sun and how hard you work to make the world a better place. You make me so much better. I can't wait to go in there with you and tell everyone this isn't a dinner party. That they're actually at our wedding. And I know you said you didn't need an engagement ring, but I saw this and wanted you to have it."

He reached for her hand and pulled out the most beautiful ring she'd ever seen. It was colourful and quirky like she was. Traditional and classic like Owen. An exquisite blend of everything that made their love so special.

"Now, you've already said that you'll marry me." His voice was deeper, huskier. "But I'm going to ask again because I love hearing you say yes."

Alice wiped her eyes.

"Will you be mine forever, honey?"

It had been the easiest yes of her life when Owen had asked if she ever saw herself getting married again. He'd said he didn't care about a piece of paper; all he'd wanted was her.

But Alice cared.

She wanted a ring on his finger. One on hers. A celebration of their love with the people they loved.

She just didn't want the spectacle of a big wedding, and luckily, neither did Owen.

Her arms wound around his neck. "Forever and always."

"Then let's go get married."

WATTLE IT BE?

BILLIE'S THE ONE WOMAN WYATT CAN'T HAVE.

AND SHE'S THE ONLY ONE HE WANTS.

No one knows more secrets than a bartender. Just ask Wyatt Andrews. The manager of the Wattle Junction Hotel has plenty of his own and hears about everything that happens in the small town. Determined to make up for his past mistakes, there's nothing he won't do for his family or community. Which is why he reluctantly agrees to take part in a charity bachelor auction.

Billie Winnick loves everything about Wattle Junction, the magical place she's lived in all her life. In the wake of some surprising career news, Billie vows to start checking things off her bucket list. First thing: taking chances and going after what she wants by bidding on Wyatt. The tax deductible donation is just a bonus.

Thrown together by two meddling matriarchs for a romantic date, will Wyatt and Billie finally give in to their simmering chemistry?

ABOUT THE AUTHOR

Emma Mugglestone is a Queenslander who lives in Melbourne, Australia with her family and dogs. When she's not writing contemporary romances filled with small town charm and swoony characters, she can be found chasing sunrises, binge reading rom-coms like it's an Olympic sport and trying to remember her passwords.

Connect with Emma at www.emmamugglestone.com

ACKNOWLEDGMENTS

(Get cosy, team, we're going to be here for a while.)

They say it takes a village to raise a child and I can attest that the same is true for writing and publishing a book. A huge number of people have helped me bring *The Reality of Us* into the world and I'm truly so grateful.

Thank you so much to:

- Sam Palencia at Ink & Laurel for the beautiful cover that is more perfect than I could've ever imagined.

- Penny Carroll for her supreme structural editing skills and support. Owen and Alice are so much better for your care and advice.

- Jo Speirs from Nurturing Words for her brilliant proof-reading skills and not judging me for throwing commas and em dashes around like confetti. I'll try to be better.

- Sarah Richhelm from The Beta House Collective who was the very first professional I ever showed the manuscript to. You provided such amazing and insightful feedback and became a wonderful writing friend.

- Romance Writers of Australia, especially the Aspiring eLoop under the care and guidance of D.D. Line, for intro-ducing me to so many amazing writers who have become my friends.

- Everyone who beta read a version of this manuscript. It's a long list and I'm so appreciative of the feedback you gave me and this story: Holly Brunnbauer, Melanie Smythe, Elouise Tynan, Stephanie Hazeltine, Alison Middleton,

Kylie Michelle, Antonella Licciardi, Carrie Clarke, Karen Lieversz, Renae Black, Victoria Brown, Julie Weaver, Claire Hunter and Hannah Carson.

- I'm so lucky to be part of two very special writing groups and they deserve a special shout out. To my anthology gals—Elle, Steph and Ali—you are all the best and our group chat is always the most unhinged, encouraging and super fun notification I get each day. And to Carrie, Karen and Antonella who kept me accountable with weekly check-ins and support, you gals rock.

- To my wonderful family and special friends who always ask about my writing and encourage me to chase after my dreams.

- To Luke, Hamish and Annabel, thank you for understanding why this was so important to me and never wavering in your support and love. This is the culmination of years of work and it's so much sweeter to celebrate with you all by my side. Please don't ask me for a snack on release day.

- My final thanks is always to you, the reader. To know that you gave Owen and Alice's story a chance means the world to me. Welcoming you to Wattle Junction has been a pleasure, and I hope you visit again soon.

Em x

ALSO BY EMMA MUGGLESTONE

The Wattle Junction Series

Wattle It Be?

The Story of Us

Anthologies

Anyone But Him (Finding Home,

Jawson Ranch Book 1)

All I Want For Chris-mas (Finding Christmas,

Jawson Ranch Book 2)